MW01138387

THE

OF
UNINTENDED
CONSEQUENCES

Cover and interior design by Jacqueline Cook.

ISBN: 978-1-7366203-4-2 (Paperback)
ISBN: 978-1-7366203-5-9 (e-book)

10 9 8 7 6 5 4 3 2 1

BISAC Subject Headings:
FIC050000 FICTION / Crime
FIC030000 FICTION / Thrillers / Suspense
FIC069000 FICTION / City Life

Address all correspondence to:
Fireship Press, LLC
P.O. Box 68412
Tucson, AZ 85737
fireshipinfo@gmail.com

Or visit our website at:
www.fireshippress.com

For my kitchen cohorts, Kelly, Laura and Marsi

THE *Law* OF UNINTENDED CONSEQUENCES

G. DAVIES JANDREY

Cortero
An Imprint of FIRESHIP PRESS

There is a crack in everything.
That's how the light gets in.

—Leonard Cohen, "Anthem"

CHAPTER 1

No Rent, No Roof, No Refuge

Sunday, May 26

Scratching his stubbled chin, Davie Woodward pulled back the curtain. The Mexican at the door was wearing a bulletproof vest stamped front and back with the word "constable" in big block letters. He pounded on the door again.

"You have 30 minutes to vacate the premises, Mr. Woodward," the constable said, then stepped back from the door.

Davie patted the Colt 45 snugged in the holster at his hip. "Another goddamn Mexican." The landlady of the sagging adobe that had been made into a duplex was a Mexican. She barely spoke English, for Christ's sake. Because of the goddamn Mexicans, landscaping jobs were so scarce that at the end of each month there was nothing left to put aside. He was waiting for call backs on five job applications he'd filled out last week and four from the week before. And now this guy, this constable… What the hell was a constable anyway and what right did he have to tell him to fucking vacate the premises? Heart racing, he washed his hands over his face. Vacate to where?

His wife, Garnet, sat on the couch, caressing the swollen belly, which contrasted sharply with her otherwise gaunt appearance. When she started to get big, the manager at Pizza Shack began cutting back her hours until her job was hardly worth the bus fare. Now there was nothing for her to do but wait for the baby. Rising from the couch with a grunt, she went to the window and put her hand on his shoulder. "Davie, let's just pack up and go."

Fists balled, he roughly shrugged off her hand and immediately regretted it. He would never do to Garnet what his father had done to his mother and to him. Never. They'd been together for three years, married less than one, and now the baby. Seemed he'd been working his ass off but could never get ahead. He rubbed his chest. It felt like he couldn't get enough air.

A police car pulled into the parking lot and Davie glared as a big, fat black cop climbed out. Backup, Davie assumed, as he watched the two men conferring. He pulled his baseball cap off and ran his fingers through his shaggy, brown hair. "Not right, Garnet. Not right," he said, but she'd already gone into the bedroom to pack up their belongings. There wasn't that much. The duplex was furnished, if you could call the old sprung couch, chipped dinette set and a recliner that no longer reclined, furniture. Even the mattress on the bedroom floor wasn't theirs.

The trouble had started when they came home after celebrating Garnet's birthday at the Chinese buffet down the road to find that the water heater had sprung a leak. Soon after, they noticed black mold creeping up along the floorboards. Felicia Ramirez, the landlady, kept putting them off, even when Garnet, with her asthma, started to have trouble breathing. Davie reported the mold to the health department, but still nothing. Finally, he told Ramirez that he wouldn't pay the rent until she did something to solve the problem.

Then came the eviction notice. Davie had the money, tried to give it to her, but Ramirez refused to take it; said they had trashed the place and had to be out in 10 days.

When he went to court to fight the eviction, Davie thought it was obvious that the whole thing was retaliation because he'd reported the mold. But the judge asked only one question: "Did you pay the rent?"

That was it. Didn't matter about the mold, didn't matter that he'd tried to pay up but the landlady wouldn't accept it, didn't matter that they had seven months left on their lease. It was the law, the judge said. In less than five minutes it was over.

Shaking his head, Davie closed the curtain. He just didn't get it. It was okay that the shyster of a slum landlord, who was probably not even a U.S. citizen, was charging big bucks for roach infested substandard housing, but it was not okay for a U.S. citizen to hold out on the rent until something was done to fix a known health hazard. And mold wasn't the only thing wrong, not by a long shot. There were cockroaches in the kitchen and bathroom, and when you flushed the toilet a black sludge gurgled up from the shower drain. Ramirez never even replaced the water heater. Davie was already out hundreds of dollars and it was not his fault. He felt like his head was about to explode.

And where were they going to get the money for a new place? Not only did they still have to pay the rent owed, Ramirez blamed them for the broken water heater and water damage to the drywall. She refused to return their security deposit, and they were stuck with the court costs. Right now, there was no money for a new security deposit and the first month's rent on another shit-hole. He punched the wall leaving a satisfying dent in the drywall. They could try pulling that money out of his ass.

Garnet emerged from the bedroom toting a garbage bag of clothing.

He reached for her arm as she walked by and gave it a gentle tug. "Sorry about all this, babe."

"Where are we gonna to go?"

"I'll take you to your sister's."

"But she…"

"Won't have me. I know. I'll camp out in the truck. When I find us a place, I'll come get you. It won't be long, I promise," he said, though he didn't believe it.

Eyes brimming, Garnet headed outside to put her things in their truck, an old faded green Dodge Ram already loaded with assorted landscaping equipment. "You better get your things together," she said over her shoulder. "I'll do the kitchen."

He nodded, but didn't move.

"This job sucks, man," Constable Frank Nuñez was saying to Officer Torrance Stedman. "His wife's as big as a house. Did you see her?"

"Yeah."

"I mean, it's the law, it's my job, but sometimes…" He tipped his hat back and rubbed his buzzed head with his knuckles. "My wife's due next month. I really feel for the guy."

"Yeah." Fact was, Stedman knew very well what it was like to be a paycheck away from disaster.

"It's hard to believe." Nuñez pointed his chin at the faded duplex. "The Westside is now prime real estate. With all the white folks moving into the neighborhood, Ramirez could sell this property as is for a chunk of cash. Could be why she's in such a rush to get them out. Sucks, man, but what can you do about it?"

Stedman nodded. "Heads up," he whispered. "Here he comes and he's carrying." He eyed the man's days-old beard, the straggly hair, noted the hunting knife in a scabbard strapped to his leg, the Colt 45 on his hip and tried to assess the danger. "Let me handle this one, Frank," he said, stepping forward.

"Afternoon, Mr. Woodward. I'm real sorry for your troubles." Stedman had learned that a simple apology can save time, effort and sometimes lives.

"I've got the rent money." He reached in his pocket and pulled out his wallet. "Take it. We need more time to find another place."

"Sorry man, I can't accept your rent money. We've got court orders and, right or wrong, you've got 30 minutes."

The hot afternoon sun was making Stedman's skin itch. He scratched the back of his neck. "I know it's too late for advice, but the same thing happened to my daughter not so long ago. She withheld the rent because of a gas leak, then got an eviction notice. I was pretty damn mad, went with her to court to fight it. But it seems the law requires that the renter give written notice before withholding rent. She was SOL as they say." He shook his head. "Doesn't seem right, but it's the law." The man looked at him as if he were speaking a foreign language. "Just thought you might want to know in case this ever happens to you again."

Stedman paused to scratch his ear. "Oh, yeah, one other thing, man. Never tell the judge you didn't pay the rent. Tell him anything but that. Once you say those words, he stops listening cause nothing else matters before the law."

"Then the law is fucked."

"In this case, I have to agree." Stedman studied the ground for a moment. "Hey, I noticed your wife's gonna have a baby soon. Can I help you load up your belongings?"

After dropping his wife off at her sister's, Davie had picked up a six-pack of Bud and a Whopper and fries at Burger King then headed to a spot out in the desert where he used to take Garnet before they moved in together.

Though it was not yet solid dark, the sun and the fast food were gone and the doves and quail were settling in for the night. He'd just opened his last beer, thinking he'd be needing another six-pack, when a flashy red Camaro came bumping down the dirt road. The driver, a Mexican kid, his girl snuggled next to him, carefully skirted the deep ruts to avoid bottoming out. Davie sipped his beer as he watched them pull onto the narrow track that led to the wash. He'd been down that track, been down there with Garnet, her and a few others, and knew just what they'd be up to.

Nice car, that Camaro, vintage. Davie wondered what the little wetback did to get the money to buy it. Suddenly furious, he chugged the last of his beer and crushed the can in his fist.

•••

Three women, Pappy, Elaine and Brittany, were sitting in the shadows beneath the giant bronze statue of Pancho Villa on his rearing stallion. The only thing they had in common was poor prospects, but last summer they'd banded together for safety after the murders of two homeless women.

Pappy and Elaine were seasoned survivors of addiction and abuse. At least for now, Brittany had survived a voice that sometimes urged her to step in front of a SunTran bus. Before she'd been consumed by her singular affliction, Brittany had been an English major at the University of Arizona. It was she who once dubbed them the Weird Sisters, after the three hags in Macbeth. The name had an odd appeal and stuck.

All night the women had been waiting: waiting for the temperature to drop below 90 degrees, waiting for the stores, then the restaurants, then the bars to close, waiting for a bit of quiet and dark to rest in.

When it was as quiet and dark as it was going to get, they ambled, no reason to hurry, to the corner of Pennington and Stone to the public library. They passed a big red metal sculpture, part jungle gym, part Chinese pagoda. Brittany used to think it awkward and out of character for Tucson, but more recently, she had come to appreciate its splash of color. They passed the library itself. To the west of the building was a parklike setting with actual green grass and an assortment of thirsty looking trees.

Their destination was a pepper tree with a wide canopy that grew in a strip of decomposed granite between two low block walls. It was darker under there and quieter. A sign read "Hummingbird Hollow." Brittany thought it too quaint for the ultramodern building with its concrete planters filled with aloes and cacti—plants one would certainly not find in a cozy hollow—but the sign would capture the imagination of a child. She liked to think that during the day, some mom and her kid might sit on the wall and read in the shade.

Beneath the tree it was darker, cooler, quieter and the ground more forgiving. Pappy, calves bulging below her baggy basketball shorts, began to unload her backpack, Elaine her roller bag. Brittany hesitated a moment to make sure they were not under surveillance then slipped off her pack. In an orderly fashion they spread their gear next to the wall where it was darkest.

First, they laid out the blankets. Pappy's, a rough wool army surplus, always went on the bottom as insulation. Next was Elaine's worn cotton quilt for a bit of padding. Last was the maroon fleece. According to Brittany, it was a gift from the government for allowing them to implant a computer chip into her brain so that they could monitor her creativity. Just before the first delivery trucks started to clatter down the street, the temperature would fall below eighty. With the humidity at three percent and a bit of breeze, the women would want to pull the soft fleece over their legs.

Pappy, a solidly built woman of middle age, reached into the side pocket of her pack and pulled out a knee sock full of rocks. She could whirl it above her head with force and menace while spewing invectives of such vehemence and originality that she'd never had to hit anyone with it. Even though Elaine wasn't that much younger than her and Brittainy not much younger than Elaine, Pappy thought of them as *her girls* and felt as protective of them as a mama bobcat of her kits. Pappy put the sock on the ground next to her pack.

Brittany produced a sharp number 2 pencil with a makeshift hilt of duct tape. Before the voices had begun to compete for her attention, every spring break, while her more stable peers got drunk on the beaches along the Sea of Cortez, she had reread "The Lord of the Rings" and so dubbed her little weapon Sting. Once Brittany had used it on a would-be rapist. Although she had been aiming for his eye, she was pretty certain that she'd merely provided her attacker with a third nostril – all the better to smell his own shit with, she would sometimes boast. She put the pencil in her pants pocket for easy access, then sat her narrow butt on the wall and listened for approaching footsteps or the crackle of an agent's radio.

Elaine began to braid her hair. Thick and near auburn, it was the last of her beauty. She secured it with a rubber band then pulled out a single, stiletto-heeled red patent leather shoe. A relic of better times, she figured the heel could be an effective deterrent. She waved the shoe about now. "To keep away the cockroaches," she said, referring to the men who prey upon the homeless. Men who raped them, or bludgeoned them with a baseball bat just to see what was inside their backpacks or perhaps just to see how it felt to bludgeon someone with a baseball bat.

Despite the heat, the women didn't remove a single layer of clothing, not even their shoes. Fight or flight, they needed to be prepared for both. Could be there was someone out there right now, watching and waiting for one of them to go off by herself to pee. Well, they knew better.

When everything was just right, they snugged their packs against the wall and settled down for what was left of the night, each trying to maintain a slice of space between their bodies; it was still so hot. Exhausted, they stared into the branches of the pepper tree, a black filigree against an opaque sky, and waited for sleep to come.

Brittany, who became Brittany the day she ran away from home, some 10 years ago, suddenly sat up. "Let he who is without sin, cast the first stone."

"What?" Pappy was clearly annoyed.

"What, what?" asked Brittany.

"You just said something about sin."

Brittany shrugged. "Not me."

Though Pappy was used to Brittany's non sequiturs, pique always affected her like a double espresso. Now she was wide-awake. Her father had been a Bible thumper to the bone. He'd versed her well in sin, so she had an opinion. "My guess is that not even Christ himself could have thrown that stone," she observed. "The deadly sins – sloth, envy, pride, greed, gluttony, wrath and lust – who the hell hasn't sinned?"

"So, what about stealing?" Long ago Brittany had shoplifted a package of bikini panties in assorted florals. "And why should greed, gluttony, sloth, envy, pride, wrath and ... what's the last one?"

"Lust," Elaine offered.

"Why are those sins worse than committing murder or rape?"

Now propped on an elbow, Pappy warmed to the topic. "Just think about it." Her tone implied the additional word *stupid*. "The *deadlies* are at the root of all of other sins."

Brittany chewed that over for a moment. When she'd stolen those panties, she had committed the sin of envy for sure, and probably wrath as well. She'd been very angry at her mother that day.

"So, nobody's innocent, then." Elaine found a degree of comfort in the notion. In her day, she'd committed so many lustful, greedy, gluttonous acts she could not count them, and though she was the only one with a roller bag, secretly she coveted Brittany's fleece blanket.

As for Pappy, once she lost her temper, good luck finding it again. Pappy was full of wrath and proud of it. Kind of a *deadlies* two for one.

"Is it a sin to make poor choices?" Brittany asked in a near whisper. "People—my mother, social workers, counselors, doctors, politicians and generals—even heads of states have told me I make poor choices."

Pappy hooted. "Politicians and heads of state, no less. I guess they should know. But choice? More like a hand in the middle of your back shoving you towards the edge of a cliff."

"More like a knife at your throat," Brittany added.

"Excuses, excuses," said Elaine. "If you don't accept responsibility for your actions, you'll never…"

"True, but fuck you anyway," Pappy said, though she was no longer angry. It occurred to her that there was really only one sin at the root of every evil in their lives. It wasn't sloth or envy or any of the others; it was poverty. She and Elaine were born and reared in it. Poor Brittany committed the sin of poverty in the midst of the voices, sincere and angry, wheedling, loving and seemingly wise voices that whispered in her ear.

After a few quiet moments, there was a dry fluttering, Brittany's lips gently flapping in sleep. The woman was always the first to fall. Elaine was next. Pappy could tell by the faint whistle with her every exhale.

Pappy leaned back against her pack, counting backward from 100 until she could no longer keep her eyes open, then coming from a planter, a dry, exhausted squeak. "What the hell?" Her voice was tight with exasperation.

Again, the faint mew. "Sounds like a kitten," Elaine said. She produced a little flashlight from her roller bag and shined it toward the planter. Two eyes reflected the light. She struggled to her feet and peered into the concrete bowl filled with aloes. "Hey baby. Look at you." She extracted a very small, very grimy kitten and held it aloft.

"Holy shit," Pappy whispered. It was almost a prayer. "Is that the only one?"

Elaine scanned the planter with her flashlight. "Looks like it. Poor baby." Elaine stroked the kitten with her index finger. "Where's your mom?"

"It looks like it's going to die," said Pappy.

The women began to search through pockets, zippered compartments and various plastic bags.

Several minutes passed. Pappy threw down two packets of grape jelly and a tiny container of peanut butter squirreled away from this morning's breakfast at the Las Hermanas Women's Hostel. "That's it for me."

Elaine added three packets of non-dairy creamer, two packets of mayo and one of mustard, also compliments of Las Hermanas.

Brittany produced five packets of sugar, two of salt. In silence, they studied the small mound of condiments, absorbing the fact that between the three of them they didn't have enough to keep a kitten alive.

"Well, we can mix the jam and the creamer and add water," Brittany suggested. "Anybody got a little bowl or something?"

"Hang on." Elaine searched through her roller bag once again. "It's in here somewhere." She continued her search, pulling out panties, tampons, toothbrush and paste and a small cake of unused hotel soap. "Aha!" Elaine set a plastic container next to the packets. "For my dentures."

"What dentures?" Pappy snapped.

"I used to have dentures."

"What happened to them?"

"They went with the grocery cart that went with the son of a bitch who stole it."

"So how come the container didn't go with the dentures?"

"Because it was in my pocket holding the joint I was going to share with my then boyfriend."

"Why weren't you wearing the dentures?"

"They hurt like hell."

"Oh," Pappy said. "Well, just pour a little water in it, why don't you?" She watched as this was accomplished. "Now add the creamer."

"I know. I know," said Elaine. "Don't be so bossy." She added the creamer, then the sugar and a bit of grape jelly, mixed it with her finger, added a little more water then set it before the kitten. For a moment the kitten wobbled forward then collapsed.

"Put a little on your finger to get it started," Brittany suggested.

Elaine dipped her finger into the mix and offered it to the kitten. No luck.

"Let me try." With her pinky, Elaine scooped up a little jam and held it under the kitten's nose. "Come on, baby. Try this." The kitten didn't even lift its head. "Oh, God. It's going to die."

"Here, give it to me." Pappy reached out for the kitten. "Come to Pappy." Sitting cross-legged she took charge of the kitten, dipping a corner of her tee shirt into the mixture then stuffing it into the kitten's mouth.

"You're going to choke it," Brittany cried.

"Oh, hold your water." Pappy pressed the tee shirt corner a little deeper into the kitten's mouth and it began to suck.

•••

A man in worn, lace-less running shoes, tongues lapping, sat on a concrete bench. His back was resting against the concrete table, arms spread, feet propped on a big roller bag. The bill of his cap was pulled low over his brow. He might have been sleeping. It was late. Most of the homeless men and women camping in Santa Rita Park had already settled into their nests of accumulated debris.

A small figure slipping by not 30 feet from where he sat, drew the man's attention. Last night, and the night before that, he'd watched the boy crawl beneath an oleander hedge like some little animal. He could easily imagine the boy's terror as he hid there in the dirt. Yes, he knew exactly what it was like to hide, fear banging around his ribcage like a trapped squirrel. Used to be that the fear got so bad sometimes he thought he might die from it. Eventually, he'd found ways to manage it.

Tonight, the man had brought a Coke, an orange and little bag of cookies, things that wouldn't spoil in the heat. Later, he would set them down by the hedge, not too close to the boy. He didn't want to scare him.

•••

Gripping the cool dirt that surrounded him in his small brown fists, the boy awoke with a start. So, this is what it is to be dead, he thought and closed his eyes again. His stomach rumbled. All his life he'd heard tales of hungry ghosts. Was he one of those now? Moments later the boy was roused by rain sifting through his hiding place beneath a hedge covered in white blossoms. If he could feel rain, he must not be dead yet.

After several minutes, the rain that he remembered was not rain, ceased. It struck him as strange to water dead grass, but there were so many strange things in this country. Inhaling the fragrance of the dampened blossoms, he peered out from beneath the hedge. The people gathered in their makeshift shelters were no more than humps in the grass. Some were harmless, some not.

It must have been well after midnight, though it was hard to tell. It was never totally dark, not like it was in his town, where at night you could not see the path to the latrine, but had to feel its worn surface with the soles of your feet. No, he knew how to move in the dark; it was in the light of day that he had trouble navigating.

During the day, he always kept a close eye on the comings and goings of those around him, appraising. An opportunity to perform some heroic deed would be best. He'd heard that if you saved a life, the authorities might show mercy. Every day he looked for such a chance; pulling a mother and child from a burning car would be good, but so far, no such opportunity had presented itself.

Walking toward his hiding place was a familiar figure, nothing more than a tall silhouette against the opaque sky. The only one still about, he pulled a large suitcase on wheels. It must hold many possessions, the boy supposed, because the man struggled to maneuver it across the uneven ground. When he passed the hedge, he placed a paper bag on the ground.

The boy did not move. He had learned not to trust men who gave him gifts. Nothing was free. The boy waited until the man was out of sight to retrieve the bag. Inside was an orange, a Coke and a packet of cookies. He ate the orange and the cookies immediately. The Coke he'd save for later.

It wasn't long before the man returned, now pushing the cart easily across the grass. When he was gone, the boy crawled out from beneath the hedge. Despite the water, the grass was brittle beneath his feet as he tightly laced the shoes that were two sizes too big. The sky was beginning to lighten and he needed to hurry to find his next meal, the one he would eat while drinking the Coke.

CHAPTER 2

A Modern Mother at Work

Monday, May 28

It was still mostly dark outside as Marie nursed the baby, rocking back and forth and humming an old Beatles tune. She was an alto with a mellow vibrato, a surprisingly beautiful voice coming from such a plain, broad face. In fact, Marie was broad at all points, shoulders, waist, hips equally broad, and she was tall. A boy she had a crush on in high school once likened her to a walking refrigerator.

Her mother, who was still pretty and petite at age 70, claimed that Marie took after her father. According to her mother, he'd been a big, good looking devil. But Marie was just large, thick and plain as an adobe brick.

They'd separated before she was born. Marie always wondered if he had run off with another woman. That's what she would have done, had she been married to her mother.

Marie could hear Nick shuffling around in the kitchen. She gazed down at the baby. A hefty 8 pounds 10 ounces at birth, Nichole was big and sweet like her namesake, who was also built like a refrigerator. The other babies had been small. Francis barely weighted 5 pounds. Catherine, Claire and Mary Ann each weighed in at less than 6 pounds, Teresa just over. The girls, at least, had been cranky for months. She often wondered what kind of a baby Francis had been, what kind of a child? Now a man, would he resemble her?

Marie switched Nichole to her left breast, then peered out the French doors that led to a little patio and a hot tub, the scene of the last conception. Smiling, she recalled that night. A July monsoon had ripped through town, sending the temperature plummeting to a cool 68 degrees. The storm was moving on, lightning still pulsed in the distance, the wind had calmed and the rain had gentled. Sleepless, they had slipped out to the hot tub with half a bottle of Chardonnay that had been in the fridge for weeks, the cold wine on their tongues, the cold rain on their shoulders.

She smiled down at Nichole, sucking hard on her nipple. Apparently, hot, chlorinated water was not an effective spermicide.

Over the stucco wall, the Tucson Mountains were silhouetted against the mauve, predawn sky. Though she was still exhausted most of the time, this early morning feeding was the sweetest time of day.

"Hey Jude," she sang. "Don't be afraid. Take a sad song and make it be-e-e-ter." In high school, she had been actively recruited for the choir. Now singing her babies asleep and "Happy Birthday" were all she had the heart for.

Marie closed her eyes. When she opened them, the rising sun was turning the mountains to copper. She looked down at her now slumbering babe, pale eyelids traced with delicate blue veins. She stroked the head, which was covered with pale fuzz, lightly circling the fontanelle with her index finger. Yes. Nichole was the easiest baby. If fed and dry, she would stare into the face of whoever was holding her with placid interest, then fall into the dreamless sleep of the innocent, or if she did dream, it could only be of warm and tender arms and her mother's milk. At seven weeks, that was all she knew.

"Dear lord," Marie prayed, "Please don't let her grow up to look like me."

The teakettle whistled. Soon Nick, her true sweetheart and soul mate, would have the oatmeal on the table. Sighing, she slipped her little finger into Nichole's perfect mouth, popping the strong suction, and eased herself out of the rocker.

•••

The entire complicated apparatus fit inside the capacious bra she'd purchased to house it. Pricey, but well-engineered, the device came with a small battery pack, charger, two pumps, two flex tubes, milk bags, cleaning brushes and customized flanges that all fit neatly into a flowered plastic carrying case when not in use. Periodically, Detective Marie Stransky would hear a faint hum, then feel the machine draw the milk from her breasts. She'd been testing it out for the past week and now that she was used to it, the tugging sensation was reassuring, although it did make her feel like a Guernsey.

She checked the app on her Apple watch. One point two ounces, it read for the left breast. One point five for the right. The two bags that captured her milk were also contained within her bra. Each held 4 ounces, and they were supposed to be spill-proof. When the right bag was full her watch would chime. So far so good, she thought, as she logged onto the computer.

Every morning, there were the activity and call logs from the night before to go over as well as reports on current investigations to review. There had been a recent rash of drive-by shootings, a motorcycle cop from neighboring Marana had been deliberately run over and was in critical condition, but there was nothing there that particularly concerned her.

Marie looked at her watch. Not yet 7 a.m. She had time to ease into the day. The butt of her Glock 18 resting in the pancake holster positioned just to the back of her hip was jabbing painfully into the baby fat that lapped over her belt. She'd gained 44 pounds with Nichole and still had 38 to lose. How was that even possible when the baby had weighed 8 pounds 10 ounces at birth?

Despite her chronic fatigue, a gun butt poking into her waist was a great motivator to get out to the gym Nick had set up in the garage. Every day she promised herself that she would start working out again; every evening she found a dozen good reasons why she could not.

She adjusted her belt, set the alarm on her watch for 15 minutes then Googled *puppies*.

Minutes later, Officer Torrance Stedman leaned in, filling the entrance to her cubical with his dark mass. "Morning, Marie. My, my, already hard at work I see."

Startled, Marie quickly closed the YouTube video of a little lab puppy fending off a rubber ducky. "Morning yourself, Torrance."

Stedman took a tissue from a box on Marie's desk and started to polish his glasses. They had sturdy black frames and lent his round face a scholarly aspect.

"And how are the girls?" Marie asked, referring to Stedman's daughter and granddaughter.

"Good. And you and yours?"

"Everybody's fine, thanks, just a little overwhelmed with the new baby and all. So, what brings you in so early?"

"You mean what brings me in so late."

"Up all night? Poor you."

Ignoring the sarcasm, he replaced his glasses. "Anyway, I was just about to go off duty when I heard a call on a homicide victim, female, found in Santa Rita Park."

"Oh yeah?"

"They're taping the scene right now. I thought I'd stop by and have a look before I go home. Figured you'd be on it." Stedman glanced around the cubicle. "What's that humming noise?"

Grabbing her briefcase, Marie looked at him blankly. "What humming noise?"

•••

Marie started to sweat the moment she closed the door of the patrol car. "Crank up that AC, Torrance." As Marie waited for the air to blow cold, she considered her old friend. They'd been partners, she and Torrance, until he was busted back to patrol for failure to obtain a search warrant.

Thing was, Torrance firmly believed that in certain circumstances rules were best ignored and one's sense of right and wrong and the risk to civilians needed to be factored first into actions taken. What he did not factor in was his own personal interest. Had he done that, he'd have waited for the search warrant. Sure, he'd still be a detective, but a woman and her kids would probably be dead.

Marie knew the inquiry was all so much bullshit, born mainly out of Lieutenant Carl Lindgrin's very thin white skin. Lindgrin, who headed the homicide unit, had been a fairly competent cop, but was a miserable human being who seemed to derive pleasure from making others miserable as well. She'd always wondered how he was chosen to head the unit. They say cream rises to the top. Well, so does sewer gas.

When Torrance was demoted, she'd done what she could to support him, which hadn't been much given that she'd been pregnant with number three and was going through her own little hell at the hands of Lindgrin.

Twenty-second Street was clogged with morning traffic and the June air was brown with exhaust and dust as Stedman and Marie plodded across the stiff grass toward a bleacher where a knot of police officers stood around a rectangle of yellow tape. Though it was still early, their dark clothes absorbed the sun and perspiration dotted their brows. Wearing a crisp, specially tailored, torso hugging shirt that was popular among the young and the fit, the crime scene technician, Officer Audrey Wallace, was bagging assorted plastic water bottles, Styrofoam clamshells and Big Gulps that were piled up around the overflowing trash barrel. Undaunted by the heat, she waved cheerily at the two newcomers then stuffed a stiff terrycloth wash rag smeared with something that might be feces into its own paper bag. Not far from the barrel was an enormous hedge of oleanders covered in white blossoms, their sweet aroma competing with the stench of garbage and urine.

Marie smiled as the officer lifted up the yellow tape so they could enter the crime scene. "Hey, Freddy, what's up?"

"Same old, same old." Sergeant Freddy Felix, clipboard in hand, checked his watch then added their names to the list of arrivals at the crime scene. "All we need now is the gal with the gurney."

Stedman followed Marie under the tape and the two stepped closer to the body. It was wrapped in a beach towel and lay in the blessed shade beneath the bleacher.

"Any witnesses?"

Felix shrugged. "One of those Vets on Patrol called it in. He looked down at the clipboard. "Oliver Kemp, but he said he didn't see or hear anything peculiar. I told him to wait over there." He nodded toward a group of onlookers standing in the shade of an Aleppo pine.

Stedman pressed his lips together. Veterans on Patrol, also known as the VOP, had established a military style tent camp for homeless vets on the north side of the park and took it upon themselves to patrol the area, which was a hangout for drug users and dealers as well as the homeless. Armed, the patrols also scoured the outlying desert and the washes in search of vets who might be in need. Stedman wasn't opposed to them, but as a vet who'd seen action in Iraq himself, he was skeptical. Maybe they did some good, but it seemed to him that they were mostly just a bunch of poorly adjusted dudes in camouflage trying to recapture the adrenalin high of their glory days.

"And what about those other folks?" Stedman tossed his head in the direction of the pine. "Anybody step forward?"

"You know how it is. Everybody wants to know; nobody wants to tell." Sergeant Felix's stomach growled loudly. "Sorry. I was about to take my dinner break when the call came in."

Marie reached into her briefcase and pulled out a box of apple juice and a packet of peanut butter crackers.

"Oh. I really don't ..."

"Take them," Marie directed.

"Well, thanks." The sergeant ripped open the cellophane and popped a cracker into his mouth.

Marie walked around the towel-wrapped body, viewing it from all angles, then extracted two pairs of latex gloves from her briefcase. She handed one pair to Stedman then tugged on the other, careful not to catch it on the elaborate wedding set that sparkled incongruently on the blunt ring finger of her left hand.

"Let's see what we've got," she said, kneeling beside the body. Marie sat on her haunches then gently pulled back the towel, on which a large pink flamingo stood on one leg beneath a palm tree.

Most obvious was the wide ligature-type mark on the victim's throat. A trickle of dried blood ran from her nose down the side of her cheek. She wore a tie-dye tank top that was scrunched up on one side exposing a small, pale breast. The distressed denim stretch-jeans she wore were unzipped. A leather thong sandal was on her right foot. The other sandal, its strap broken, lay next to the body. Beneath a thick layer of foundation, Marie noted a trace of adolescent acne across the forehead and in the hollows of her cheeks. Her brows had been plucked into painfully thin arches. The girl's rich brown hair was pulled into a ponytail.

Resisting the urge to pull the tank top down over the breast, Marie turned the head slightly, noting resistance. "Rigor in the face and the neck," she observed, then moved on to the ligature mark extended around the base of the skull. She imagined the killer had used something handy, perhaps his belt.

Stedman's glasses skidded down his nose. He pushed them back in place with a knuckle, then eased his bulk down beside Marie. With a gloved hand he picked up the girl's right arm. It was still flaccid. On the underside of the wrist was a small, round burn. "See that?"

Marie nodded.

Stedman eased the arm back down. "Looks like she hasn't been dead that long."

"Less than 10 hours anyway." Marie looked at her watch. "It's exactly 7:23 now, so that would put the time of death no later than midnight. We'll know better after the medical examiner gets the internal body temp."

He took a notebook from his shirt pocket and jotted the time down. "Fucking hot out here and it's not even 8 o'clock yet."

Marie tapped her watch. "Says it's 93 at the airport."

Stedman wrote that down too. "Hey, is that an Apple Smartwatch?"

"Yeah. Nick gave it to me for my birthday. You should get one."

"Nice, but not my style."

"Too techie for the old dinosaur?"

He shrugged. It was true. He didn't take to technology, didn't fight it, but when he could avoid it, he did. Much to the amusement of his granddaughter, he still had a flip phone.

"You still seeing Abby?"

"Yup."

She nodded. Since Torrance had met Abby on a case, Marie didn't quite approve of their relationship, and he knew it. It was clearly not up for discussion, she figured, as she scanned the body. Noting the chipped neon orange polish covering the woman's finger and toenails, she sighed. "How old do you think?"

"Could be 15, could be 25," he said. "If she's homeless, she hasn't been for long, not with skin like that."

"Notice anything else?"

"Yeah, her pants are on inside out."

"You know what I'm thinking?"

"You're thinking she was dumped."

"That and …"

"You're thinking it's a pretty fucked up world we live in."

"Yeah and…"

"You're thinking he's back."

A breeze had started up and Marie drew the towel back over the girl to keep hair and fiber evidence from blowing away.

Stedman lumbered to his feet then held out his hand.

"Thanks, Torrance," Marie said, allowing herself an assist. "I've got to get back into shape."

"You and me both," he said, scanning the ground for drag marks. There were none that he could see. The girl was slight of build, the dry grass unyielding.

"Where's all her stuff, I wonder?" Marie scanned the area looking for a purse or a backpack. "Officer Wallace," she called to the crime scene tech. "Sorry to ask in this heat, but would you look through those other garbage cans as well?" She swept her arm in a broad arc to include the cans that were well beyond the immediate crime scene. "We're looking for a purse, or a backpack maybe."

"No problem," the young woman said and jogged away.

Shaking her head, Marie pulled off her gloves then approached the crowd. The vet immediately peeled off from the others. He was a tall, rangy man in his mid-forties wearing head to toe camouflage complete with sidearm. By his ruddy complexion and conspicuous absence of teeth, it was apparent that he was no stranger to homelessness himself.

"Detective Marie Stransky," she said, extending her hand. "And this is Officer Torrance Stedman."

"Oliver Kemp, ma'am, Veterans of Patrol." He shook her hand then the hand of Stedman. "One of us vets is here on site 24-7-365."

"Hmm, think of that." She tapped the record function on her watch. "Did you know the victim, Mr. Kemp?"

"Never seen her around here before." He squinted into the sun. "That is before I found the … victim."

"And what time was that?"

"Approximately 0630 hours, just as I was finishing my patrol. After determining that the victim was deceased I…"

Marie's eyebrows shot up. "You touched the body?"

"Just to see if it was … ah … warm or cold. I didn't disturb it or nothing." He pulled back his shoulders a bit. "As a vet, I'm no stranger to death. Anyway, she wasn't there when I surveilled the area at approximately 0130 hours, so I guess …"

"I see." She took out two water bottles from her briefcase. "Man, it's hot," she said, handing one to Kemp. She waited until he took a swig from the bottle. "Would you spell your name for me, sir?"

While Marie recorded Kemp's account, Stedman looked over the crowd. They were mostly men. One angular fellow, hair stiff with dirt and dried sweat, lounged against a conveyance, sort of like a dolly with makeshift wooden sides. It was stuffed to the brim with plastic garbage bags. So much stuff, Stedman thought. He wondered what each bag might contain and how the man determined what items he could not live without. Guy's probably mental, he supposed, lugging around a lot of junk that was worthless, but somehow essential.

Officer Wallace waved from the farthest garbage can then jogged back to the crime scene, holding her prize in a gloved hand, a small pink, kitty-shaped bag.

Gratified to see the sweat darkening the woman's armpits, and shirt back, Marie handed her a bottle of water. "It's not cold, but it's wet."

The officer drank while Marie pulled on clean gloves then unzipped the bag. Inside was the implement of the tortured brows, a tube of foundation, mascara, eyebrow pencil and liner, lipstick, a tampon, three twenties and a five rolled into a tube, assorted change and a little bracelet – a series of plump hearts dangling from a silver chain. It was broken. Marie opened the lipstick. A bright red, it was well used. She dropped it back into the kitty bag then handed it back to the officer.

Just as Stedman and Marie were about to go back to the patrol car, Meg Gupta from the Pima County medical examiner's office was muscling a collapsed gurney across the grass. She gave them a cheery smile, displaying a mouthful of lovely white teeth. "But it's a dry heat," she said in the clipped English of a Mumbai import. "Don't you just love it?"

Marie flapped her jacket a bit. "Not so much, Meg." She pulled a zip-lock bag from her briefcase. Inside was an empty plastic water bottle.

"What's that?" Stedman asked.

"Kemp's DNA. Turns out, the guy's a litterbug."

"I'm guessing Kemp's not our guy, but you never know."

"Not until you do, anyway." She wrote the vet's name on the bag with a Sharpie and handed it to Gupta. "Please give this to Officer Wallace."

"Sure. Probably see you later then."

Later would be at the medical examiner's office where Marie would observe while a forensic pathologist disassembled the body from sum to parts.

•••

Stedman cranked up the AC, while Marie stood in the shade of a pine. When the hot air blew cold he gave Marie the thumbs up and she climbed in then adjusted the vent so that the air hit her face, wiping her sweat-drenched bangs back from her forehead. This morning she had carefully blown her hair dry then used a curling iron to give it a little umph. She probed an inside pocket of her briefcase and pulled out a couple of bobby pins. "So, by Kemp's account the victim was dumped sometime between 1:30 and 6:30 this morning," she said, pinning her hair back from her face. "My guess is that shortly after death, she was dragged, probably into a car."

"Or possibly out of a car."

"Or both, then somehow transported to the bleachers. But, here's the big question. Why …"

"Did he put her jeans back on her."

"Exactly." Marie extracted two more bottles of water from her briefcase and handed one to Stedman. "Could be he thought a clothed body would be less conspicuous than a naked one."

Stedman twisted the cap off the bottle. "Yeah, it wouldn't seem strange to see someone lying under the bleacher wrapped in a beach towel, at least not at Santa Rita Park. Still, I fail to see the advantage, given the time and trouble it would take to dress a corpse." He paused to take a swig of water. "Maybe he had some weird concern for her modesty."

"Somehow that's really disturbing." Marie gulped down half the bottle of water then wiped her mouth on the back of her hand. "Well, we'll see what Ramona has to say, but it sure looks like he's back."

"So, you want me to drop you off at the ME's office or back at the station?"

"The station. I left my lunch there. It's seems counterintuitive, but I learned long ago not to go to an autopsy on an empty stomach."

Stedman nodded, then cocked his head. "There it is again."

"There's what again?"

"That humming."

"I don't hear anything," Marie said, straight-faced. "You know, Torrance, maybe you need to get your hearing tested."

•••

The smell of overheated coffee pervaded the break room as Marie examined the sad contents of her lunchbox. In support of her weight loss campaign, Nick had provided 6 ounces of nonfat strawberry yogurt to dip her sliced apple in and one hard-boiled egg, no salt.

She set the items on a paper towel and sighed. Just as she began to peel the egg, Ed Johnson, a recent transfer from the burglary unit, charged into the room, bringing with him the unmistakable aroma of a Reuben sandwich. He grunted in her direction before diving in to his sandwich. Marie acknowledge him with a wave of her hand then closed her eyes. After a moment, she packed the yogurt, the apple slices and the egg back into her lunchbox. Though she didn't have much use for the new homicide detective, it wasn't Ed, but the smell of the Reuben sandwich that drove her from the room. Before exiting, she snatched the salt container from the counter. "Need this, Ed?"

"No, go right ahead."

"Thanks," she said, and dropped it into her lunchbox.

By the time Marie had eaten and replaced the full bags in her breast pump with empties, the sheet-wrapped body was already waiting its turn outside the autopsy room.

Dr. Ramona Antone pushed through the swinging doors. She was in her mid-forties with a heavy coil of blue-black hair secured to the back of her head with a large plastic clamp. Born out in Sells on the O'odham reservation, the doctor had studied forensic medicine at the university then stayed on in Tucson despite the traffic she claimed to hate.

The doctor smiled when she saw her. "Hey, Marie. It's been awhile." She was both taller and broader than Marie, yet she sailed across the room like the only cloud in a wide blue sky. "So, what did you end up naming the newbie?"

Marie returned the woman's smile. "Nichole."

"Nice. And how are you feeling?"

"Exhausted."

She nodded her sympathy. "Ah, yes. I can identify." She pointed her chin at the body on the metal gurney. "So, this one's yours?"

"Yup."

"Okay." She glanced at her watch. "I hate to rush, but its nearly 2. When humanly possible, I like to be on the road no later than 4, otherwise crosstown traffic is a bitch."

The autopsy room, though well ventilated, sometimes smelled of vomit, or fecal matter or more subtly of charred bone and blood. But mercifully this afternoon, all Marie could discern was the sharp order of antiseptic. She settled her hips against a counter and took a deep breath.

Slowly, Dr. Antone unwrapped the sheet and the beach towel, then began circling the body. "Chart says the rectal body temperature taken in situ at 0842 was 31.3 degrees centigrade."

Marie did a quick mental calculation, subtracting 31 from 37, the normal body temperature, then dividing by 1.5, the amount of heat lost per hour. "That would put the time of death at about 4 a.m., but given the degree of rigor ..."

"What was the ambient temperature when the rectal temp was taken?"

"Oh yeah. It was 90 at least."

"So, the body would have stopped cooling at some point. May have even started to warm back up. I'll get a better internal temperature, but in this heat even that's not going to be much help determining time of death." She raised the victim's right arm, tried to flex the elbow. Complete rigor.

Marie checked her watch. "It's 1:52 now, so that puts the time of death somewhere between 11 pm and 2 am.

"Broadly."

"Well, it makes better sense. The guy who discovered the body, one of those Veterans on Patrol, said it wasn't there when he canvassed the area at 1:30."

"Hey, Marie. Did you notice the little red dots on the forehead and eyelids?"

Marie stepped closer to the body.

"Petechiae, they're called – broken capillaries. In the case of strangulation like this, they appear on the forehead, cheek, eyelids." She continued the external examination. "Okay. And these bruises on the torso just below the armpits. I'd say she was dragged." Head cocked to one side, the woman studied the bruises for another moment. Head cocked to the other, she squinted at the rivulet of dried blood running from the nose. Carefully, she measured the width of the band around the girl's neck. Carefully, she checked the girl's hands, noting the burn on the inside of the right wrist. Carefully, gently, she scraped beneath each chipped orange fingernail, depositing the debris in a small plastic bag. "Her pants are inside out."

"I noticed."

"By the way, I baked brownies yesterday. They're in the coffee room, if you want some."

"I'm on a diet."

"Yeah. The battle of the baby fat," Dr. Antone said, as she slowly peeled off the jeans. "No unders." She removed the rest of the girl's clothing with great care, placing it in a large plastic evidence bag. The sheet and the flamingo towel went into separate bags so they could be examined for fibers and hairs not belonging to the victim. Dr. Antone took a moment to record her observations on the computer then examined the vaginal and anal cavities, taking swabs from each.

"Well?"

"No blood, no tearing, no apparent semen," she said and went to get the tools she would need for the internal examination.

Before the doctor began the autopsy, Marie suspended any notion that the body on the gurney was a once lithe and living creature, somebody's daughter, somebody's friend – a skill honed by painful experience.

An hour later, the victim's skull had been flipped back and the brain removed weighed and sampled, the internal organs had also been removed and weighed, and fluid samples had been taken from the heart, liver and bladder. An assistant was called to reassemble the parts into a semblance of the whole.

Marie hurried out before this last phase began. At the front entrance, she turned on her heel and went back to the coffee room, where she grabbed two brownies. They were gone before she got back to the Ford Explorer.

CHAPTER 3

There But for God's Grace

Wednesday, June 9

As directed by her Smart Watch, Marie Stransky took the Valencia exit off of I-19 and continued west toward the Santa Cruz River, which once flowed south into Sonora, Mexico. Except during the wettest storms of the summer monsoon, this section of the river was dry, had been for over 70 years.

Two days ago, a group of Veterans on Patrol discovered an abandoned camp and concluded that it had been used by sex traffickers to exploit children. Immediately, they posted the claim on Facebook along with a video of the site that went viral. Already the Tucson Police Department had reports that extremist militia types armed with AR-15 rifles had begun to assemble in Tucson, ostensibly to rout out the Mexican cartel responsible.

This type of crime was not her priority, but here she was. It had been one of the hottest Mays on record and now June was promising to be another record breaker. The temperature reading on her dash was already 98 degrees, and bushwhacking through a mesquite *bosque* was not how Marie wanted to spend the morning. She wondered if at this very moment, Carl Lindgrin was sitting on his wide butt in his air-conditioned office laughing.

As usual she was the last to arrive. She spotted Torrance, also on Lindgrin's shit list, hunkered beneath a scraggly mesquite with Sergeant Oscar Gutierrez and the crime tech, Officer Audrey Wallace, her uniform, as ever, well-pressed. Stedman waved as she hauled herself out of the Ford Explorer. She took off her jacket, folded it neatly in half and placed it on the seat.

Marie was wearing one of her maternity blouses. It had long sleeves, and was made of some kind of stiff, wrinkle resistant material that she managed to wrinkle nonetheless. Feeling dowdy and unkempt, she smoothed it out as best she could and plodded toward the mesquite. With every step, her badge, hanging from a lanyard around her neck, tapped on her chest like an accusatory finger. She slung it over her shoulder.

"Morning, Marie," Stedman said. "How you doing?"

"Could be cooler." She pulled a hat from her briefcase and shoved it on her head. A wide brimmed canvas affair with a flap that protected the back of her neck, it made her look like a dowager on safari. She nodded in the direction of the two officers. "Morning, guys."

Stedman pointed vaguely toward the river. "They've already located the camp."

"That's a relief. So, we'll just follow them."

They started out, Gutierrez in the lead and Marie bringing up the rear. In less than a minute, her sleeve snagged on a catclaw. Pesky desert shrubs, they were everywhere. She struggled to unhook herself from the aptly named plant, leaving a small rent in the fabric. Six paces later, another catclaw snatched the hat off her head She disengaged it then stuffed the hat back into her briefcase. As she hurried to catch up, she was snagged once again, this time by the hair. "Ouch, damn it!" She fiddled with her hair, but the more she fiddled, the more entangled it got. Finally, she took out the bobby pins that kept it out of her eyes and teased the strands out of the catclaw. When she was finally free, the rest of the group were nowhere to be seen. "Hey," she yelled. "Hey, wait for me."

"Over here," Stedman responded.

Over where, she thought. As she proceeded toward the river, she grazed the leg of her pants on a prickly pear cactus. It occurred to her then that she was tromping through prime rattlesnake habitat. Reflexively she palmed the butt of her Glock 10 resting in the holster on the belt beneath her blouse alongside her radio and two extra magazines of ammunition.

Rattlers were masters of camouflage. She studied the ground. Even if she saw one she wouldn't fire her weapon. At the sound of a gunshot, Torrance would come busting out of the brush like a charging rhino —she'd seen him do it—and nobody, especially Torrance, should have to move that fast in this heat.

After several minutes of rising panic, she saw them. The camp was set up under a canopy of mesquite trees just above the riverbank where it would not likely be inundated by a flash flood. Wallace was snapping pictures of the conglomeration of trash fashioned into furnishings. There was a torn blanket, a stiff and yellowed porn magazine and an assortment of cans, mostly beer, tuna, chili and stewed tomatoes – someone had a fondness for anchovies. Leaning against the trunk of a mesquite was a makeshift kitchen. There was even a latrine complete with toilet seat. Wallace lifted the lid and snapped a picture down into the pit.

The most unusual amenity was a plastic septic tank. Turned on its side, half-buried in the sandy soil and covered with a tarp, Marie presumed it was shelter from the heat and the rains yet to come. There were a few plastic toys and a pair of children's shoes, which was troubling but not so unusual. Homeless women sometimes had children with them. Canvas straps had been fastened to the trees and that gave her pause. Pushing the sweaty hair back from her face she asked no one in particular, "What do you make of these?"

"The VOP thought they were restraints," Stedman offered. "More likely something to hang gear from. That would be my guess, anyway. I imagine javelinas, coyotes and pack rats would make short work of anything left on the ground, not to mention the ants." He pointed to a line of harvester ants hauling bits of debris back to their nest.

Wallace snapped several pictures of the straps and the children's shoes.

Marie pulled a bottle of water from her briefcase. "Water anyone?"

"Please," Wallace said, reaching for the bottle.

"Anyone else? No?" Marie took an already half-empty bottle from her briefcase and drank deeply.

"Looks like this camp's been abandoned for a while."

Wallace began to collect material from the ground around those straps and inside the septic tank. Marie, who did not like standing around while others worked, put on a pair of gloves, untied the canvas straps and dropped them into an evidence bag. The towel and the children's shoes went into separate bags. When she bent over to collect the beer cans, she heard the hum of her breast pump and felt the familiar tug. Suddenly, she was light-headed and allowed herself to sink quietly to the ground.

"Are you okay, Detective?" Wallace asked.

"Fine," Marie responded. "Just taking a little break. She sucked her water bottle dry and opened a fresh one. "Be sure to drink your water, Wallace. You don't want to get dehydrated."

Sighing deeply, Marie took the needle-nose pliers from her briefcase and began to pluck the prickly pear's tiny spines from her pant leg. She'd salvaged those pliers from a jewelry making kit that had once belonged to Catherine for the exact purpose of plucking spines out of things: dog paws, fingers, butts—she had backed into a prickly pear more than once—and pant legs.

Marie scanned the area from her ground-level perspective. Squalid, to be sure, but she didn't see any used condoms or drug paraphernalia. The porn magazine was of the adult variety and relatively tame. "We'll see what the crime lab comes up with, but I don't see much evidence of criminal activity. Torrance, what do you think?"

Stedman shook his head. "I think this is a hell of a way to live," he said, but was thinking, *There but for God's grace go I.*

CHAPTER 4

A Mother Knows

Wednesday, June 9

By the time Marie got back to headquarters it was past noon. The activity and call logs from last night still waited as did the reports on current investigations, and she needed to fill out an incident report. They can wait a little longer, she thought, and took out her cell phone.

It took half a dozen rings for Nick to answer. "It's me," she said.

"Hi, me."

"So, how's it going?"

"Got Catherine up and off to horse camp without any grumbling. I think she might be in love."

"With a horse or what?"

"Hmm. I didn't think to ask, but she was pretty enthusiastic for Catherine. Claire's spending the morning at the library with Chutney and her mom."

Marie chuckled. "Chelsey?"

"That's the one. Ronda has a cold, so Mary Ann is home today. At the moment she and Teresa … hold on a sec."

While Marie waited, she scrolled through last night's call logs. Other than the homicide at Santa Rita Park, there was nothing of particular interest to her.

"They're watching Mr. Rogers reruns. And Nichole is right here. Want to say hi?"

"Hi, sweet pea. Mama misses you. Tell Daddy I'll bring home dinner and I love him bunches," she said and hung up.

Marie went to the unsolved homicide file to revisit the two homeless women who were murdered last summer. The bodies were found on July 12 and August 4. One was discovered in an alley beneath an old carpet, the other in back of Llantera Gomez, which sold used tires. Both locations were within less than a mile radius of Santa Rita Park. Both women had ligature marks circling their necks, both had anal penetration, both had a single cigarette burn on the inside of the right wrist, and both had fentanyl in their bloodstreams. Neither was ever identified. She closed the file.

And now another. She applied her rule: Two homicides with similar MOs might be coincidence; three meant serial killings. Where had the killer been? Like a reverse snowbird, he seemed to prefer summer in Tucson to winter. And those burns to the wrist, what did they say about him? Well, for the moment, there was nothing to do but wait for the coroner's report.

Marie took a banana from her briefcase and turned her attention to current investigations. One in particular stood out. Over the weekend, a man sweeping the arroyos with a metal detector had found the partly decomposed remains of a woman in Julian Wash on the southwest edge of Barrio Viejo. Cause of death, a gunshot to the back. She peeled the banana as she looked at the pictures taken at the scene. The victim, who appeared to be Hispanic, was lying face-down, long dark hair spilling over the sand. From the extensive damage to the woman's torso, Marie figured her assailant had used a large caliber weapon. She took a bite of the banana and scrolled to another picture. The woman was wearing one of those blouses with the peekaboo cutouts at the shoulders, short shorts and high-wedged heels, not the kind of shoes you'd wear to stroll down a sandy wash.

She was about to dismiss it as a gang related killing and not one of her priorities when she scrolled to a close-up shot of a small tattoo peeking through the cutout on the victim's blouse. It was a unicorn inside a heart. A gangbanger would not likely sport such a tattoo.

The woman had yet to be identified. Marie's throat constricted painfully as she pictured a mother wondering what had become of her little girl. Quickly, she read through the description of the body, then scanned missing person reports from the past two weeks. One stood out as a possibility. Xochitl Salcedo, a 17-year-old Mexican American. Her mother, Gloria Salcedo, had reported her missing 10 days ago. The girl had left her home in the afternoon for the El Rio Library where she was a summer intern and never returned. There was no mention of a tattoo and Marie wondered how the girl had managed to keep it hidden from her mother.

Putting her banana aside, Marie took a screenshot of the tattoo, printed it out along with the least gruesome photograph then headed for the office of Carl Lindgrin.

The lieutenant, steel gray hair was slicked back with what looked to be Gorilla Snot. On his desk was a framed photo of himself with the governor, and a toppled stack of manila folders. Lindgrin, it seemed, was always at his desk, which might explain his disagreeable nature. He didn't look up when Marie knocked on the open door.

"What is it, Stransky?"

"Afternoon, Carl."

"What is it, Stransky?"

"So, I was just looking through outstanding investigations and this one caught my eye." She placed the photos before him. "Anyway, I took a moment to go through missing persons and I think we may have a possible match."

"Oh yeah?" Lindgrin pushed back his chair. "And you want to check it out."

"That's what I was thinking."

"Not your priority, Stransky."

"Has the case been assigned?"

"No, but ..."

"At the moment, I'm waiting on a coroner report so I have the time to show these to the person, the possible mom of the victim, who filed the report." Marie didn't want to appear too eager. From experience, she knew that if she revealed what she really wanted to do, he'd do his best to keep her from doing it.

Lindgrin looked her up and down, his lips pulled into a little smirk. "Haven't you got enough on your plate?"

It took Stransky a moment to realize he wasn't talking about her caseload. "Pardon me?"

"How long has it been?"

"Since when?" She wasn't going to make this easy for him.

"Don't go stupid on me, Stransky. Since the last baby, what is it, number 17?"

"Number five and it's been seven weeks."

"That long. Well, with the extra weight you're still packing, I'd like to see you run 300 yards let alone a mile and a half."

He was referring to the part of the police academy fitness test that all cadets had to pass. Lindgrin had a pretty good muffin top going for him and she doubted that he could pass it himself. She started to point that out, but long ago she'd learned to keep to the script. "Point taken," she said without batting an eye. "Now, what about the girl?"

He swiveled his helmet head around the room then surveyed the ceiling? "What's that humming noise?"

"Sounds like one of the neon lights is about to go out," she said pointing to the ceiling. "So, the girl?"

He waved his hand as if shooing a fly. "Probably just some Mexican gangbanger's bitch who cheated on her *vato*, but if that rings your chimes be my guest."

Since she'd gotten what she wanted, she quickly scooped up the photos then left the office. She'd been bullied by a pro. By comparison, Lindgrin was an amateur.

•••

Marie pulled the black Ford Explorer into the shade of a mesquite tree. Why the hell did the TPD always buy black cars? It was murder in the summer. For a moment, she studied the house where the missing Xochitl Salcedo most likely spent her last night. One of the many modest adobes typical of Barrio Hollywood, it was painted a fleshy tan that mimicked the color of the packed dirt that comprised the front yard, a simple brick shrine harboring the Virgin of Guadalupe the only adornment. Off to the side of the house was an old Tuff Shed, its door slouching off the hinge. Marie's Spanish was limited, at best, and she hoped Señora Salcedo spoke English. Sighing, she got out of the car.

As Marie made her way across the yard, the only sound was the wet soughing and rattle of the swamp cooler on the roof. Reflexively, she made the sign of the cross as she passed the shrine. Though she had made dozens of next of kin notifications, they never got any easier. Taking a deep breath, she knocked on the screen door.

It took a few moments before Gloria Salcedo opened the door.

"*Buenas tardes, Señora.* I'm detective Marie Stransky." She held out the badge on its lanyard so the woman could see it. "I'd like to speak to the mother of Xochitl Salcedo."

At the mention of her daughter's name, the woman collapsed.

•••

"Take your time, Mrs. Salcedo." Marie handed the woman a bottle of water from her briefcase, then slipped the photos back into the manila envelope.

Gloria Salcedo took a sip of water then a great shuddering breath. "I knew she was dead. My friends kept telling me, 'Don't worry; she's run off to Mexico with her boyfriend. She'll be back,' they said. But a mother knows. Xochitl was a good girl. She'd never do anything like that." The woman paused to sweep the tears from her face. "A mother knows. A mother always knows."

"Can you tell me the name of her boyfriend?"

"Jorgé Montenegro. He wanted to marry Xochitl, but her father and I said no. 'You're too young,' we told her. Plus, we didn't really trust the boy, a little macho type up from Hermosillo, or thereabouts, who thought Xochitl was his personal property. We told her she couldn't go with him anymore, but ... She told me she was going to the library."

"What time was that?"

"Afternoon, I don't remember exactly. She never came home." The woman shook her head and buried her face in her hands. "It was him, Jorgé; he killed her."

"What makes you think so, ma'am?"

"Xochitl was smart, a good student. In the fall she was going to start at the U. of A. Jorgé barely graduated high school. He had pretty good pay as a janitor someplace, I forget where, but basically, he was going nowhere. I think he knew that once Xochitl started school, well. He wasn't good enough for her, wasn't smart enough. He didn't want to lose her so he killed her and ran back to Mexico." She rocked back and forth in her chair. "That's what I think."

According to Gloria Salcedo, Jorgé Montenegro lived with his mother and two siblings.

•••

The house was not far from the Salcedo's, but decades separated the old adobe from the graceless brick house that stood behind a cyclone fence. The only concession to Barrio Hollywood was a chinaberry tree sitting in the middle of the front yard. In the spring the tree would be covered in fragrant sprays of lavender. Now there were clusters of berries, pale and hard as porcelain.

The gate was open, so no dogs, Marie thought as she crossed the yard. The metal front door was the kind someone who is afraid of a home invasion might install. Was Jorgé Montenegro a gang member? She banged with her fist.

A woman opened the door a crack, a look of suspicion on her face. She seemed too young to be the mother of a 19-year-old boy. A toddler peeked from behind her legs.

"*Buenas tardes, Señora.*" Smiling, Marie held out her badge. "Detective Marie Stransky. *Habla inglés?*"

The woman nodded.

"I'm looking for Jorgé Montenegro." The woman opened the door and stepped back. "*Esta muerto?*" Her hand flew to her mouth. "He's dead, isn't he?"

"Not to my knowledge."

"*Momentito. Ven mijita.*" She swept up the toddler and carried her out of the room.

After a few moments she came back with a terry dishtowel in hand. "Please come in." The woman led the way into a small, neat kitchen and pulled out a chair at the dinette. "*Sientese*, please sit."

Marie took a chair. There was a photo of a young man with dark hair combed straight back from his forehead and a sweet smile pinned to the refrigerator door with a Virgin of Guadalupe magnet. "Is that your son?"

"Yes, that is my Jorgé for his graduation."

"Handsome boy. You said you thought he was dead. What makes you say so?"

The woman wiped her eyes with the towel. "He been gone now for …" she stopped to think. "Nine, ten days. Jorgé leave the house to meet Xochitl, his girlfriend, and never come back. We have family in Mexico, San Ignacio, so I think he run there with Xochitl so they be together. Xochitl's parents think Jorgé is no good enough, but they are in love, so…." She paused to wipe her face again. "But he no call to tell me. I call my sister and …"

"I see," Marie said, nodding her head. "Did you file a missing person report?"

"No, I, *pues, tengo miedo.*" The woman buried her face in the towel.

Marie didn't have to ask the woman what she was afraid of. She figured that Señora Montenegro, and possibly her son as well, were undocumented and feared deportation. Marie waited a few minutes while she cried into the dishcloth.

Finally, the woman looked up. "He is no with my sister and he is dead." She placed her hand over her heart. "I know it here."

"Señora Montenegro, was your son ever involved with a gang?"

"*Nunca.* Jorgé is a good boy, always he work. When his father get sent back to Mexico, he help me out and take good care of his little sister and brother. He has a job and he … *pues*, he never quit from that job. The pay is very good. He just bought a car, a Camaro, old, *pero* … nice red car."

There had been no mention of a red Camaro, or any abandoned car in the vicinity of Julian Wash. "Did he take his car when he went to meet Xochitl?"

"Of course. He very proud of that car."

"I see. Señora Montenegro, did you know that Xochitl's mother reported her missing 10 days ago?"

The woman shook her head. "Xochitl's mother and me, we do not talk. Never meet. Like I say, we wasn't good enough for her."

"What about friends?" Marie took out her notebook and began to jot down names. There weren't that many.

Señora Montenegro once again buried her face in the towel. After a few moments she looked up, brown eyes red-rimmed and shimmering. "Now my son is dead. Dead! Will you find him for me?"

"I'm going to try, Señora." Marie rose from the chair.

The woman put her hand on Marie's arm. "Let me ask you, Señora. Do you have children?"

"Yes, I do."

"*Entonces sabe.* You know how it is with your children. *Siempre, la madre sabe.* Always, the mother knows."

•••

Marie turned the Ford Explorer north onto Silverbell Road. A small ice chest rested on the passenger seat. Inside were four 4-ounce packages of breast milk.

All afternoon she had been puzzling over the murder of Xochitl Salcedo. Had her boyfriend killed her and run back to Mexico as Gloria Salcedo believed, or had he too been a victim? Señora Montenegro believed her son wasn't involved with gangs, but just because she believed that didn't make it so. She made a mental note to check out his friends; there were only two that his mother had first and last names for, not unusual. She only knew three of Catherine's friends' last names and that was only because back in elementary school, the girls and mothers spent a couple of Saturdays together selling Girl Scout cookies.

Both mothers had claimed to know in their hearts that their children were dead. A mother always knows, they had insisted. Well, this mother didn't know. Didn't know how or where her son was. Didn't know if he was happy or sad. Was he dead or alive? Her heart told her nothing.

His name was Francis. For 18 years, she'd received her son's school photo and a little progress report. There was never a return address, but they were postmarked Phoenix. It was part of the agreement she'd made with the man and woman who adopted him 21 years ago. The last letter came just after his 18th birthday, also agreed upon. His parents were to have given Francis her contact information. Marie's hope was that the boy would contact her, but he hadn't. For the last three years she could only wonder. She liked to imagine him in college. This year, he might have graduated, perhaps with a BA in biology or mathematics. Marie been good at math and science when she was in high school.

If he were in some sort of trouble, or worse, dead, wouldn't some sort of mother's sixth sense register the fact in her heart? But, of course, she had never mothered him. No, logic dictated that the most likely reason she had not heard from him was that he simply was not interested in connecting with the woman who gave him up 21 years ago. She didn't need a sixth sense to know that.

She turned in to Bianchi's Pizza. While waiting at the drive-by window for her order—two large pizzas, one with everything, the other with nothing but pepperoni, which Marie could easily peel off from a couple of slices because Catherine was currently not eating meat—she thought of the young lovers. Both Jorgé and Xochitl had disappeared on the same day. Had they been together? Most likely. Was there another body yet to be found in that wash? Maybe.

The AC wasn't running cold enough and rivulets of sweat ran down the sides of her face as she considered the next step. Tomorrow she'd simply lay the facts out to Lindgrin and hope he would conclude that they should dispatch Cosmo to search the area where Xochitl's body had been found.

•••

Marie picked up her excellent Japanese chopping blade. Nick had given it to her their first Christmas. She cherished it in a way most women might cherish an expensive piece of jewelry. The blade sliced easily through the soft flesh of a ripe tomato in a totally satisfying way. And it curved upward toward the tip, which gave it an easy rocking motion. Marie loved chopping, which required just the right amount of attention to distract her from the day's events.

With the flat of the blade, she scooped up the tomato, the only vegetable that they could all agree on, and tossed it into the salad bowl with the romaine. Everything else went into separate bowls to be added at the table.

Earlier, she'd nursed Nichole, who was now asleep in her carrier on the kitchen counter. For the next 14 hours, Marie was free of the sucking machine, as she had come to call it, tomorrow's breast milk was in the fridge, the pizza was keeping warm in the oven and all seemed right with her little world.

The landline rang. This call could only be her mother. The woman seemed to sense when Marie was having a rare quiet moment to herself, then did her best to disturb it. Reluctantly, she picked up.

"It's just me," her mother said with a sigh. Marie peeled and chopped a cucumber as she listened to her mother's catalogue of complaints. There was the dentist who was putting in a crown, the neighbor's barking dog and hence the neighbor, the aching big toe that kept her awake at night. The litany went on and on.

"And how are you?" Her mother asked at last.

"Good. Everyone's good, Mom." Marie's answer led to an additional five-minute monologue. Had her mother always been so self-centered? Marie thought not. As a child, Marie had felt securely at the center of her mother's world. Though the woman had never been one for hugs and kisses, Marie had been well-fed, appropriately dressed and taught to be well-mannered. Her mother closely monitored her homework, taught her to wash and iron her own clothes, the rudiments of sewing and house cleaning. Marie was certain that in her mother's mind all those things equated with love. And she had set a strong example.

Whenever a crisis arose, small or large, Marie would ask herself what would her mother do and then do the opposite.

Guido, the mystery dog, shambled into the kitchen, nosed his food bowl around and gazed at her balefully. Four years ago, he had appeared on their doorstep as a little black puppy, totally helpless and irresistible and now weighed some 90 pounds. He butted her leg with his big, blocky head.

"Excuse me, Mother." She put her hand over the receiver then yelled, "Claire, get in here and feed your dog." In reality, the dog was hers since she'd been the one to advocate for its adoption. "So, Mother, I guess I better let you go. I have to finish up dinner. Yes, yes. You too."

A sturdy 8-year-old baring a strong resemblance to her mother skated into the kitchen on stocking feet, scooped three cups of kibble from the enormous bag stashed in the pantry into the dog's bowl, then skated out again.

Marie put the cucumber into its own bowl. "Catherine," she called. "Come set the table, please." She waited a few beats. "Catherine!" Marie began to reduce half a small red onion to a mince. After she scrapped the result into another bowl, Marie put down the knife. "Damn it," she whispered.

Catherine, who was sprawled on her bedroom floor with her iPad, didn't look up when her mother came into the room. Though her eldest daughter was not beautiful, she was athletic and graceful, with thick near-black hair, a gift from her father. Thanks to his ministrations, it was caught in a long braid that snaked down her back to the point where her butt began its outward curve.

Marie shook her head. "Come set the table, Catherine." Her voice was level, but firm.

"Be there in a minute," her daughter said.

"Salad's ready, pizza's hot, everybody's hungry. I need you to set the table now," she said, and with one swift movement snatched the iPad out of the girl's hand.

"That's so rude," Catherine complained.

"So is ignoring me when I need your help. Now get in there and set the table if you want this back any time before the monsoons."

The girl sighed loudly then peeled her lanky body off the floor.

Back in the kitchen, Marie took up her blade and started to julienne a carrot. "So, Catherine, how was horse camp today?"

The girl shrugged, still too put out to reward her mother with conversation.

"Your father said that you like the horse you were assigned." This was a fabrication, but Marie was determined not to be ignored, bad precedent. "I forgot his name."

"Her name."

"Right. So?"

"Her name is Windy."

"Windy, that's cute. And what kind of a horse is Windy; I mean what color?"

"Brown, Mom, brown as poop," she said slapping down the last piece of silverware. "And she farts all the time, which is why she's called Windy."

"Hmm. And this is a horse you like?"

"She's fine. May I have my iPad back now ... please?"

Catherine had begged them to let her go to horse camp. It was not cheap. Was it too much to expect a little hassle-free cooperation in exchange? Marie was way too tired to deal with her daughter's snarky attitude and was tempted to simply ignore it, but from past experience with this one, she knew that rarely played out well.

Taking a deep breath, she leveled her gaze at her daughter. "You know, Catherine, we are a big, busy household. Everyone has to pull their weight. Your dad weighs the most, so he pulls the heaviest load, working, taking care of you kids and the house. Then me. I go to work and I make most of the money we all enjoy spending and I help dad with the cooking. You're next, then Claire and Mary Ann. Even Teresa is expected to behave at the table, which is hard work for her."

"And Nichole ..."

"Gets a free ride for now, of course."

"Speaking of babies..." Catherine took a moment to realign the silverware in relation to the paper napkins. "You know, Mom, there is such a thing as abstinence."

Marie's jaw dropped. How did this conversation morph from horses to birth control? For a moment she searched her own repertory of snarky retorts, but thought better of it. She studied her daughter who was carefully rearranging the silverware once again. She was no longer the noodle she once was. Now her waist nipped in a bit, and budding breasts were just discernible beneath her tee shirt.

Marie determined that her best course was honesty. "Yes, I know all about abstinence. For one thing, it doesn't work that well as a mode of birth control, not when you are truly in love, and so we now have Nichole."

"I'm not saying I don't love Nichole," Catherine said in a voice that sounded a lot like reason. "But in case you haven't noticed we live in a three-bedroom house."

"Is this about wanting your own bedroom?"

"No! Well, of course, I'd like my own bedroom, but that's like so not going to happen the way things are going. Besides … I don't know. It gets embarrassing. Most mothers your age have stopped having babies. It's like the world knows you and Dad are like so doing it."

"So doing it? You mean having sex?"

"Mother!"

"Okay." She took another moment to gather her thoughts. "In addition to loving your father, there is another reason why I keep having babies."

For the first time in some minutes, Catherine looked directly at her mother. "Well?"

Marie set her blade down. "Well… It was a long time ago, long before I met your father. I made a promise to God to accept all the children he'd give me without interference."

"Does Dad know about this?"

"Of course, Dad knows!"

"Is this your Catholic thing?"

"Yes and no. Well, not exactly."

"What kind of an answer is that?"

"The best one I can give on such short notice."

"But why did you promise God?"

Marie sighed. "Listen, sweetie, you deserve an honest answer and I promise to give you one the moment you turn 16."

"Sixteen? Why do I have to wait five years to find out why we're all sleeping in bunk beds."

"You're right. That's totally arbitrary." She put the salad bowl on the table. "I'll tell you when you start your period, okay? We'll have lots to discuss then and I don't think it's so far away."

"How do you know?"

"Some things a mother just knows, okay? Now dinner's ready. Please get Dad—he's in the garage doing his workout—and tell your sisters to come to the table. Oh, and Catherine?" Smiling, she handed her daughter the iPad. "Don't forget this. And Catherine …"

"What now?"

"I love you, honey."

"Love you too, Mom," the girl said without enthusiasm.

•••

Nick was working in his office—an alcove off the kitchen—editing copy for Science in Review, a bibliographic journal for mathematicians, physicists, statisticians and logicians. It was part-time and paid poorly, but the hours were flexible and he could do if from home. From Marie's point of view, his real job was house husband, but she never said those words to Nick, who could be a bit prickly when it came to his work.

After reading Mary Ann and Teresa to sleep, Marie had been hoping for a Netflix night, "The Girl With the Dragon Tattoo," but by 8, even the manic Lisbeth Salander couldn't keep her awake. Before she could go to bed, she needed to check on the girls and feed Nichole.

And then there was Nick. He'd been making all the little gestures that indicated he wanted to make love. He'd been so patient and she knew she should, but she simply didn't have the energy. In the past, Marie had pretty much snapped back after six weeks. Not this time. This time she just felt … well … old. At 38, she was too young to feel so old. "Damn it," she hissed as she hauled herself up from the couch and trundled down the hall.

Ostensibly, Catherine and Claire were in their room reading. Marie knocked on their door, a courtesy her mother had never afforded her. "May I come in?"

It was Claire who opened the door. Her times tables flash cards were spread over the floor. She had still not mastered her sixes, sevens and eights. Being the diligent but math-challenged child that she was, she wanted to learn them before she started summer school the following week.

"How's it going?" Marie asked.

"Good. Catherine made me this concentration game with the combinations that I still need to learn." She slapped down the cards, ordering them from one to 12. "See? I flip one over, and try to get a match."

Catherine, who'd been reading in a nest of pillows on the top bunk while plugged in to her music, hopped down so she could demonstrate how the game was played. She flipped over two cards: 8x8 and 64. "See? I got a match. The one who gets the most matches wins."

"It's nice of you to help your sister, sweetie." She hugged Catherine to her side. "So, what's the book?"

"Suggested summer reading."

"What suggested summer reading in particular?"

"*Oliver Twist*. It's boring." Catherine turned over two more cards and got another match.

Satisfied that both girls were appropriately occupied, she kissed each good night and started for the kitchen to say her good nights to Nick. Not wanting to interrupt his train of thought, she massaged his shoulders in silence for a few moments as he finished editing the page he was on. He had broad shoulders and his shaggy dark hair almost touched them. A relatively new tattoo with a Polynesian motif encircled his meaty right bicep. Of late, Nick had become almost handsome. Recently he'd grown a beard, which covered most of the old acne scars and the slightly receding chin that had saved him from being snapped up by some pretty girl. Seeing him now, people probably wondered why he'd chosen her.

"Umm, feels nice," he said.

Marie kissed his ear. "I don't think Catherine is really into horse camp."

"What?" he said without taking his eyes off the screen. "She loves it."

"Didn't sound like it to me, and all that money."

"That's just you and Catherine butting heads."

Butting heads? Offended, Marie was about to protest when Nick reached around and grasped the bulgy part of her thigh.

"You know what I've been thinking?"

"What?" she answered with a tired little smile.

"Why don't you go out to the garage and do a little workout. Just a few reps to start out with."

This was not the suggestion she was expecting. "Not tonight, honey." It occurred to her to add, *I have a headache.*

"Come on. You can do a few reps."

"But it's 90 degrees out there."

"Turn on the floor fan, then just push through it. The humidity is what, four percent? Once you start sweating you'll cool right off."

There was just the slightest edge of impatience in his voice. It was the edge that made her dig in her heels.

"I put in a 15-hour day, produced nearly a quart of milk and I simply do not have the energy." Her voice was louder and harsher than she intended.

"Just 10 minutes on the elliptical for starters. You'll ... feel better if you do."

Feel better or look better, she wondered. But of course, he was right. She needed to get back in shape and she knew exactly how to do it: 10 minutes a day the first week, 15 the second and so on until she reached 60 minutes, at which point she could cut back her workout to three days a week. Still, she had to suppress the urge to punch him.

Without another word she turned on her heel and pounded off to the garage. Not one minute more than 10, she vowed.

CHAPTER 5

Thoughts on God and Motive

Thursday, June 10

It was just past 7 a.m. when Marie arrived at the top of Julian Wash west of I-10. The Pima Rescue and Recovery K-9 unit and a squad car were already parked in the wildcat parking lot at the end of the dirt road. A quarter mile away from the nearest house, the lot was mostly stubby, dry grasses, flattened creosote and broken beer bottles. There were a few Palo Verde trees, which would remain leafless until the onset of the monsoon rains, still a month away. All and all, it was a pretty bleak spot by daylight, but Stransky could imagine young lovers parked there at night. Would anyone hear a gunshot over a radio blaring jaw-rattling bass while some *vato* was putting it to his *ruca*? If they did, would it be unusual enough to remember?

Marie didn't recognize the two young officers leaning against the squad car. New hires, she figured. "Good morning, guys."

Standing at attention, they replied in near unison. "Morning, ma'am."

Fresh out of the Academy, she figured. "I'm Detective Marie Stransky and you are?"

The taller of the two stepped forward. "Officer Noah Gutierriez and this is Officer Stanley Bakey."

"Good to meet you both," she said. "You ready for this?"

Nodding solemnly, the two replied once again in near unison, "Yes, ma'am."

Cute, Marie thought, and so young they made her bones creak.

Marie waved at the woman still standing by the K-9 recovery unit. She had worked with JC Brennen and her golden retriever, Cosmo, before. At Stransky's approach, Brennen opened the back of the air-conditioned unit and the affable Cosmo leaped out with a joyous woof.

"Hey, JC" Marie ruffled the dog's fur a bit. "You ready for some action, Cosmo?"

"How's it going Marie?" said Brennen, a stout youngish woman with buzzed hair the same color as the dog's.

"Good, JC It's going good." Marie, who'd been up since 5, saw no point in honesty here.

Brennen had been adamant about getting an early start to avoid the heat. Cadaver sniffing dogs, whose training could take up to two years, were a valuable commodity. In addition, Cosmo was also a sweetheart, and, at 8 years of age, a bit elderly for the business at hand. Brennen didn't want him heat-stressed.

With her chin, Stransky pointed toward a series of braided paths leading to the wash. "The body of a young woman was found in the wash two days ago, so there's that, but there might be a second body that was missed. Either way, Cosmo won't be disappointed."

Brennen, clearly anxious to get started, attached a leash to Cosmo's halter. "Find it," she commanded, and the dog was off.

Marie and the officers followed Brennen and Cosmo down a narrow rocky path, which became increasingly precipitous and rugged as they neared the wash. At the bottom, mesquite trees provided a tracery of green and a bit of respite from the drilling sun. Marie held back a bit, not wanting to expend any extra energy, as Cosmo, ears pricked, snuffled back and forth across the sandy expanse, searching for the strongest whiff of decay. A pair of lovelorn white-winged doves calling from somewhere in the brush were undeterred by the multiple feet crunching over decomposed granite.

After a few minutes, Cosmo turned and barked at Brennen, once, twice, three times. They'd come to the spot where Xochitl's body had been found. "Good boy. Good Cosmo," Brennen said, caressing the dog's head. "Find it," she commanded once again.

Within minutes, Marie heard Cosmo's bark and hurried to catch up. The stench of decay intensified and she pulled the handkerchief she'd earlier sprinkled with baby powder out of her pants pocket and held it to her nose.

Jorgé Montenegro's body lay face-down in the wash. Unlike Xochitl, he'd been shot in the head.

"Well, I guess that's it." Brennen said, tossing Cosmo an old tennis ball. The dog mouthed his reward, tail wagging.

•••

Once again, Marie pulled the Ford Explorer up to the brick home of Florencia Montenegro to confirm what the woman already knew. For a few moments she sat gathering her thoughts. What were the possibilities? Jorgé Montenegro had taken a bullet to the side of his head. Who were Jorgé's friends and enemies? Had Jorgé been targeted or was this a random act. If so, had Xochitl been a target as well or was she simply collateral damage? Jorgé's body had been found in the bottom of the wash some distance from the path where Xochitl had been found. Had she tried to escape after her lover had been shot? Despite his mother's belief that Jorgé was a good boy, was he? He'd recently bought a very nice car. Was he dealing drugs? Were these two homicides gang related or something else? Did he know his killer?

Marie could imagine a stranger discovering the young lovers parked at the end of the dirt track, but what would have been the motive? Xochitl had not been raped. Not theft. In Jorgé's wallet there was $72 and an uncashed paycheck for $432.73. And what had become of Jorgé's pride and joy, the red Camaro? Had they been killed because someone wanted the flashy but well-used car? Hard to imagine. Beyond tired, Marie pulled herself out of the car and trudged across the yard. Señora Montenegro opened the door before she had a chance to knock.

•••

After leaving the Montenegro home, Marie needed a little down time to try to pull some threads together. Numb with grief, Florencia Montenegro had been unable to give her much additional information beyond the name of his employer. She'd get to him soon enough. At the moment, she needed something cool.

She raised her left wrist. "Hey Siri, where's the nearest Dairy Queen?"

•••

In spite of the cold air blowing directly at her ice cream, Marie had to lap at the sides of the cone to keep the soft serve from running down her hand. The task didn't interfere with her thread gathering, however, as she considered the murder of the two young lovers.

One reason she had become a cop in the first place was because she had always wanted to know the reason behind abhorrent behavior. The newspapers only told the things people did. Rarely did they say why they did them. Reasons equated with order and order equated with God. If there weren't reasons then where was God? Random killings, to her mind, did not exist. Every murder had a motive, no matter how indirect. Usually, the superficial motive was pretty obvious. Jealousy, for instance, was a common motive, as were lust, rage and greed. There was rarely just a single motive, but the common denominator, Marie believed, was fear: fear of failure, fear of loss, fear of judgment, displacement, humiliation, retaliation.

Less obvious were the mitigating factors that preceded motive, often by years and years, like physical, sexual and emotional abuse, neglect, domestic violence, alcohol and drug addiction. And the absolute absence of hope. Adverse Childhood Experiences, as they were called by defense lawyers trying to get a lighter sentence for the guilty as charged. Though the Carl Lindgrins of the world would laugh at her, Marie truly believed that murderers were the consequences of past events they had little, if any, control over.

Marie was once on a case where three daughters had been imprisoned, starved and beaten by their parents. Why would anyone do that? The father's motive was never clear, but the mother's motive was fear, plain and simple. Though she was never beaten or starved, she was terrified that her husband would turn on her if she did not obey him. Still, as a mother. Marie had a hard time with that one. A mother's first duty was to protect her children. And what would those girls grow into as adults?

Pensively, Marie tongued the quickly melting ice cream. So, motive. If she could figure out the motive behind the murder of Xochitl Salcedo and Jorgé Montenegro, she would be closer to finding the person who had committed it. Could have been a simple auto theft gone wrong. Could have been a carjacking. Carjackings often led to homicides. In the case of the young lovers, Marie could not discern an obvious motive and that was deeply disturbing to her.

•••

Back at her desk, Marie began the summary of the morning's events. Briefly, she wrote a chronology and description of her involvement at the scene of Jorgé Montenegro's murder. After that, she donned a pair of latex gloves and began to go through the property taken from the boy's body by the crime tech. There wasn't much: a comb, a clean and pressed white handkerchief, a wallet, empty save for the cash, the check and a picture of Xochitl in the clear plastic space usually reserved for a driver's license. If Jorgé had a driver's license it was not in his wallet.

Palms pressed together prayer-like, Marie studied the photo. In it, Xochitl was wearing what appeared to be a prom dress, or perhaps it was the dress she'd worn for her quinceañera. Yes, Xochitl was the type of girl who would have had the traditional coming out party when she turned 15. Smiling at the camera, she was a girl without a care. Pre Jorgé Montenegro?

She pushed the picture back into the slot, then dropped wallet, assorted pocket change, the comb and handkerchief into the evidence bag. After she finished her report, she'd return the bag to the property room. From there it would go to forensics for analysis, though Marie doubted they'd find any latent prints, doubted that the perpetrator had even touched the boy's wallet. When the analysis was complete, the boy's belongings would be turned over to Señora Montenegro. It would take just long enough to tear open the gaping wound that had sealed over the mother's heart.

"Gang related," she whispered, though there was no one around to hear. Reluctantly she had to conclude that Jorgé, maybe even Xochitl, guilty or innocent, must have seriously pissed off a very bad actor.

Marie turned to her computer for a look at the TPD's archives. She entered Female/Mexican American/shot. There were a disturbing number of hits.

CHAPTER 6

Armed and Demented

Friday, June 11

Torrance Stedman set his Starbuck's iced Mocha Frappuccino on the edge of the desk then checked his email. Quickly he scanned one Marie had sent him from her iPad, after her morning briefing with Lindgrin and the homicide team. Bless that girl's heart, he thought as he opened the first attachment. She always kept him in the loop.

According to Ramona Antone, this latest victim was between 15 and 25 years old, 5 feet 7 1/4 inches tall and weighed 122 pounds. Estimated time of death between 2200 and 0100 hours. In addition to the burn on her wrist, her arms and legs were crisscrossed with faint scars, consistent with self-cutting. Consistent with strangulation, were the petechial hemorrhaging in both eyes. The anal cavity showed signs of trauma, but vaginal, anal and oral swabs came up negative for semen.

No semen, Torrance thought. Our guy could have used a condom or perhaps he sodomized her with some object.

Sipping his Frappuccino, he opened a second attachment. He studied the photo. Turned out their Santa Rita Park homicide victim was a 16-year-old runaway from a group home. Her name was Sierra Horton and she'd been out on the streets less than a week. In the photo, perhaps taken when she was 12 or 13, a younger Sierra was holding a plush SpongeBob SquarePants. She was a pretty ordinary looking little girl, with blue eyes, limp bangs swept to the side and a toothy grin. Little girls who end up in group homes have complicated histories. Stedman wondered if her mother and father even knew she'd been missing.

Consistent with other victims, the toxicology report from the crime lab showed significant amounts of both alcohol and OxyContin and a trace of fentanyl in Sierra's system. There was nothing, no blood or skin under her fingernails, to indicate self-defense. He supposed she'd been out cold at the onset of the attack.

Most serial killers operated in familiar territory. This one was no different. All his victims had been found within a two-mile radius of Santa Rita Park. All had drugs, alcohol in their systems. Did the killer lure them with drugs and attack once they were incapacitated or was he an opportunist, just waiting in any of a number of places where the homeless gather for some woman to fall into a deep, drug induced sleep. Was he known to his victims, or did he stalk them at a distance?

Stedman's thoughts turned to his daughter, Cara, who now had a daughter of her own. Back when she was 15 or 16 she'd run away from home. It was just after he and Clarisse had split and Cara was madder than hell at both of them. He'd personally witnessed what could happen to a pretty young girl on the streets and he and Clarisse had both been terrified. Luckily, Cara got spooked – she never told him by who or what – and came on home in tears and full of apologies. What would he have done if she'd ended up like little Sierra? He took off his glasses and massaged his eyes.

Could have happened. He hadn't been the greatest of fathers. He hadn't been the greatest of husbands either. Fact was, if he'd done a better job of it, Clarisse wouldn't have looked elsewhere. Both his daughter and his granddaughter, Lynnetta, were living with him at the moment, so at least Cara had forgiven him.

He moved the attachments into his file of ongoing investigations and deleted the email before starting the rest of the day. He'd been assigned to patrol the Ronstadt Transfer Center specifically, and downtown in general.

•••

Stedman had the little notebook he carried in his breast pocket in hand. Unlike Marie, who talked into her watch like Dick Tracy, he was happy with his pencil and notebook. The fact that he even knew Dick Tracy talked into his watch made him a dinosaur, but his notebook was a useful tool. He always made a show of jotting down the specifics in the personal shorthand he had developed over the years. It helped him write up the report later. More important, it seemed to calm things down, reassured folks that they were being heard.

•••

"Soon as they saw me take out my cell and dial 911," the man was saying, "the punks took off."

They'd been standing in the shade of the arched entry to the Ronstadt Transit Center, Stedman and a skinny, muscle-shirted man with a sleeve of tattoos on his right arm and a face the color of stewed tomatoes.

"It's pretty hot out here, sir," Stedman said. "Can I get you a bottle of water from my squad car?"

"No man, I'm good, but I'm telling you the security here is fucked up. I'm just sitting there waiting for number10 and some gangbanger types hit me up for cigarettes. When I say no, one of the punks pulls a knife on me. Right away comes the security guy, says he don't want to get cops involved and that we just need to chill out and stay away from each other. And I'm like, what the fuck! I'm just minding my own business and it's okay that some punk pulls a knife on me? I don't think so."

Stedman couldn't help but notice that the tattoos were characters from "Where the Wild Things Are." He'd been reading that book to Lynnetta just the other night.

"Security says he just wants to keep the peace. I'm telling you straight out, I'm gonna start carrying my own peacekeeper, see how that works out for the mother fucking security guy."

"Well, I guess I better have a talk with the man."

"I guess you better."

"Hey, nice tats, by the way. 'Where the Wild Things Are,' right?"

The guy looked down the length of his arm and smiled. "Yeah, my son's favorite book, well was. He's in junior high now; thinks he's a man." He shrugs. "What can I say, kids change, but tats are forever."

"Kids grow up fast these days." Stedman put his notebook away. "You sure you don't need a bottle of water?"

The guy's face had gone from tomato red to normal white guy red. "No man, I'm good."

•••

Stedman had just come out of the Circle K when he got the call. Seems a woman was armed with a shotgun and threatening her son. He set his Big Gulp Pepsi in the cup holder of the squad, set the Reese's Peanut Butter Cups on the passenger seat and took off, lights whirling.

Nearly simultaneously, three squads pulled up in front of the modest stucco home. An older model Ford sedan sat in the carport. Rosebushes, alternating yellow and pink, flanked the brick path leading up to the front door. A black man stepped out from behind the sedan, arms waving in the air.

Stedman took a big sip of his Pepsi then got out of the car. After conferring with the other officers, it was determined that this was a job for Stedman. For a moment he studied the house. The drapes were drawn tight. Had he not known better, he would have assumed that no one was home. The sun burned the top of his head right through his hat as he made his way up the drive to the shade of the carport.

"Afternoon, Mr. Harold," he said taking out his notebook. "What's your mama up to now?"

The older man shook his head. His face was beaded with sweat and his grizzled hair glistened with it. "She's got a 12-gauge shotgun. Says she's going to blow my nuts off if I don't leave her be."

"Your mama said that?"

"Hard to believe out of the mouth of a church going woman."

"How'd your mama get ahold of a shotgun?"

"Belonged to my daddy. I haven't seen it since … long before he passed and that was well, let's see, 28 years ago. I'm older now than he was when he died."

"Is that so? Well, your daddy was a fine man."

"Yes, he was." He took out a handkerchief from his back pocket and mopped his brow. "You know, Torrance, I wouldn't have thought Mama capable, you know, of …"

"So, what got her so capable all of a sudden?"

"She's getting up in years, 92 next month."

"Hard to believe." Stedman clearly remembered the feisty old lady. When he was a child, she was one of those women who ran the neighborhood, always organizing a carnival or bake sale for the church or the school or someone in need and bullying everyone into taking part. A bossy, but good friend and neighbor, he recalled. In the past few years, she had gone from bossy to downright mean on occasion. Just a couple of months ago, he'd been called to the house because the old lady threw a rock at a passerby who dared to venture up her walk to smell one of her roses.

"Up till 90," Mr. Harold was saying, "she was doing all right, but once she hit 91… well things began to roll downhill. She fell down twice just last week and she doesn't keep things clean like she should. Denise and I been taking turns coming over after work – Mama won't have a stranger come and clean and cook for her. We tried that. And she won't move in with us. Tried that too. We're afraid she might take a fall and break her hip."

Nodding his head, Stedman wondered if breaking a hip would be such a bad outcome under the circumstances.

Mr. Harold continued. "So, we been trying to talk her into going into one of those homes, you know, a nice safe place where she can get three meals a day and not have to worry about anything but going to church and her TV programs. I told her, 'Mama you deserve a rest.' She said, 'Son, I can rest in heaven. I ain't going to some blankety-blank old folks' home.' I won't repeat her exact words. 'Now leave me the blankety-blank be,' she says. And I tell her, 'Mama, the way you're going you might not get to heaven.' And that's when she went and got the shotgun. Can you believe that?"

Stedman shook his head. "Hard to believe."

Minutes later, Stedman was knocking on the kitchen door. When there was no answer, he opened it a crack. He could hear the television blaring from a back room.

"Ms. Harold? Ms. Harold? It's Torrance Stedman, Ms. Harold. May I come in, ma'am?"

There was no answer. One thing he did not want to do was surprise a mean old lady wielding a shotgun. He raised his voice. "Ms. Harold, it's Torrance Stedman, ma'am." Removing his hat, he proceeded cautiously through the small kitchen still fragrant with this morning's bacon and down the darkened hallway. "Ms. Harold?"

She was sitting on her bed, legs straight out, the old 12-gauge shotgun across her lap. "It's me, Torrance, Ms. Harold. May I come in?"

"Torrance Stedman? My, but you've gotten fat."

"Too true, Ms. Harold."

She'd always been portly. Now the skin, stretched tight across her high cheekbones, seemed burnished. She patted her white hair, which she wore in wide cornrows that had frizzed out at the root ends. He imagined those cornrows had been imposed upon her by her daughter-in-law. Back in the day, she'd straightened her hair like all the ladies of an age. Clearly embarrassed, she ran her fingers along a row. "I didn't expect company."

"Well, I was in the neighborhood and just thought I'd stop by, see how you're were doing?"

"Really?" She raised a skeptical brow, then pointed to a floral print chair. "Well, have a seat, Torrance. I'd offer you some ice tea, but I'm in the middle of my program. I never miss the *The Good News*." She seemed to have forgotten that there was a shotgun across her lap.

"That's quite all right, ma'am." He sat and they watched in companionable silence as the Reverend Leland Carver entreated, threatened and cajoled his devoted viewers to turn toward Jesus and away from sin.

After a few minutes, Stedman cleared his throat. "My, my, isn't that the old shotgun your husband used to hunt deer with? I remember him so well. When my daddy was laid off work, more than once, Mr. Harold brought mama a big old hunk of deer meat." He chuckled. "Until Daddy went back to work, we had fried deer, deer stew, deer chili, you name it. We did not go hungry for meat. A fine man, your husband."

As if stroking a cat, the old lady ran her knobby old fingers over the shotgun's stock. It was still smooth, but the bluing on the barrel was almost worn off.

"That old shotgun sure brings back memories. May I see it?"

"No, Torrance, you may not. And you can tell that son of mine that I will blow his nuts off and yours too if you try to put me in some old folks' home. Now you best leave me be."

She turned her attention back to *The Good News*. For a few moments she was lost in her program then seemed to doze. Stedman was about to reach for the shotgun, when her eyes snapped open and she clapped her hands. "Do you remember that time you and Eddie went bowling and you dropped the ball on his foot. You had to half-carry him out to the car."

Stedman remembered the incident well. It had been his father who'd been bowling with Edward Harold that night, but he didn't feel the need to point that out. "The bones in that foot were shattered," he said, shaking his head. "It's a wonder he was ever able to walk on it again."

"And what about the time the two of you ran out of gas on the way back from Douglas and had to hitchhike home. Two black men. It took you 12 hours to catch a twenty minute ride. Remember that? And then there was the time you two thought you could make a peach cobbler. I don't know where you got those peaches, but they were water-starved little things and hard as rocks."

He laughed. "I don't remember the peaches, but that sounds about right. Now, let me ask you this. How in the world do you get your roses to bloom in this heat?"

An hour later, Stedman came out of the house. Mr. Harold was still in the carport, sitting on a paint bucket. He stood when he saw the shotgun. "Well, well, can you believe that!"

Stedman handed the old man the shotgun. "I took the shells out."

"How did you manage it, Torrance?"

"It seems the problem is the roses. She won't leave without them."

•••

By the time Stedman got back to his squad, his Big Gulp was warm and the peanut butter cups melted. He turned the AC on high and aimed a vent at the peanut butter cups, then looked at his watch. While he waited, he wrote down the details of his encounter with Ms. Harold then radioed dispatch to clear the call. By the time he finished, the peanut butter cups were cool enough to unwrap.

When she pulled into the drive of the first person on her list, it was 5:45, almost dinnertime, the best time, she figured, to catch a teenage boy at home.

As Jorgé's mother had explained, her son's friend, Norberto Navarro, lived just down the block in the pink house, the only pink house. It was a squat but cheery slump block ranch house with a tidy yard and a pot of geraniums on either side of the front door. She knocked and a little girl about Mary Ann's age answered, a squirmy puppy tucked under one arm.

"Hello, little lady," Marie said.

Immediately, the child ran off screaming, "Mamá!"

Moments later a heavy woman appeared, wiping her hands on a paper napkin.

"*Buenas tardes, Señora.*"

"What is it you want?" the woman said in unaccented English.

Marie handed her a card. "I'm Detective Marie Stransky. May I speak to Roberto Navarro?"

"Is this about Jorgé?"

"Yes, ma'am, it is."

"He knows nothing about it."

"May I speak with him, please?"

The woman looked at her long and hard. "Come inside, well." She gestured toward the living room then yelled, "Beto, there's a detective here wants to talk to you about Jorgé." The woman nodded toward the couch and Marie sat down.

A serious looking young man wheeled into the room; the little girl and her puppy were sitting in the space where his left leg should have been. Mama Bear perched on the arm of an upholstered chair, thick arms folded across her chest, mouth a tight line.

"Hi, Beto." Marie began. "I'm Detective Marie Stransky." She got up and handed him a card. "I'm so sorry for the loss of your friend. It must be hard."

The boy nodded.

"What can you tell me about Jorgé?"

•••

Before heading home, Marie checked the odometer and made note of the mileage on her watch. There was hell to pay should she forget to enter her mileage on her activity sheet.

Eventually Mama Bear had relaxed her guard and opened up. Beto Navarro, it turned out, had lost his leg to bone cancer when he was 8. Probably one of the only positive outcomes of the war in Iraq was improved prosthetic devices, but even though both mom and dad worked full time, the Navarros didn't have insurance and couldn't afford one.

As it turned out, neither Beto Navarro nor his friend Billy Huerta, whom she'd just finished interviewing, had much to say. Fighting back tears, both boys affirmed Señora Montenegro's claim that Jorgé was a good, hardworking kid who had nothing to do with gangs. He loved Xochitl and would never do anything to harm her, they'd both insisted. Marie had no reason to doubt them, but that didn't mean the pair weren't victims of gang violence.

As she pulled onto Grande, she wondered how much a prosthetic leg would cost and how hard it was to set up a Go Fund Me account.

CHAPTER 7

Strays

Tuesday, June 15

She'd been waiting for him since midnight. Her skinny butt was sore from sitting on the concrete table and she was feeling edgy and sick. Running both hands though her tangle of curly hair, she wondered how much longer she could wait. The bastard had probably been jiving her, hoping she'd do him before she got her pills. Well, at least he hadn't gotten what he wanted.

She was about to light one last cigarette when she heard the click of his roller bag on the sidewalk. Relieved, she smiled when he finally came to sit beside her.

•••

It was still dark when the boy emerged from the shelter of the oleanders. He skirted around the others who were still deep asleep as he made his way across the park and onto 22nd Street. He was hungry. He was always hungry and he needed to hurry if he was going to be first.

The sky was beginning to lighten as the boy hoisted himself into the dumpster behind the 7-Eleven and began sorting through the trash, tossing the occasional aluminum can over the side. Discarded was a stack of flattened corrugated cardboard. Over the side it went. Sometimes people threw away sandwiches, bottles of juice, energy drinks, cups of coffee with cream and sugar only partially consumed. So much waste, he was thinking when he heard the sound of wheels on asphalt. He peeked over the edge of the dumpster. It was him, the man who'd left the cookies, the orange and the Coke. He couldn't say when that was, one day was so much like another. He crouched down and waited.

He could hear the man unzipping his big wheeled suitcase then much grunting. The boy could just see the top of the man's head as he pushed a big black plastic garbage bag into the dumpster. Heard the man zip up the suitcase. Heard the click, click, click as he wheeled it away.

Like a spider monkey, the boy scrabbled over the trash on all fours. The bag was sturdy. It would be useful and perhaps inside there would be clothing, even food. Hopeful, he untied the knot, careful not to tear the bag. The first thing he saw was a foot covered with a dirty white sock.

•••

Marie hastily wiped the toast crumbs from her mouth and poured the rest of her coffee into an aluminum Starbucks to-go cup. Though she'd been up since 5, she was fighting to get out the door on time. Just as she was pulling on her jacket, Nick came pounding in, a tearful Mary Ann in his arms.

"Here," he said, plunking the wailing 4-year-old down. "You comb her hair. Apparently, I pull."

The brush was still caught in the child's hair. "Apparently, you do."

Nick gave her the "fuck you" look and pounded back out of the kitchen.

There was no avoiding it. She was going to be late. Again. Sighing deeply, she pulled her daughter onto her lap and began extricating the brush from the fine brown hair so like her own, poor child.

"Hold still, sweetie, so I don't pull."

Usually, Nick had no trouble with hair combing and brush extrication, which was fairly routine, but this morning he'd been grumpy and impatient. She didn't have the time to get to the bottom of that, if indeed there was a bottom. Sometimes Nick was just grumpy for no apparent reason. Well, of course with five girls, there were five potential reasons for him to be grumpy on any given morning, six, if she counted herself. She knew he loved his girls, but sometimes it was hard for him to relate to them, hard for him to relate to her sometimes, as if the female psyche were uncharted territory.

Mary Ann wiggled her butt. "Hold still, sweetie. Mommy's almost got the brush out."

Well, she couldn't put it all on him. She was not such a great communicator either, but at least she knew it.

"Mommy, you're pulling!"

"Sorry, honey. Almost done."

Communication didn't used to be a problem. Their connection had always been more physical than verbal, more intellectual than emotional. That used to work for them. Now she found his cluelessness annoying.

Lately, she wondered if he might be on the high end of the autism spectrum. It was comforting to think that cluelessness was simply built into his genes and that there was nothing she could do about it.

Once Marie had freed the brush, she used her fingers to unknot her daughter's hair. Once unknotted, she quickly brushed and braided it, securing each skinny little braid with a plastic flower clip.

"There you go, sweetie. All pretty now." She kissed the girl on the cheek and went to find her grumpy husband so she could kiss him as well.

He was scanning the New York Times on his iPad, a second cup of coffee perched on the arm of the chair. Rarely did she have the leisure for a second cup of coffee, and never time for the Times. Suddenly, Marie felt a bit grumpy herself. Still, she leaned in for the goodbye kiss.

"We need to talk," he said, offering a cheek instead of lips.

"Right now?"

"Well, when you get home." He closed the lid on his iPad, and turned to look at her. "You need to start thinking about what you're going to do about birth control; obviously, condoms are not the answer." He opened the lid then shut it again. "Since we can't afford another baby, we can't resume sexual relations until the issue is resolved."

"Sexual relations? Issue? And all these years I thought we've been making love."

"Don't change the subject."

"Okay." She took a deep breath to regain her equilibrium. "Look, I didn't intend to have six kids when I made that promise to God. It's just that …"

"You made that promise when you were, what, 16?"

"Seventeen."

"And now you're 38. Isn't it time for a little reevaluation, Marie? Jesus, you could have six more babies before you're done."

The absence of the word *we* in that sentence stung like a swat with a wet towel. "**I** could have six more babies before **I'm** done? Where are you going to be?"

"Marie, **I** am not going to father any more children, period!"

Instead of responding, she turned on her heel and marched out the door.

•••

Now that was just plain stupid and juvenile, Marie was thinking as she merged into the heavy traffic on I-10. Usually, she was able to avoid the morning rush hour. Thanks to Mary Ann's hair, she was now in the thick of it, and thanks to Nick, well beyond grumpy. And birth control! As if it were her sole obligation. Well, for all practical purposes, it was, but his tone!

The call came in just as traffic stalled at Grant Road. A body had been found in a dumpster. It had been what? Over two weeks since Sierra Horton's murder. Most likely this one was Marie's priority too. Though a dead body was hardly an emergency, Marie turned on her siren and squeezed the Ford Explorer into the left lane.

She took a sip of coffee, sighed, took another sip and winced. For this most recent weight-loss campaign, she'd given up the luxury of cream and sugar, and her coffee was not only too hot, but too bitter. She did a sequence of Lamaze breathing that she'd learned 12 years ago in preparation for Catherine's birth. Weaving in and out of traffic, she sucked in air through her nose then blew it out through her lips is a series of breathy hoo, hoo, hoo, hoos. It wasn't working.

"Can't resume sexual relations until the issue is resolved," she said, wagging her head. She was still very pissed.

By the time she arrived at the 7-Eleven at 22nd and Park, a half-dozen other officers were already in place. Torrance, Audrey Wallace, looking cool and crisp, and Meg Gupta from the medical examiner's office were among them. Marie noticed a small man sitting in the shade of the 7-Eleven, head in hands.

"Morning," she said then pointed her chin at the little man. "He's the one who found the body?"

Stedman nodded. "But there's a problem."

"Oh yeah?"

"He can't talk."

"Can't or won't?"

"Can't. He's got no tongue." Stedman let that sink in for a moment. "I think he's an immigrant, probably an illegal. I'm thinking from one of those places, El Salvador maybe, where gangs cut out people's tongues for whatever reason suits them, MS-13 or somebody. Anyway, he's pretty shook up."

Marie didn't bother to remind him that the Mara Salvatrucha or MS-13 as they were called, originated in LA rather than El Salvador, not that it mattered. They were everywhere now. "Do you think he understands English?"

Frowning, Stedman shook his head.

Marie walked over to the man, then squatted. "Sir?"

He looked up, his eyes bloodshot and shiny with tears, and she realized he was more boy than man. His hair reached below his shoulders; that and his gaunt face and ragged fingernails gave him a feral appearance. Marie could see his collarbones clearly outlined beneath the dirty, oversized tee shirt he was wearing. "*Tienes hambre?*"

The boy studied her face, his expression weary, but did not respond. She patted her stomach and touched her mouth in what she reckoned was the universal sign for hunger. Nodding his head, he smiled. Not only was the boy tongueless, but toothless as well. She reached into her briefcase. There were two granola bars, a slightly bruised banana and a small carton of apple juice. She rooted around some more and came up with an additional carton of juice and a couple of butterscotch candies.

Stransky watched the boy as he ate, watched how he took sips of juice with each bite, somehow adapting to the absence of teeth and much of his tongue. There were no visible tattoos, so he was probably not a gang member himself. He looked to be no more than 16, maybe that was just because he was so small, but certainly even if he were using meth, he was too young to have lost all his teeth. More likely they were knocked out by the same people who cut out his tongue.

She took out a packet of baby wipes from her briefcase, demonstrated how to use them, then turned her attention to the crowd around the dumpster. There wasn't a whole lot she could do. Even if she were able, she wouldn't crawl up into the dumpster. She'd just have to wait until Wallace, balanced on the edge of the dumpster like a pigeon on a telephone wire, finished taking photos, and Gupta, standing at the ready with her gurney, finished her business.

Stedman emerged from the 7-Eleven holding a maple bar wrapped in a napkin. "Want half?" he asked.

"No thanks ... well, maybe just a bite." She chewed for a minute, swallowed, then licked her lips. "The clerk inside was the one who called, I take it. Have you interviewed him?"

"Says his shift began at 10 p.m. Says he's seen the kid around before, but doesn't know him. Says he saw nothing, heard nothing, knows nothing. The kid just walked in about 5 a.m. real excited, pointing to the dumpster. Figured something was up. Took a gander, saw the foot and called 911."

"According to ..." Stedman looked at his notebook, "James Knotch, all hours of the night, there's homeless guys on the street. Maybe one of them dumped her. Anyway, Mr. Knotch says his shift ended at 7 a.m. He's not getting overtime and just wants to go home. I gave him my card and told him he could go."

"Okay. So, what do we know?"

"Female, apparently strangled, other than that, not much yet. What about our little man over there?"

"Doesn't seem to speak English or Spanish. My guess, the boy's from somewhere in Central America, like you said. I understand that there are indigenous folks there who don't speak Spanish. And not only is he missing his tongue, he has no teeth."

Stedman winced. "Gangs, huh? Maybe he snitched. What I'd like to know is why he stuck around. If you were in the country illegally would you wait around for the cops?"

Marie shook her head. "Maybe he's like … what's the PC expression these days?"

"Intellectually challenged?"

"Yeah that. Or maybe he got tired of living out of dumpsters. Whatever, he needs a proper meal, medical care and a lawyer to handle his asylum claim."

Forty minutes later, Marie was studying the woman on the gurney. A Caucasian between 20 and 30 years old, she'd guess. Rigor mortis had set in. Marie looked at her watch, 8:45. That would put the time of death at least eight hours earlier, say between 10 and 1. The victim had the coarse complexion of someone who'd been out on the streets for a while. She was slender and her hair spilled off the sides of the gurney in chestnut spirals. Needle tracks, both old and new, pocked the pale crooks of each elbow. Her pants were unzipped, but this time they were right side out. The woman's blouse had been ripped open exposing her naked torso. Unlike the other victims, bite marks, deep enough to draw blood, ringed each nipple. Stransky took a tape measure from her briefcase. The ligature marks on her neck were 2.9 centimeters wide. She turned over the right wrist. As expected, there was a small round burn. She'd have to wait for the coroner's report to determine if the woman had been raped or sodomized. Whatever, she'd been in that dumpster a while and stank like … well, like the inside of a dumpster.

"I guess that's it for now," Stransky said stepping aside so Meg Gupta could zip up the body bag.

"Have you had breakfast yet?" Stedman asked.

"Yeah, but a second cup of coffee wouldn't hurt." She started to scroll through the contacts on her watch. "What was that guy's name, the one who got Leticia Obregon a snitch visa?"

"Started with an S. Stocky, Stockman, something."

"Stokey Stokelund, here it is. Maybe he can meet us."

"What do you have in mind? The boy wasn't a witness."

"We don't know that for sure. Certainly, Stokelund doesn't know that. Anyway, I'm thinking I can say the boy is a possible witness and get Stokelund to release him on his own recognizance."

"Let's say Stokelund gets an OR for him, then what? You gonna take him home to your family?"

"Just to breakfast. But he needs medical attention and a safe place to stay. Once that's accomplished, I'll call Eva Chacon at the Coalición de Derechos Humanos, let her deal with him from there. It should be obvious to any immigration judge that the kid deserves asylum."

"You think? Well, good luck with that."

•••

The three sat in a corner booth of Omar's at the Triple T truck stop—Stokelund's request. Marie pulled out hand sanitizer from her briefcase, squirted a bit in the palm of her hand then passed it to Stedman, who did the same before passing it to the boy, who politely refused with an outward palm.

"He probably thinks it's hand lotion," Stedman offered.

She shrugged then dug out two more bottles, one red salsa, one green, and doused her poached eggs with some of each. "Poblano?"

"I'll take the green," Stedman said, then carefully dotted it over his sausage gravy and biscuits.

She handed the bottles to the boy who was sitting next to her. He examined each then selected the red, which he sprinkled liberally over the chorizo and eggs Marie had ordered for him. The boy had already downed a large glass of orange juice.

The server refilled their coffee cups. "*Quiere mas jugo de naranja?*" she said, addressing the boy.

"Please," Marie answered for him. To compensate for the sad little poached eggs in front of her, she stirred double sugar and cream into her coffee. She glanced at the door and waved as a large, well-muscled man strode toward their table, modest beer belly straining the last three buttons of his sharply pressed shirt.

"Hey, Stokey. How are you doing?" She offered her hand. "You remember Officer Torrance Stedman."

"Morning," the agent said curtly, as he shook each proffered hand.

Before sitting, he removed his cap, revealing a head as smooth and shiny as golden delicious apple. He nodded toward the boy, who was looking down at his plate as if willing himself invisible.

"This the IA who witnessed the murder?"

"We haven't been able to interview him, so we don't know for a fact that he's an illegal."

"Then how do you know he witnessed the murder?"

"We don't think he witnessed the murder, but he was the one who found the body in the dumpster. We have reason to believe that he may have been inside the dumpster when the body was dumped and may be able to identify the killer."

The boy leaned into her ever so slightly and she gave his knee a reassuring pat. At that moment, Marie heard the gentle hum then felt the tug of the breast pump. Without changing her expression, she added, "That would make this boy a witness. Of course, a humanitarian visa would be preferable. The boy is obviously a candidate for asylum."

Torrance shot her a look. She raised one brow.

Stokey looked skeptical. "If he'd wanted asylum, he should have turned himself in at the border."

"Given the fact that he can't speak ..."

"Makes no difference," he said flatly.

Marie handed the agent a menu. "You want to order something? It's on our dime."

The waitress appeared with coffee then pulled out her order pad. Without looking at the menu, Stokey said, "I'll have the chimichanga *a la bandera, por favor."*

Marie pictured the deep-fried burrito covered in guacamole, sour cream and salsa, then sighed with resignation. "Make that two, please."

Their vehicles were parked next to each other. "So, now you think the kid actually saw the killer throw the body into the dumpster?" Stedman said, leaning his butt against the door of his car.

"It's possible."

"Well, I don't think the man was buying it."

"I admit it was a reach, but so far, the kid is all we've got. And I certainly don't want to see him deported. By the way, I've been thinking about the woman in the dumpster. How much to you think she weighed, 110, 120 pounds, right?"

"I'd say so."

"You're a pretty big guy, could you lift 120 pounds of dead weight into a dumpster?"

"Not without a stepladder and a lot of noisy grunting. So, our guy is big."

"I'm betting on tall and well built. How tall, you think?"

"Better than 6 feet and maybe into weightlifting."

"Whoa!" Stedman pointed to the street. "Look there!"

"What?" She followed his gaze. A little dog was panting in the median, cars whizzing both fore and aft.

"He's going to get killed or cause an accident or both, poor little mutt." He headed into the street.

Marie watched Stedman bring the traffic to a standstill. As if someone had just delivered a blow to her chest, she was short of breath.

Poor little mutt, he had called her. She could hear him clearly, as though he were standing right next to her almost whispering.

Your voice lacks passion. Voice is all about passion, but what would a poor little mutt like you know about that? He caressed her cheek then and she leaned her face into the palm of his hand.

She had been 16 and that was the first time he'd ever touched her. It had been awhile since she'd thought about that. She walked to the back of the car and threw up her big greasy breakfast. Just as well.

By the time Stedman had returned, dog in arms, the color was returning to her face. She took a bottle of Scope from her briefcase, took a swig, swished and spat.

The dog looked to be one-part Chihuahua, one-part doxie and one-part pincushion. He was a she and had no collar.

"What are you going to do with that?"

"Take her home to Lynnetta. She's been begging for a dog. What should I call her?"

Bess, Trixie, Sheba, Marie was thinking. *Anything but poor little mutt.*

•••

It was mid-afternoon by the time Marie got back to the station. Still feeling a little shaky and empty, she took a bottle of water and a granola bar from her briefcase. Quickly, she unwrapped the bar and nibbled as she logged on to the department data system.

She'd been reluctant to let the boy go with Stokelund, but she had no choice in the matter. The Border Patrol agent had promised to call her when he'd finished processing him. Though Stokelund hadn't bought the witness thing, under the circumstances, he was willing to try to swing a snitch visa for him.

Quickly, Marie bypassed the call log reports on current investigations. By now she figured there would also be a coroner's report on Jorgé Montenegro.

Two days ago, a border patrol agent had found the partially burned remains of Jorgé's Camaro in the desert a couple of miles south of Julian Wash. The tires and the upholstery had been slashed, but it had not been stripped, which eliminated theft as a motive. It could still have been a carjacking gone south, but that kind of destruction takes time. And who brutalizes a car like that anyway? Someone filled with rage and hate, she imagined.

The coroner's report was there. According to Ramona Antone, he'd been dead for approximately 14 days. She looked at the calendar on her watch and counted back. That would mean they'd both been killed on or about May 27, a Sunday, the last time the lovers had been seen alive. She scanned through photos of the boy's body, taken both at the scene and on the coroner's table. They weren't pretty. The side of his head was completely blown away, his face, what was left of it, unrecognizable as the handsome kid in the picture on Señora Montenegro's refrigerator.

A single casing from a Colt semiautomatic pistol had been recovered at the scene. Stransky figured they must have missed one. A 45-caliber round was a big, slow velocity bullet with a large impact. The gun that blew the fist-sized hole in Xochitl's back was undoubtedly the same that took off a major part of Jorgé's head.

If she recalled correctly, the Colt was a military sidearm used up to and through the Vietnam War. Every old soldier loved the Colt 45.

Old soldiers, there were plenty of those around. Since the Vets on Patrol had broadcast on Facebook that Tucson was a hotbed of child sex trafficking, various militia types had descended on the town. Just last week the VOP came upon a skull while patrolling an area west of Tucson, a known migrant and drug smuggling corridor. Over the past 15 or 20 years, dozens of human remains had been found in the vicinity, yet somehow, the VOP had determined that it belonged to a 9-year-old child. Later the medical examiner declared it was the skull of an adult, likely some unlucky migrant. This made perfect sense to everyone but the VOP and the militia that had gathered around them.

Okay, so the Colt 45 might be the weapon of choice by a vet, but if the murderer was a militia member or one of the VOP, what would be a possible motive? Hate crime?

Marie heard the little three-note chime and checked her watch. The right bag on her breast pump had reached capacity.

In the bathroom, she quickly slipped the breast pump from her bra, removed the full and nearly full packets of milk, popped them into her ice chest, and put in their replacements. The whole operation took less than two minutes.

On her way back to her desk, Marie passed the vending machine. Just keep on walking, she told herself. Told herself she'd just eaten a granola bar and didn't need a Butterfinger. When she was almost to her desk, she turned and retraced her steps.

Back at her station, Marie unwrapped the Butterfinger. After one more look at the pictures of Jorgé Montenegro, she took out her cell phone from her briefcase, took a photo and emailed it to Torrance.

Hispanic boy, possibly illegal, and his girlfriend, a Mexican American killed in Julian Wash on or about 5/27. Murder weapon a Colt 45. On 6/13 the boy's Camaro was found burned 2 miles south of J. wash. Gang related? Vets on Patrol? Crazy militia member? Hate crime? Your thoughts.

•••

The floor fan was trained on her and set to high, blowing her hair back from her face and the sweat into her ears. Marie looked at her watch. Five more minutes left on the elliptical.

After exactly five minutes, she stepped off the machine and onto the digital scale Nick had bought her last Christmas. It read 187.4, exactly .7 pounds less than last week. After the births of Catherine, Claire and Mary Ann, it seemed like she'd gotten fit pretty quickly, losing most of the baby fat and regaining her stamina within two months. But Teresa and Nichole were like this double whammy. She'd never lost all the weight she'd gained with Teresa before she got pregnant with Nichole. Fact was, Marie hadn't seen her toes in nearly two years. Sighing, she looked at her watch, set the alarm for 15 minutes and got back onto the elliptical.

Five more minutes into her workout, an image of Xochitl came to her unbidden. She was dressed for her quinceañera. The girl had been found first. Jorgé had been found some distance farther up the wash. She assumed that both were killed with the same weapon. Marie imagined he'd been first. Xochitl must have tried to run away. In those impossible shoes, she had made it maybe a hundred feet. Had the killer thought to let her go then changed his mind? Or was he just playing with her, allowing her to think for a few desperate moments that she could escape?

•••

After her shower, Marie pulled on a pair of Nick's old boxers and one of his tee shirts, her bedtime apparel, and quickly dried her hair. One more feeding and she was done for the day.

Nick was still at his desk. Poor guy, she thought. As she passed his chair, she trailed her hand across his shoulders. "How much longer?"

"It'll be awhile," he said without looking up. "I want to finish editing this chapter so I can send it off. By the way, have you given any consideration to the question of birth control?"

The formality of his tone took her aback. "As a matter of fact, I have."

"So?"

"I think we need to get rid of the hot tub."

"What? The hot tub? You think this is funny, Marie?"

Actually, she did. Trying to suppress a smile, she massaged his neck.

When he rolled his shoulders, shrugging off her hands, she knew she was in trouble. "Really, honey, I've been giving it a lot of thought," she lied.

"A lot of thought? And what did you conclude, Marie?"

The acid in his tone left her speechless, that and the fact the she had come to no conclusion at all.

•••

Always eager at the breast, Nichole didn't seem to notice the quality of her milk, which must be curdled. Blindsided, Marie was both angry and hurt by Nick's sudden hostility. This was to be their last child, the *or else* implicit. No discussion. Well, to be fair, he'd given warning, while she, silly woman, had been preoccupied with the murder of two kids and a few homeless women.

Guido padded in and dropped his head onto Marie's knee signaling his need to go out. "In a minute." She scratched behind his ears and he settled down with a great sigh.

Logically she knew she didn't need to keep that promise to God. What did God care about how many babies she had? They weren't being raised Catholic; they weren't being raised anything. If she were to be honest, it wasn't logic at play here but magical thinking. If she kept her promise, then her son would forgive her and contact her. Not logical, not realistic, but she clung to the notion nevertheless. Now she was feeling hollowed out, done in, bereft and so angry. What made it worse was that no matter how hard she tried, she couldn't blame Nick for any of it. Well, there was all that hostility. That seemed over the top.

CHAPTER 8

It's Not the Way They Look at You;
It's the Way They Don't

Thursday, June 17

The Weird Sisters made their way toward the bus stop. Perched on the top of Elaine's roller bag was a small mesh carrier, courtesy of Las Hermanas, the only shelter in town where pets were allowed. Inside, the kitten, which turned out to be a calico once the grime was wiped off, rode sleek and pert as a little pasha. She was now called Precious, Gumba or Lil' Bit, depending on who was doing the calling.

"What do you think they'll serve for breakfast?" Elaine asked no one in particular.

"The usual: oatmeal or cold cereal, hard-boiled eggs, toast, peanut butter and jelly, bananas if they've got 'em," Pappy answered, swiveling her baseball cap from front to back to keep the sun from beating down on her neck.

"Sometimes there are doughnuts," Brittany added.

"Sure, if you like day-old," said Elaine.

"What do you expect for free?" Pappy was clearly irritated as much by the rising heat as Elaine's lack of gratitude. "You want fresh doughnuts, get a job."

"I'd love to have a job, any job." Elaine looked at Pappy, smiling broadly. "Would you hire me?"

"No! You don't have any teeth."

"Right, that's why I don't have the five bucks for fresh doughnuts."

Adjusting the strap on her backpack, Brittany persisted, her tone almost reverent, "The Hospitality House sometimes serves bacon and eggs, toast and potatoes."

"Yeah, well. Good luck getting in there. Besides, they wouldn't allow Gumba." The green light at Congress had begun the countdown and Pappy picked up her pace.

For several minutes the woman trudged on in single file toward the bus stop, sweating though their layered clothes. It was the morning rush hour and the streets and sidewalks were busy. Men in ties and women in impossibly high heels or little pointy flats strode along with purpose. Deftly, they wove around the women as if they were stanchions on a downhill slalom.

The three stopped at a red light. Brittany swiped at the sweat now running down her neck. "Yesterday a man drove up in a car and asked if I wanted a ride," she said.

"Didn't happen, Brit," Pappy said flatly. "You were with us all day."

"Well, maybe it wasn't yesterday," she said, fast talking to preclude further interruption. "But it's 111 out, so of course I want a ride. He gives me a bottle of Fuji water to drink and the next thing I know, I'm Gorilla-taped to a metal table. Men and women in white coats and those masks people in white coats wear – there were at least a dozen, standing around the table. The table's cold and hard under me and I am naked. And this one woman wearing Ray-Ban aviator sunglasses says, 'This is going to pinch a bit,' and I see that they've made an incision in my breast so they can insert a microchip to monitor my every move so they can siphon off my creative juices."

"It's okay, Brit," Elaine reached for her hand. "We won't let anybody siphon off your juices. Not while we're around. Right Pappy?"

"You bet."

"I reported it to the cops. I even showed them the incision in my breast, and nothing. They didn't care."

"Sometimes, cops are like that," Pappy observed.

"Yeah. It brought up a lot of sediment," Brittany said.

"Sediment?" Pappy asked.

"Emotions and stuff."

"You mean sentiment?"

"No. Sediment. Those bad bits that fall to the bottom. Whenever something scary happens, like the woman in the Ray-Bans, they get stirred up and float to the surface. You never can get rid of all the sediment."

"Makes sense to me," Elaine said.

The light turned green and the women, resolute, crossed the street gazing straight ahead. At Las Hermanas there would be air conditioning, food, a laundry and a shower waiting. If they ever had any, they could even check their email. While Brittany did the laundry, Pappy and Elaine would attend a 12-step meeting. That was today's plan. Every day there must be a plan.

•••

Garnet Woodward threw the pack onto the passenger seat then turned the key in the ignition. She studied the directions she'd jotted down then checked the gas gauge. Still a quarter of a tank left. Usually, Garnet took the bus whenever she needed to go anywhere and this was only the third time she'd gotten behind the wheel of the truck. Sitting up perfectly straight so she could see over the steering wheel, she slowly depressed the clutch, then fumbled the gearshift into what she hoped was first. Holding her breath, she released the clutch while pressing on the gas pedal and the truck lurched forward. She determined that it was best to take I-10, less need to shift gears. And it would take less time. Her sister didn't like it when she had to take care of the baby.

•••

Dated June 16, Ramona Antone's autopsy report on the dumpster victim was waiting for Marie when she came into the station. Now she read it for the third time. Jane Doe number 4 died on June 9 sometime between 0100 and 0300 hours. She was 5 feet 3 inches tall, weighed 118 pounds, was 25 to 32 years old and had had recent sexual activity both vaginal and anal, with anal tearing. High amounts of both alcohol and fentanyl were in the blood sample. Hair and fibers not belonging to the victim were collected. She wore no underpants beneath her jeans and none were found at the scene.

Marie considered that for a moment. Maybe the woman didn't ware underpants. Maybe the Santa Rita Stalker, as the Daily Star had dubbed him, hadn't bothered to put them back on or maybe he kept them to enjoy later. Sometimes Marie didn't like the way her mind worked.

In addition to a ligature mark, 10 centimeters in width, around her neck, there was a burn on the inside of her right wrist. Like Sierra Horton, no blood or skin was found beneath her nails. Unlike the teen, the cause of death was an overdose of fentanyl rather than strangulation. Did the attack take place after the woman was dead or while she was dying? Didn't the killer realize the woman was already dead? If not, why not? Is so, why the overkill?

Marie made a few notes. Victims: Anal penetration, absence of semen in one case, bite marks to breast in another. The killer: Possibly impotent. Tall, muscular, likely. Belt, a possible murder weapon. Why does he re-dress his victims? Why the burns? To determine awareness? Necrophilia? She underlined the last word.

Marie studied the photographs taken at the medical examiner's. She had not been able to find anyone matching number 4 among the missing person reports dating back for the past five years. Though her skin was coarsened by life on the streets, she'd been young and pretty not so long ago. It was hard to believe no one missed her. As yet, no one had come forward to say that their daughter, sister, wife, lover, friend had not come home.

Marie had run her fingerprints and photo though the local and federal databases, but there'd been no hits. The Star, by policy, would not run pictures of dead people, so that was out. The body and clothing had been reasonably clean. Even if she'd been homeless, she'd had access to a shower and laundry. The autopsy report indicated that her liver looked a little gray. Though the woman had been actively using both drugs and alcohol at the time of her death, she might have gone through a round of rehab. So, Marie would parade the photo around the homeless shelters and the Primavera Foundation, maybe Old Pueblo Community Services, though, in cases of violent death, it was sometimes hard to make a positive ID. Still, someone, somewhere had known this woman.

If the body remained unidentified, she'd be buried by the state and no one would ever know or care but Marie.

Marie copied the report and the photo onto her iPad then emailed them to Torrance. She looked at her watch: 8:10. She better get moving. Breast pump humming, she selected a photo of the victim with a sheet tucked up under her chin and sent it to her phone. There was no point putting it off. Santa Rita Park was the logical place to start, and it wasn't getting any cooler out.

As she was walking out of the building, her phone rang, Eva Chacon of Derechos Humanos.

"What's up, Eva?" Marie listened while the woman quickly brought her up to date on the Honduran boy. He now had a name, Jacinto Escobedo.

As she got into the car, Marie shook her head, resisting the scene that had begun to unspool in her mind.

Feeling queasy, she ramped up the AC high enough to blow her hair back and took a few deep breaths before putting the Ford Explorer in gear then waited another minute before pulling out of the TPD lot and then south on Stone Avenue.

According to Eva, a medical exam revealed that not only had Jacinto's tongue been cut out and his teeth pulled, but his eardrums had been punctured, perhaps with a wire coat hanger. How had Jacinto survived such violence, not only physically but with his humanity intact? She recalled him leaning into her at the restaurant, trusting, like a child might. How did this boy find the strength to travel some 2,000 miles to a place both foreign and unwelcoming?

And what kind of person would do such a thing, not killing the boy outright, but leaving him so damaged as to practically guarantee a death, slow and painful both physically and psychologically. Who could be so evil? Marie had encountered crimes committed by people who were crazy, tortured, desperate, angry, jealous and stupid, but evil? Evil was rare.

Once it was determined that Jacinto was deaf, Eva had tried to communicate with him through writing. Turned out that Jacinto could read and write Spanish well enough to tell his story.

He was the youngest of five children. His older brother, Rigoberto, who had been coerced into joining a gang, apparently snitched, Eva had told her. Jacinto didn't know anything more than that. Presumably, his brother escaped into Guatemala and then headed north. The gang took their revenge on Jacinto.

After the boy recovered, if you ever recover from such a thing, his mother had insisted that he and his sister, Ascensión, follow their brother north. Somewhere along the way, they became separated. Eva wasn't able to determine how that happed or where his sister might be now. Jacinto couldn't or wouldn't say how he got into the United States or how long he'd been here.

According to Eva, all asylum claims must be made upon entry. Obviously, Jacinto had not done that. And no, ICE was not known for flexibility. Since the fear of gang violence was no longer considered in asylum claims, Jacinto would likely be deported back to Honduras.

"We'll see about that!" Marie said, as she made a U-turn on 22nd Street and headed north toward midtown and Posada de la Luz instead of east to Santa Rita Park. Jacinto was a key witness to at least one murder, she would claim. Who was to say he was not?

A waystation for migrants who'd been granted temporary asylum, Posada de la Luz was one of the places ICE agents regularly dumped families when released from detention. Typically, they'd be there a couple of days while arrangements were made to join family members elsewhere. Jacinto had been staying there for the past week while Eva Chacon figured out what to do with him next. Now that Marie knew he could write, there were some questions she wanted answered.

She knocked on the door of the inconspicuous little house in a slightly shabby central Tucson neighborhood that would, no doubt, soon be transformed into the next yuppy enclave. As she waited, she could hear a child crying. After several minutes, a placid, but weary looking young woman answered the door.

"Good morning," Marie said holding out her badge. "I'm Detective Marie Stransky and I'd like to speak with, or rather … is there someone here that can help me communicate with Jacinto Escobedo? I have some questions I'd like to ask him."

"I can do that if you don't mind waiting a few minutes. One of our families is about to go to the airport and that's always a little chaotic."

"I can wait. And your name?"

"Tricia Delgado," she said, stepping aside. "Please come in."

The living room was cluttered with furniture and toys. A playpen was set up in the middle of the floor. The aroma of fried chorizo hung in the air from the morning's meal. Marie's own breakfast had consisted of a small bowl of nonfat plain yogurt topped with frozen blueberries and Splenda. She looked at her watch. Her lunch of tomato slices and cottage cheese was still hours away.

In the kitchen, Tricia was speaking in rapid Spanish to a woman washing dishes. Marie understood the words *hurry, leave it* and *airport*. On the dining table was a platter with the remains of breakfast: a pool of beans, some rice and a small pile of eggs scrambled with the chorizo. She looked at it with longing.

"Have a seat," Trisha called from the kitchen.

Marie sank down into the worn sofa, her knees folded almost to her chin. After a few minutes, she got up and took the platter to the kitchen. "You forgot this."

"Thanks." Trisha took the plate from her hand. "We're in such a rush this morning."

Marie watched in horror as Trisha scraped the food into the garbage pail. At that moment, a dark spark plug of a man appeared at the kitchen door. He was carrying a boy who looked to be about 4 years old. The little guy seemed unable to hold up his head and there was something strange about his hands. Cerebral palsy, Stransky figured.

"*Listo,* Ramón?" Trisha asked.

"*Si. Listo.*"

The woman who had been washing dishes grabbed her purse from the back of a chair. She waited while Ramón gave Trisha an awkward hug and then the three were gone.

Trisha nodded toward the space just vacated by the man and his son. "He carried that child all the way from Guatemala, every mile of it on foot."

"Where's he going?"

"To family in Atlanta."

Marie nodded. How would they manage, she wondered. Under the circumstances, facing airport security seemed as daunting a task as walking all the way from Guatemala. "So how do they get through security?"

"Sometimes it's dicey. Alma, the woman who was washing dishes, will take them to the gate and wait with them until they board."

"The airport allows that?"

"Yes, but sometimes there's a hassle." She picked up a toy off the floor and threw it into the crib. "Jacinto's out weeding the backyard. I'll call him."

With his hair buzzed, clean clothes, nails trimmed and cheeks filled out by good food, the boy who sat across from her now bore only a slight resemblance to the one slumped in the shade of the 7-Eleven just last week. Only his expression, eyes weary and wide with apprehension, was the same.

Trisha jotted down a few words on a tablet and showed it to Jacinto. As he read them, some of the tension left his shoulders.

"He doesn't write well, so I suspect he doesn't read very well either. It works best if you ask short questions requiring simple answers."

Marie needed only a moment to formulate her first question. "Did you see who put the woman in the dumpster?"

Trish wrote the words in Spanish then turned the tablet toward Jacinto.

Marie watched as Jacinto slowly penned his answer. *Si, un hombre.*

"Did you know this man?"

"No, pero, yo he le visto de ves en quando en el parque."

She didn't need the words translated. The boy had seen the man in the park before.

"Can you describe him?"

He read the translation and shrugged. *"Es grande y rubio".*

Okay, he was tall and blond. "Did he have a beard?" she asked.

"No lo recuerdo," was his response.

Marie was skeptical. You'd think he'd remember if the man had a beard or not. "Was he muscular, thin, fat?"

Once again, he did not remember.

"Would you recognize him if you saw him again?"

"No se."

No need for translation there. Jacinto was shutting down. Marie reached over and patted his shoulder then took the pen from his hand and wrote, *"No tienes miedo. Estas seguro aqui."* Even as she wrote the words, she knew she could only guarantee his safety from the killer. Deportation was another matter.

He took a deep breath then wrote for some time, then drew a sketch of a boy hiding in a hedge and a man pulling a large roller bag. On another sheet of paper, he drew a more detailed sketch of what looked to be bleachers, crime scene tape surrounding a figure on the ground, police officers and a woman who might well be herself. In a third picture, he drew the dumpster. Once again there was the man with the roller bag. When he finally finished, he looked up at her, the slightest smile on his lips.

She kissed the tip of her index finger and touched it to his cheek, then tucked the drawings into her briefcase.

As she threaded her way in and around the heavy noontime traffic, Marie considered the interview with Jacinto. From his hiding spot in the bushes, he had seen a man pulling a large suitcase on wheels, as he called it, across the grounds at the park. Jacinto wrote that the suitcase had appeared heavy. They were pretty sturdy, those roller bags, sturdy enough to carry a 120-pound body.

Jacinto had described the man as tall, which might not mean much. The boy, who barely reached her shoulder, would think most people tall. Jacinto didn't know what day or what time that was, but it was before dawn when everyone else was asleep. Later that same morning, he'd seen the crowd of people around the yellow tape. Marie had shown him the picture of Sierra Horton. He had never seen her before. But yes, Jacinto was certain that the man he'd seen in the park was the same man who threw the body into the dumpster.

Smiling, Marie turned onto 22nd Street. Jacinto's snitch visa would be good for a very long time. It might take months to catch the killer, and given the current justice system, years before they got a conviction. There would be plenty of time to prepare a case for asylum.

She needed to call Stokey and Eva Chacon at Derechos Humanos. And she couldn't wait to tell Torrance.

Before she left Posada de la Luz, Marie had asked Jacinto one final question. After long consideration, he answered it with a shrug. Probably she would never know why the boy had not simply run away when confronted with the body in the dumpster. Under the circumstances, that's what she would have done.

The sun drilled into the top of Marie's head as she crossed the brown grass at Santa Rita Park once again. An assembly of ragtag men stood in the shade of an Aleppo pine. A number of them were tall, most had carts or some sort of makeshift conveyance piled high with what looked like debris to Marie. No one would meet her gaze. She looked around for Oliver Kemp or any Vet on Patrol, but none was about. So much for 24-7-365.

Armed with the photo of victim number 4, Marie ignored her discomfort and strode over to the nearest man. Despite the hot sun, he had a blanket wrapped around his tall, thin frame like a Masai warrior. A red cloth was twisted around his head and tilted at a rakish angle. He seemed mesmerized by some object in the distance, the majestic Rincon Mountains, perhaps, or possibly the traffic light at Park and 22nd.

"Excuse me, sir," she began.

After a few moments, he turned the full force of his bloodshot gaze upon her. "My lady, how can I be of assistance to you this fine morning?"

She flashed her badge. "I'm Detective Marie Stransky." She held out her hand.

He deigned to smile, but did not take the proffered hand. "And I am Cicero." He seemed to wait a beat as if listening for confirmation, then added. "Yes, I am Cicero."

Or possible just crazy, Marie thought, adjusting her posture from authority figure to supplicant. Lowering her chin and rounding her shoulders a bit, she continued. "Sir, I've come to you today because I need your help identifying a woman whose body was found near here on June 10. If you would be kind enough to look at a photo." She held up her phone and pointed to the photo of number four.

The man took the phone from her hand and brought it close to his face. "Hmm. She is white. I am afraid all white women appear the same to me. There are skinny white women and fat, old white women, and young. To me that is the only difference. But perhaps one of my colleagues could be of help." He led her by the elbow to a picnic table beneath an Aleppo pine, then took off with her phone, she hoped, to consult with his fellows.

The interviews with the willing few took no more than 10 minutes. Several of the men thought they might have seen the victim around. Two knew her to turn tricks for drugs. One, a tall guy who called himself Crazy Eight, said her name was Roxy – he didn't know her last name. He was sorry, but not surprised, that she was dead. Marie gave him a bottle of water, but he tucked it into his cart rather than drink and toss it.

Still standing with his blanket wrapped around him, Cicero had been waiting patiently nearby. Marie waved to him. He smiled and waved back, her cell phone still in his hand.

"What will you give me for this very fine phone?" he asked.

Two juice boxes and a granola bar later, Marie was on her way. It seemed a pretty good bargain. She had her phone and number four had a name – Roxy, short for Roxanne possibly, or just as likely a name she'd chosen to call herself when she became a person no one would miss. She was sorry not to have gotten a DNA sample from Crazy Eight, but she'd surreptitiously snapped his picture with her phone, so

94

that was good. All good.

It was nearly noon and Marie had one more stop to make. Las Hermanas Women's Hostel was within striking distance of Santa Rita Park.

•••

Unlike other shelters, where the homeless must leave after an early breakfast, the women at Las Hermanas, both overnighters and women sleeping on the streets, could stay during the day. Now that temperatures were upwards of 105, many women would come in to get relief from the heat, catch a shower and a meal.

Women in twos and threes were sitting around the half-dozen tables in the dining area. Some were chatting; others were more guarded, eating in silent concentration. Marie was allowed to circulate among the women, cell phone picture of Roxy in hand.

After canvasing the dining room and the laundry, Marie went into the day room, which doubled as a dormitory at night. Some guests were napping or reading within little habitations made up of their stuff. Some were grooming, some talking, others simply watching.

Marie was surprised to see a number of dogs, big and small, on leashes or in crates. A little elfin thing with wiry black hair and teeth in a jumble was perched atop a wire cart stacked high with the usual assortment of bundles and bags. At her approach, the dog growled, apparently taking great offence at this stranger in their midst.

"Hush," her owner commanded. She'd been using an orange stick to push the cuticles back from her fingernails. "Please ignore her rude behavior. She's a guard dog in a lapdog's body." The woman scratched the dog's ears, but it continued to growl. "I'm Cynthia and this is Tootsie."

"I'm Marie," she said, taking the soft hand the woman offered. Cynthia was older than most of the other guests, perhaps in her late 60s, slender, almost fragile, and well-groomed. Marie wondered what events led to her fall from grace.

She showed Cynthia her cell phone with Roxie's picture. "I'm wondering if you might have known this woman."

"Pretty." She touched the screen gently with the tip of her well-manicured finger, then shook her head. "Sorry, dear, I can't help you."

"Thanks anyway." Marie was about to add, 'have a great day,' but thought better of it. This woman's great days were long behind her. Tootsie was still growling as Marie moved on to a table where three women were eating their lunch in the day room since animals were not allowed in the dining area. One of the three was holding a calico kitten, offering it tiny bits of bologna from her sandwich.

"She doesn't like bologna, I told you," another woman was saying. The third stared quietly into space.

Smiling, Marie held up her badge. "Sorry to interrupt your lunch, ladies. I'm Detective Marie Stransky and I'm trying to identify this woman."

Three heads snapped up in unison. They were Pappy, Elaine and Brittany, she was told.

Pappy, clearly the oldest of the trio, studied the picture. "Nope. We've never seen her." Apparently, she was the spokesperson for the group.

"Thanks, anyway," Marie said. As she turned to leave her breast pump started to hum.

Eyes wide, Brittany shot up from her chair. "Oh my God, that sound."

"Oh dear," said Elaine.

"But she has the power," Brittany yanked up her shirt. "Look at this." She pointed to a spot on her bare breast. "A computer chip. They're monitoring my every move."

Marie leaned in closer to the small, pale breast, then closer still. Sure enough, there was a tiny mark a shade whiter than the rest of the breast, a scar perhaps or a stretch mark.

Brittany pulled her shirt down, her voice thinning to a whine. "I need a lawyer, or if you could just call the FBI. No, don't do that. They may be involved too."

Shaking her head, Elaine looked directly at Marie and drew her finger across her throat. Pappy simply rolled her eyes. Marie quickly got the picture and apologized once again for the interruption.

It wasn't long before she had spoken to every willing woman in the room. As with the men at the park, a few had been acquainted with the woman known as Roxy, Roxanne or Rocky. The name varied, but all agreed that she was into drugs and that it had only been a matter of time before something very bad happened to her. Their fatalism did not surprise Marie. Women without options often felt their lives were out of their hands. In other words, shit happens. Deal with it.

One woman stood out, however. Her name was Flor. A fading beauty with a tangle of light brown hair, she looked a bit like number 4. As Flor studied the photo, tears began to fall.

"Did you know this woman?"

"Yes. She was …" She pressed her index finger to her lips, as if to keep them from trembling.

Marie lightly touched the woman's shoulder. "Take your time."

"Let's just say a friend." Flor took a deep breath. "She liked to be called Rocky, like in that old movie with what's his name, that Stallone guy? She thought she was tough, unbeatable."

"Do you know her real name?"

"Roxanne Bellacosta. That's an Italian name, you know." She half-sat, half-collapsed, crossed-legged on the floor.

Marie eased her bulk down, first one knee, then the other, then her butt so she could face Flor.

"It could have been me. Not that long ago, it could have been me. Rocky didn't want to … I couldn't make her … you know. Wasn't ready to give up the drugs. But things had gotten really, really bad on the street. I guess I just didn't want to die."

"Do you know if she had any family?"

"Oh yeah. She had a couple of kids in foster care, a mother and a brother, but I don't know where."

"Did you ever see her with a tall, blond man, possibly homeless, who might have been supplying her with drugs?"

She shrugged. "Tall and homeless? There are a lot of tall, homeless guys out there. Besides, I haven't seen Rocky for … well, it seems like a very long time."

Marie took out a packet of tissues from her briefcase and handed them to Flor.

"Thanks," she said, blotting away the mascara that streaked her cheeks.

With both hands, she pushed her hair back from her face. "Listen, I need a smoke. I don't suppose you…"

"Sorry."

"So, are we done here?"

Marie nodded. "If you remember something, anything at all, that might be of help." She struggled to her feet then handed Flor her card.

•••

"I'm home," Marie sang from the kitchen. Only Guido came to greet her. She patted his head and scratched beneath his jowls. "Anybody home?" When there was no response, she smiled. Nick must be picking up the girls, Nichole in tow. If she was lucky, she'd have a few minutes before chaos descended. She stowed her breast milk in the fridge, turned the oven to 350, then went to their bedroom.

After locking her Glock and mace in the gun safe, she exchanged her pants suit for a pair of cutoffs and a tee shirt. Next, she began the daily breast pump maintenance, filling the sink with warm water and a squirt of antibiotic soap. Using the tiny brush that came with the apparatus, she scrubbed out the flanges and tubes, set them to dry on the back of the toilet then plugged the cups and her cell phone into their respective chargers.

"Damn," she whispered, slapping her forehead with her palm. She'd meant to call her OBGYN for an appointment. She been vacillating between having her tubes tied and going on birth control pills. The permanence of a tubal ligation gave her pause, but unlike with birth control pills, sperm and egg would never meet and there would not be the monthly possibility of a baby being swept from her body like old dishwater. Well, tomorrow she'd make the appointment for sure. In the meantime, she'd give it more thought.

Forty minutes later, the aroma of chicken legs slathered in bottled barbecue sauce filled the kitchen. She took an enormous bag of tater tots from the freezer, counted out eight tots each for Nick and Catherine, six for Claire and four each for Mary Ann and Teresa – she would abstain – then put them into the oven with the chicken.

She had finished arranging tomato wedges on a plate and was just beginning to slice a cucumber when she looked at the clock, nearly 6:30. A wave of anxiety and irritation passed over her. Where were Nick and the kids? She was about to call his cell when Guido's bark announced their arrival.

Relief just seemed to heighten her anger. She took a deep breath. "Hi, guys." She could hear Nichole screaming as the parade of children filed through the back door. "How come so late?"

"*Frozen*," Claire said, placing the baby's diaper bag on the kitchen table.

Nick was the last through the door. "She's madder than hell," he said.

For a moment, Marie thought he was referring to her. "Why are you so late and where's Catherine?"

"Didn't you get my message?" he said, plunking the baby carrier next to the diaper bag.

"No."

"Well, I left you a message."

"Really? How could I have missed it?" She didn't try to mask her skepticism. "So?"

"Catherine is spending the night with one of her horse camp buddies. It was in the message. After school, Claire went home with Chutney. When I went to pick her up, they were in the middle of 'Frozen.' Nichole was sound asleep so ..." He leaned in for a kiss.

Marie took a step back. "You've been drinking beer!"

"It was getting late, so Toni ordered pizza for everybody and we had a beer. It was in the message."

Toni! she thought. The woman, a Pilates instructor and single mom with buns of steel, kept work hours at a gym that were so irregular Marie suspected she must have a very special arrangement with the boss. That, plus she was always a wee bit too happy to see Nick, always touching him, touching his hand, punching his shoulder, stroking his forearm. Marie tried to modulate her voice. "So, you drove with the kids after you'd been drinking beer."

"One beer and it's what, four blocks between here and Toni's?"

Marie snapped off the oven. "So, everyone's eaten but me?"

"Yeah, sorry about that, but it was all in the message. Jesus, I thought you'd appreciate a little alone time."

"Please don't swear in front of the kids." She picked up the screaming Nichole and sniffed. "Dirty diaper. I could smell it from across the room," she declared, then whisked the baby out of the kitchen.

Hugging the howling Nichole to her chest, Marie checked her phone messages and sure enough, Nick had left one. Now she felt angry and guilty.

She set the baby down on the changing table. Crooning softly, she whipped off the offending diaper, swabbed the tiny bottom with baby wipes then slipped on a clean disposable.

"Better now, sweetheart?" She cooed softly.

Nichole shuddered briefly then rewarded her with a smile.

By the time Marie finished feeding the baby, the kitchen was empty. She could hear Nick out in the garage lifting weights on the Power Tower he'd bought at Sears last winter, when it was 20 degrees cooler out there. She peeked into the living room where Claire and Mary Ann were watching a Muppets video, Teresa sacked out on the floor between them. She picked up the sleeping toddler. The child's eyes fluttered open and her hand slid down the front of Marie's shirt seeking her breast.

"That's just for the baby." Teresa's hand clung to her breast like a mollusk to a rock. Gently Marie pulled it off and tucked her into bed. "You're a big girl now. You eat big girl food." Teresa seemed resigned to the fact and closed her eyes without protest.

Back in the kitchen, she removed the desiccated dinner from the oven, selected two legs and a pile of tots. She ate them standing over the sink, her anger diminishing with each bite of crusty barbecue-sauced chicken and every tot. The guilt was not so easily dispatched.

She dumped the remaining tater tots in the garbage to preclude further consumption. As she neatened the kitchen, she began to compose her apology. She was sorry to have been so snappy, but it had been a long day and there was the fact of the beer. It occurred to her then that Nick might not even have noticed she was mad. He hadn't been particularly observant lately. Well, she thought, washing the sauce off her mouth, she'd soon find out.

Nick grunted as he lifted a 150-pound barbell above his chest, then, blew like a breaching whale, as he eased it back down. "Sorry about the mix-up, but ..."

"You left a message, I know." She sighed, thinking an apology that ends in *but* is really not an apology. "I'm sorry I got mad. I don't know how I missed your message." She looked at her watch and stepped onto the elliptical. She'd already doubled her workouts. "Oh, by the way. I made an appointment to see my OBGYN today. I've decided to get my tubes tied." She said the words casually, as if she made life altering decisions every day. Even if it wasn't yet true about the appointment, now that she'd said it aloud, she was committed.

"Not necessary."

"What? You changed your mind?"

"No, but I figured that since birth control upsets your Catholic sensibility ..."

"My Catholic sensibility?"

"Okay, your promise to God. Anyway, I'm having a vasectomy. It's all arranged."

"Wait! No discussion, just *I'm having a vasectomy.*"

"Well, you seemed so ... I don't know. It just occurred to me that it was the best course of action. And it's all arranged. You won't even have to miss work. Toni said she'd take me to the hospital and watch the kids and ..."

"Wait! You discussed this with Toni?"

"So?" He grunted as he heaved the weight above his chest, blew out as he brought it back down. "It's no big deal; only outpatient."

Marie stepped off of the elliptical. "A vasectomy is a big deal and it's even a bigger deal that you discussed this with Toni before telling me."

"Sorry, but it just came up and she offered."

Marie drew her hand across her forehead. "You mean, like you were sipping a beer and eating pizza while watching 'Frozen' and somehow ... Help me out here, Nick, because I can't quite see how the topic of vasectomy would just come up."

CHAPTER 9

The Right Place at the Right Time

Friday, June 18

Stedman was about to take his dinner break when the call came in: a welfare check at the Desert Agave Apartments. He knew the place well. Located just shy of midtown, many of its occupants qualified for Section 8 rent assistance, a good deal for the owner of an apartment most people would not want to live in. Simply put, Section 8 folks living at the Desert Agave were poor but lucky to have help with rent. The rest of the folks living there were just poor.

He thought of Davie Woodward. Even if he'd qualified for housing assistance, there was such a long waiting list for Section 8 that baby of his might be in preschool before he got one.

People just automatically assumed that Section 8 housing brings crime to a neighborhood, but that was not Stedman's take. No. Section 8 housing was simply more likely to be in an area where crime was already high, and the poor were more likely to be the victims than the perpetrators.

Outside a ground floor apartment, a woman who looked to be pushing 70, but sported purple streaks in her gray hair, was waving her arms. She wore flip flops and a flowered muumuu barely concealed her sagging breasts. Presumably, this was the manager. Before getting out of the car, Stedman noted the time, dinnertime, and sighed.

For a moment the woman looked at him with suspicion, then nodded her head toward the apartment. "She's not answering the door. But the baby's crying and the neighbors are complaining." She folded her arms over her breasts. "She's not the type to leave her kid alone."

"Do you have a key?"

"I do, but I didn't want to go in because, well, you never know what you're going to find and I try to mind my own business."

Stedman nodded. "Go ahead and open it."

She did, then stepped aside as if a pack of wild dogs might charge out.

A heavy-set woman was lying face-down on the floor. Stedman radioed for an ambulance, then knelt down beside her. There was a pool of something that smelled like Campbell's chicken noodle soup on the floor, spilled, he suspected, when she passed out. It made his stomach roil, part hyper-alertness, part bad associations.

Stedman placed two fingers on her neck just below her jaw. Eyes closed, he could barely feel the faint beat of her heart, then there was nothing. Immediately, he rolled her over, ripped open her shirt then tilted her head back to open the airway. He placed the heels of his hands, one upon the other, on her sternum and began compressions.

"Ah, ah, ah, ah, stayin' alive, staying alive. Ah, ah, ah, ah, stayin' alive, stayin' alive," he chanted, the sternum giving way with a pop beneath his hands with each compression. He continued the chant and the compressions, adrenaline fueling his arms, until the EMTs arrived minutes later, he didn't know how many, but his shirt was soaked through with sweat.

The baby, a toddler with a mass of matted blond hair, howled from her crib. Immediately, she held out her arms to him, way too comfortable with a stranger. "Hey little girl, hey baby," he said, picking her up.

The manager stood in the doorway. "Can you give me the woman's name?" Stedman asked.

"It's Rita Hoffman."

"And your name?"

"Florence Cardona."

He shifted the child onto his hip and wrote both names in his notebook. "And is there someone, this child's grandmother or aunt, you can call?"

"I don't know. As long as people aren't making trouble, I say what happens behind their closed door is their business, not mine." She took the baby from his arms.

"Sounds wise, but maybe you've noticed somebody coming and going?"

"Sometimes I see a man go in. He stays for a couple of hours. Don't know if he's Kitty's dad, or what. Rita never said, and of course, I don't ask. But it seems to me they're ... well, close, for lack of a better word. Anyway, like I said, I try to mind my own business."

"Yes, ma'am."

"There's an older woman, could be Rita's mom, I guess. She drops by once in a while, and Rita takes Kitty for a walk just about every morning at 9, but I don't know where she goes."

Stedman nodded. If he kept quiet long enough, Ms. Cardona might come up with something useful.

"There was a birthday party for Kitty, when was that now, two weeks ago on a Saturday or maybe it was Sunday, the man who might be the baby's dad and the older woman, who could be the grandmother, were there plus some people I'd never seen before." She kissed Kitty on the cheek, saying, "You are my sweetie baby."

"Sorry I can't be of more help," she continued. "Like I say, I try to mind ... Oh! She has a phone, it's one of the expensive kinds, smart. Don't know where she gets the money for that, but maybe you can find a number there."

The two went back into the apartment. "I imagine the phone is in her purse." Ms. Cardona set Kitty back down in the crib then rummaged through the kitchen cupboards. "This will do," she said holding out a juice box to the child. "She usually keeps her purse behind the ..." She reached behind the television. "Here it is." She handed the phone over with a triumphant smile.

"Thanks, ma'am. You've been a great help."

"You know I like to mind my own business, but Kitty doesn't usually fuss like that so I knew something must be wrong."

"Well, you saved a life today."

"I did? Imagine that," she said, then threw her arms around his middle as far as they could reach.

•••

After a medium Domino's Pizza, Stedman swung by the station. There was a message from Garnet Woodward waiting for him. Stedman clearly recalled the day she and her husband were evicted, the heat and their desperation. When was that? He took out his notebook and thumbed through it. May 27 it was. Certainly, after all this time, Garnet Woodward didn't call to say thank you, he was thinking, as he dialed her number.

"This is Officer Torrance Stedman, returning the call of Ms. Garnet Woodward."

"Officer Stedman, thanks for getting back to me so quick."

He could hear the thin, inconsolable cry of a newborn in the background and recalled that Garnet had appeared close to giving birth that day. He also recalled that Davie had been armed and angry. "Yes, ma'am. How can I help you?" he asked, and the woman began to cry.

The address Garnet Woodward gave him was in one of those big house-small lot-subdivisions in the foothills of the Tucson Mountains. A floodlight illuminated a basketball hoop that hung over the three-car garage, yet the three cars were parked in the drive. A dog, it sounded like a big one, barked behind a gate as Stedman made his way up a concrete walk that wound through assorted cacti. Two neatly trimmed Texas Ranger Sages flanked the entry.

Garnet Woodward was waiting for him at the door, her eyes still swollen and red.

·"Thanks for coming," she said stepping aside so he could enter. "Can I get you a glass of iced tea?"

"No thanks, Ms. Woodward." He welcomed the cool air as he entered the living room, which was unexceptional. An oversize leather sectional filled one side of the room, a 36-inch flat screen TV hung over a fireplace that looked as though it had never been used, and the heavy floral drapes drawn across the large front window, he imagined were never opened, remained pulled tight both day and night. A chair that matched the sectional held a basket of laundry that needed sorting. The woman picked it up and set it on the floor.

"Please sit down."

There was the sound of a television coming from the back of the house where he figured the rest of the folks who lived here were assembled. He eased himself into the soft, cool leather. "So, tell me, Ms. Woodward, how I can help you?"

"Davie, my husband, do you remember him?"

"I do, ma'am."

"Yes, well, he's been gone, missing I guess, since the day we were evicted. He left me off here, this is my sister's house, saying he'd be back as soon as he found us a place. Next morning, his truck was parked out front. I thought he'd spent the night there, but no. The keys were under the mat and his wallet was in the glove compartment with the rent money. I didn't know what to think; well, I did. I thought maybe he'd …" she started to cry again. She plucked a onesie out of the basket and held it to her face.

Stedman thought to reach over and pat her arm, then thought again. "Take your time, ma'am."

"I don't know what to do. Beth, that's my sister, well, she never liked Davie; she said he'd left me cause of the baby, but he wouldn't do that. He was real excited about the baby."

Stedman flipped through his notebook. "You say your husband has been missing since May 27th?"

"Yes sir. I thought, well, I hoped he'd at least call about the baby, but it's been over three weeks now, nine days exactly since the baby came, so… I found your card in his wallet and remembered how you helped us that day. I mean, what should I do? My sister wants the truck out of here, but it's in his name so I can't sell it unless…" She held the onesie up to her face once again. "He had that gun. Do you think he might have …? I mean, he was so down and ashamed and angry, not with me though. He never was."

"I see. You might consider filing a missing person report. Do you have a photo of your husband?"

"A photo." She looked up at the ceiling then buried her face in the onesie. After a moment she shook her head. "All our photos were lost when the water heater broke," she said, then began to sob again.

At the end of his shift, Stedman took a place at an empty desk, logged in and began to file an incident report on the welfare check. Just the bare bones stuff was all that was required; he stabbed at the keys with blunt index fingers. The visit with Garnet Woodward, he would keep to himself for now.

At the bottom of his report, he noted the odometer readings and the parking space where he'd parked his Crown Victoria in a row of identical Crown Vics, so the next cop to use it would know exactly where to find the car that matched the key.

He was about to leave, then thought better of it. Turing back to the computer, he opened the NamUs database for unidentified bodies, entered Arizona, and bam, 1,752 hits, but only a few were current. He scrolled down for matching dates, age and race. It took less than a minute to determine that Davie Woodward was not there.

Stedman needed to back up. Woodward had clearly been a very scared and angry dude that day, angry at the system in general and Mexicans in particular. He was also armed and desperate, and, well, hopeless, a recipe for violence. Suicide was an obvious conclusion, or maybe it was just the conclusion Woodward wanted folks to make.

From personal experience, Stedman knew something about feeling abused by the system, about rage and worthlessness and screwing up. And he knew, or at least thought he knew, that Davie Woodward was not the type to turn all that against himself. And the date, May 27, seemed significant beyond the eviction of the Woodwards.

There had been an email from Marie some time ago. He remembered writing the particulars in his notebook. He leafed though it now until he came to the entry.

Marie, 6/15 — Hisp. boy, illegal? gf, Mex-Am. Julian Wash
+ – 5/27. Colt 45. Vic's. burned Camaro found 6/13, 2 mils. S. J.
wash. Gang related? VOP? Militia member? Hate crime?

The date and the Colt 45 clicked. So maybe Davie Woodward had committed suicide. There was a lot of desert out there and his body had yet to be found. Maybe Davie Woodward was alive and shirking his paternal duty. Or maybe Davie Woodward, in his rage and frustration, had murdered two Mexican kids then staged his suicide. Whatever, Stedman had gone as far as he could go with this one. Any further involvement would invite Lindgrin's attention, something he wanted to avoid.

He emailed Marie. Let her chew on it.

CHAPTER 10

Words, Said and Unsaid

**Monday and Tuesday,
June 21 and 22**

She read the message from Torrance once more before deleting it. It seemed a guy named David Woodward and is wife Garnet had been evicted the same day Xochitl and Jorgé had been murdered. According to Torrance, the man had been angry and desperate, owned a Colt 45, and then disappeared after dropping his very pregnant wife at the home of her sister. Garnet Woodward was afraid her husband had committed suicide.

Marie wondered if there was a third body somewhere in Julian Wash. The date of Woodward's disappearance and the Colt 45 could be coincidence, or maybe this guy killed Jorgé and Xochitl, demolished the car, then in a fit of despair committed suicide. It could also be that Woodward killed the lovers, faked his suicide, then simply disappeared.

Marie could imagine Woodward sitting in his truck out in the desert feeling angry and victimized. Would he have gotten a six-pack to ease his pain? Likely. Then along comes two Mexican kids in a nice little Camaro and he goes ballistic. If this were the case, the motive would be clear. Xochitl and Jorgé were victims of hate, displaced rage, alcohol and more than a bit of stupidity.

She turned her attention to her other priority. The results from the sexual-assault kits were finally in. As expected, the DNA collected from the saliva on Roxanne Bellacosta's breast matched all but one of the four other victims. It did not match the DNA taken from Oliver Kemp's water bottle. No surprise there either.

What did surprise her was the number of hits from CODIS, the Combined DNA Index System. In addition to Sierra Horton and Roxanne Bellacosta, there was a match with DNA found on six other bodies spanning from 2015 to 2018: The first on record was in Pensacola in May 2015. The second was in San Diego, July 2016. The killer struck in Tucson twice in July and August of 2016, in Orlando in September of 2017, back to San Diego in May 2018, then back to Tucson in July and August of last year.

Several questions came to mind. The killer seemed to operate in hot weather. Why? Easier access? Were there other victims yet unknown? Any survivors? And where did he go in the winter, underground like the snake that he was?

It was apparent that the killer had the wherewithal to travel back and forth across the nation, which meant he was merely posing as homeless to gain access to his victims. He seemed to be following some sort of circuit and would likely be moving on soon. That, and the fact that the known victim count numbered eight, increased Marie's sense of urgency.

What they needed was a decoy to draw him out. She could think of only one person who would fit the bill. The problem, as always, would be Lindgrin. She took a moment to make a little chart showing the dates and locations of the murders, keeping it so simple that even Lindgrin could discern the pattern.

The door to his office was closed, which might mean he was playing solitaire on his iPhone, napping or actually engaged in police business.

Hoping to catch him doing something he shouldn't, she knocked, then entered without waiting for an invitation.

Lindgrin was indeed playing with his phone and clearly annoyed at her intrusion. Marie stepped back into the hall and waited a beat.

"We can handle this in-house, plus she's a slut," Lindgrin was saying.

Marie couldn't deny that. Coco La Batt was a private detective, but she was also known to turn a trick when business was slow.

"There is no one on our force right now that can do this job. Coco's smart. She's canny. She's flashy." Marie didn't want to sound too emphatic. "Our guy seems to be on some sort of circuit, Pensacola, San Diego, Tucson, Orlando, back to San Diego then Tucson, leaving one or two victims in each location." She pointed to the chart in front of him. "See?"

Lindgrin studied the chart for a moment then shoved it back at her. "If I recall, she's a user, unreliable."

"Unpredictable, maybe, but she does good work," Marie countered. "Remember last year we had her rolling around town at night in a wheelchair. She was where she was supposed to be, when she was supposed to be there, alert and sober."

Lindgrin started sorting through some files on his desk. Was he even listening? She pointed to the chart again. "It looks like he'll move on pretty soon. We need to nail him before he does, because if I'm right, he'll commit a couple more murders elsewhere then come back here."

Lindgrin sat behind his big desk unmoved. "We were at the academy together when she was calling herself Colette something or other, something Jewish. Even back then, she was a slut and a boozer."

"That's not how I remember her."

"You?" His eyebrows sprung up in surprise. "Oh right. You were there too, sort of."

Marie stuck to her script. "Like I said, we need to nail this guy and Coco …"

"Is a prostitute and a druggie."

"Just what we need."

Marie was surprised how easily Lindgrin gave in. She took out her phone and scrolled through her contacts. They'd been quasi friends since their stint in the police academy when the woman was still Colette Swartz. The two were of an age, and as the only women in the class, they bonded over their shared otherness. Back then, Marie had known nothing of the woman's penchant for cocaine and expensive shoes. Colette failed a urine drop and was kicked out midway through training.

There she was, still listed under Swartz.

•••

For once, Marie was on time. She settled back in her chair in the bar of the posh Arizona Inn and looked out the window at the vast green lawn surrounded by beds of summer annuals in reds, yellows and blues. A midtown water-sucking oasis, the Arizona Inn was a Tucson landmark and one of Coco La Batt's "favorite places on earth."

Coco La Batt. She was sexy, streetwise and devoutly single, in other words, everything Marie was not. Fact was, if it hadn't been for the drugs, Coco would likely be where Marie was now—the only female detective on the force—and Marie would be working the beat. Like it or not, appearance trumps brains. They both knew this.

It wasn't long before she stood in the doorway. Both women were aware of the eyes that followed the yellow spandex miniskirt that barely covered Coco's firm bottom as she clicked her way across the flagstone floor on black stack-heeled sandals laced to the knee. She dragged her fingers through a tangle of variegated blond curls exposing a melon slice of toned, tanned flesh between the waistband of her skirt and the hem of her V-necked, chest hugging knit top. Amazing, Marie thought, recalling the once chubby cadet from the police academy. Marie figured the woman must spend hours each week at the gym. Clearly, she didn't want all that hard work to go unnoticed.

Feeling more bovine than ever, Marie reminded herself that Coco had no children, was not likely to have children and would most likely face a sad and lonely old age some 40 years hence.

Coco kissed the air by Marie's cheek, and sat down, making a great show of crossing her smooth legs.

Within moments the waiter was there to take their order.

Marie asked for a virgin margarita.

"Make that two," Coco said, now sweeping the loose curls to one side.

Marie's eyebrows shot up.

"Sober." Coco answered the question inherent in the raised brows. "In recovery, no booze, no pills, no powder, seven months, two weeks and four days of sobriety, not that I'm counting."

"Hey, Coco. Congratulations, that's great and you look … amazing."

"Yeah, well, I have this persistent fantasy in which I'm invited to one of my family's many celebrations, bar mitzvas, weddings, anniversaries, graduations, yada yada."

Marie nodded. She felt a stab of sympathy for Coco, but would she invite a drug-addicted prostitute to join her family for Thanksgiving dinner? Maybe. If it were her daughter, absolutely. "So, how's business?"

"Which one?"

"Detective."

"I get enough gigs to make it worth keeping my license. Besides, private detective looks a whole lot sexier on my Facebook page than …"

"Than?"

Coco shook back her hair and shrugged. Her second source of income was illegal in the state of Arizona and not a subject for open conversation.

"Oh!" She took out a little alligator case from her purse. "My card."

There was no picture, just the words, *No concern too big or too small. Discreet, attentive. Call Coco, licensed private detective and more,* in black script on shiny pink and her phone number.

"Very professional," Marie said, handing the card back.

"Keep it. Maybe you'll run into someone who needs my services." She smiled wryly. "Hmmm." She looked around the room, up at the ceiling then back at Marie. "What's that humming noise?"

It was Marie's turn to shrug.

"Well, it's coming from you."

"Yeah? I guess it must be my breast pump then."

"You're wearing a breast pump?"

"Inside my bra. It runs on a battery," she said as if wearing a portable, electronic breast pump were commonplace. She was tempted to point out that she also had an Apple Watch.

"Amazing, but spare me the details. So, you had another baby? What's that, like number eight?"

"Five. A little girl, Nichole."

"How sweet," Coco said.

Marie doubted the woman's sincerity, but smiled anyway. Nichole was sweet and she wasn't about to let Colette Swartz, who had mouse-brown hair at the academy, not streaky blond, make her feel bad because she had five kids, six if she counted Francis, who might very well be applying to graduate school even as they spoke.

The waiter set their drinks on the table. Coco took a sip. "The Arizona Inn is my favorite place on earth. You can almost smell the money." For a moment she gazed out at the flowers, then sighed. "So, what's up, Ms. Famous Detective? I have to meet up with a friend in cabana 34 at 6 o'clock sharp."

Ten minutes later, the deal was sealed. The pay was good enough, the gig would easily fit in Coco's schedule, which at the moment was wide open, and she could tell her mother all about her undercover work for the TPD; maybe that would gain her access to the next family celebration.

Coco looked at her watch. "Oops. Gotta go."

"Hang on." Marie drained the last of her margarita. "It's none of my business, but I've got to ask. Where do you keep your gun?"

Coco leaned over. Between her firm, tanned breasts, Marie could just see the polished walnut butt of what could only be a LadySmith snub-nose revolver. She didn't ask if it was secured in some kind of holster or just tightly wedged, but she certainly hoped the safety was on.

•••

With all the others, Nick had gotten up and brought the baby to her, dozed while she nursed, then put the baby back in her crib. Then there would be a cuddle and a second good-night kiss. Now he seemed quite able to sleep through Nichole's wails. She got up to retrieve her babe. Really, there was no practical reason they should both be awake. Still…

All and all, it had been a pretty terrible evening and it was a relief to just sit in her rocker and nurse the baby. Both of them had been polite and careful not to intrude on each other's space. They'd hardly exchanged a complete sentence, as if talking would only make things worse. After dinner, Nick loaded the dishwasher, which was usually her job, then disappeared into the kitchen alcove to work. Was he angry at her or feeling guilty? She didn't know and had done nothing to find out. Just done her workout—it was now up to 25 minutes and she'd lost six pounds—taken a shower, checked on the kids and then turned in. She didn't know when Nick had come to bed, so careful he'd been not to wake her.

They were in trouble, she knew. She could hear Nick snoring. Well, whatever was eating at him, it wasn't keeping him awake. Marie figured she'd be sleepless for the rest of the night trying to figure out what, if anything, she could do to make things better.

Sleep my child and peace attend thee, all though the night, she crooned into the baby's ear. *Soft the drowsy hours are creeping, hill and dale in slumber steeping*

I, my loved one, watch am keeping, all through the night.

She couldn't remember the rest of the words.

Just as Marie was slipping into a doze, she felt a hand on her arm. "Mom," Catherine whispered. "Mom," a little louder.

"Hmm. What is it, honey?"

"I think I've started."

Marie almost asked, *started what*? "Oh! Okay, honey." She lumbered out of bed and followed her daughter to the bathroom, the only room in the house where they could be assured privacy.

"See?" Catherine held up her pajama bottoms. "See that spot?"

"Yeah, that's it all right. How are you feeling?"

"Okay, I guess."

Marie cupped her daughter's face in her hands and kissed her forehead. Out the window, the sky was just beginning to lighten. Marie rummaged under the sink for the box of supplies she had put together for her daughter.

"I already got it out."

"Ah, good girl, then I guess you're all set. Do you want one of these Midols?"

"Yeah, maybe." She accepted a pill. "So, now will you tell me about your promise to God?"

Marie handed her daughter a glass of water. "I'm pretty tired. How about when I get home from work?"

"Mother, you said…"

"I know, but do you really want to hear about this before you go to school?"

"I have to go to school? I thought … never mind." She sat down on the bathmat and leaned back against the tub. Marie eased herself down beside her daughter.

"Okay, so. Are you sure?"

"Yes, Mother. Go ahead."

Marie took hold of her daughter's hand. "You know that my father left my mother when I was a baby."

"Yeah. He was a you know what."

"I suppose. Anyway, that probably had something to do with … how things happened later on."

"So, what happened later on?"

"Well, when I was 16 I had a, I don't know, I guess you could call it a crush on my chorus teacher."

"How old was this man?" Guido pawed the door. Catherine let him in and he settled down with his head on Marie's knee. "Mother?" the girl prompted.

"I don't know." She scratched the dog behind his ears. "Probably old enough to be my father." It occurred to Marie then that her 11-year-old daughter, who always seemed to be a very old soul, probably already knew where this story was leading. "Anyway, I loved to sing and he paid attention to me, but he also said things that put me down."

"Like what?"

"For one, he called me a poor little mutt."

"That's how they do it, Mom. First, they act like they like you, then they make you feel bad about yourself and then they … well, take advantage of you."

"How do you know all this stuff?"

Catherine answered with a shrug. "Go on. So, this creep is paying attention to you…"

"We had sex and the rest is history."

"Mother!"

Marie sighed deeply. "Okay. So, I got pregnant. When I finally got up enough nerve to tell the chorus teacher, he looked at me and said, 'I'm sorry to hear that. Who's the father?'" Marie chuckled mirthlessly. "It was as if God had struck me dumb."

"So, then what did you do?"

"Nothing. I felt numb. I just kept going to class, going to chorus. It was like sleepwalking through someone else's bad dream. When your grandmother finally noticed – I was a big girl even then and didn't show for a long time – anyway, when she realized I was pregnant, she was furious."

"If I got pregnant you wouldn't be furious. You'd be concerned, maybe disappointed, but you wouldn't be furious."

"True, but you're too smart to make my mistake."

"You were 16, Mom. You fell into his trap because you never had a father, and Grandma Ruth, well, let's just say she has her issues."

Taken aback, Marie wondered if she'd been a bit too candid over the years about her mother's *issues*. "Once again, how do you know all this stuff?" Guido licked her hand and she resumed scratching.

"I read."

"Not from your summer reading list you don't." Marie took a deep breath. She did not want this to turn into a lecture. "Okay. Your grandmother was furious."

"Did she know that your chorus teacher had …"

"There's a word for that."

"I know what the word is."

"Intercourse?"

"Oh. Is that the scientific term? So, did Grandma Ruth ever ask who had intercoursed you?"

Marie suppressed the urge to explain that intercourse was a noun. "I told her I didn't know and she took that to mean that I'd had intercourse with more than one boy."

"Then what happened?"

"I went to a special program for unwed mothers, which was what we were called back then, run by the Sisters of Mercy."

"Was it terrible?"

"Actually, no. Once I gave up the fantasy that the chorus teacher would come and rescue me, I began to love it. I felt valued and protected. I made friends. One of the nuns, Sister Mary Ann, God bless her, I can still hear her voice. She took me under her wing and encouraged me to get my GED so I wouldn't have to go back to the same high school after the baby was born."

Catherine nodded her head. "I see. So, what happened to the baby?"

"He was adopted by a nice Catholic family who named him Francis."

"Did you ever tell Grandma Ruth the truth about who got you pregnant?"

"No."

"Don't you think you should?"

Many times, Marie had been tempted to do just that, especially when she was angry over one of the woman's failures as a mother and grandmother, but always she had restrained herself. Whether that was good or bad, she could not say. "It would just make her feel bad and wouldn't change a thing." Marie shrugged. "She'd raised me as a single mom and I think she was trying to ... to save me from the hardships she'd gone through."

"Well, despite all that hardship, you turned out pretty well."

Marie kissed the back of her daughter's hand. "Thank you, sweetheart. I'm glad you think so."

By the time Marie had answered Catherine's questions about her promise to God, why Grandma Ruth was so mean, statutes of limitations and whether or not she missed Francis, the sky was turning pink. For a while, now, they had been just sitting quietly holding hands. Who is this wise person, Marie thought, and where have they taken my daughter?

There was a distant cry barely discerned behind the closed door and then an insistent wail that could not be ignored. "There's my little alarm clock," Marie said, struggling to her feet.

"Before you go, Mom, one more question."

"Another?"

"Yeah." She held out a slim brown calf covered with sun-bleached fuzz.

"Do you think I should shave the hair on my legs now?"

"Does it bother you?"

"Not really."

"Then there's your answer."

"So, do we have to tell Dad?"

"Of course, we do. He'll be so proud of you."

"Proud? Why would he be proud? It's not as if I've actually done anything."

"Well, it's a milestone that we should celebrate."

"Then would you tell him for me?"

"Sure, and we'll fix you a special dinner. What would you like?"

For a moment Catherine considered the options. "KFC chicken with twice baked potatoes, carrot sticks and those cupcakes from Fry's, the ones with white icing and chocolate sprinkles."

"I'll tell Dad," she said, relieved to know that there was still a child in that body.

•••

"What do you mean, she started her period? How is that possible?"

"It's not only possible, it was inevitable."

"Jesus, I know that, Marie," he said, trimming his mustache. "It's just ..."

"Yeah, I know. I'm not ready either, but guess what? This is not about how old it makes us feel. It's about Catherine, who is an incredibly squared away kid, by the way. Anyway, maybe you could pat her on the knee and say something encouraging."

"Like what?"

"Like your mother told me the big news. Like, you're a great kid and I'm proud of you. Like, I hope you know that you can come to me if you need anything or just want to talk. I'm always here for you and I love you." It occurred to Marie that she should have said those very words, *I'm always here for you and I love you,* to Nick when things between them had started to slide.

"Just say something so she knows you know." Marie paused before turning on the blow dryer. "Oh yeah, I thought a special dinner was in order. Catherine wants KFC chicken, twice baked potatoes, carrots and those cupcakes you get at Fry's – the ones with the chocolate sprinkles. Unless something comes up, I've got the chicken covered. Oh, I need some cash," she said, thinking of the vending machine at the station. "Couple of bucks will do."

"Wallet's in the front pocket of my jeans."

Marie put the blow dryer back in the drawer. Nick's jeans were spread over the back of the big flower-upholstered chair that someday, when the kids were grown and she was retired, would be a place where she'd read quietly each night before going to bed.

As Marie reached into the front pocket of the jeans she was overtaken by a sudden dizzy-queasy feeling. She plopped down into the chair, head between her knees.

In my pocket there is a surprise for you, he had told her. *Reach in.*

She had. The pocket was deep and empty. He put his hand over hers. *Surprise!* he said, as he guided her hand to his erect penis.

For a few moments, she sat, eyes closed, breathing deeply through her nose, exhaling slowly through her mouth. Drenched in sweat, Marie sat up. Her only thought was that she'd have to blow her hair dry again.

•••

Garnet Woodward sat weeping on the couch, her newborn in his carrier sleeping at her feet. "Sorry, Detective …"

Marie reached in her briefcase and handed her another packet of tissues. "Just call me Marie. Can I call you Garnet?"

The woman nodded. "Sorry, Marie," she said softly.

Garnet kept looking over her shoulder. Was she afraid someone might overhear their conversation? "Is there something else going on here, Garnet?" Marie urged. She had given the woman three packets of tissues, listened to the details of her baby's birth, watched her inexpertly breastfeed the little guy, whose name was Jason or Jared, successfully resisting the urge to give lactation advice, and now she was simply tired of listening to the woman cry. "I know you're very upset and rightfully so, but you seem, I don't know, kind of scared. Is your sister treating you okay?"

"Yeah, she's treating me okay. It's just that both she and her husband, well they're Mormons. Don't drink. They never approved of Davie because he likes … he liked…" She started to cry again. "I just can't stand to hear them criticize him when he might be …"

Garnet looked up at her, eyes pleading. It was as if the woman could not bring herself to say the word *dead* and wanted Marie to finished the sentence for her. Nodding her head in feigned sympathy. Marie knew better than to put words in her mouth. It was getting late, but she'd give it one more try. "Is there anything else you'd like to tell me?"

Mopping her eyes with an already sodden tissue, Garnet shook her head.

"Okay. I'm wondering if you might want to file a missing person report. If you have a picture of your husband I could …"

"Like I told Officer Stedman, I don't have a picture. Not one. I mean, I used to have some pictures, but they got … damaged when the water heater broke. Did I tell you about the water heater?"

"Yes, the water heater, but even without a picture, you could still file a missing person report."

"But … how would that help? I mean, what would happen?"

"Well, you can give me the information about your husband, like what he looks like, where you saw him last, how long he's been missing, who his friends and relatives are. We enter all of that into a national missing persons database, then we contact relatives and associates …"

"He really doesn't have any relatives or associates other than me."

"How about people he works with?"

"He works alone."

"I see." Marie said, by which she meant that she could see that any more prodding, however gentle, was useless.

The baby, now awake, began to whimper then quickly revved it up to full howl. Marie's breast pump hummed in response. Garnet picked him up proudly, but awkwardly. She was wearing a gold charm on a chain around her neck. It slipped across her breast. Failing to locate the nipple, the baby continued his angry wail. In frustration, Garnet yanked the charm off of her neck, breaking the chain. It fell to the floor. Frowning, she tried to guide the baby's mouth to her nipple.

Once again, Marie resisted the urge to give the new mother a few tips. Sitting back, she placed a restraining finger on her lips. Finally, desperation prevailed and the little guy latched on.

Silently, the two women watched the baby nurse. "That's a sweet little guy you've got there."

Garnet smiled weakly, tears starting again. "I broke my necklace."

Marie bent to retrieve it. "It can be fixed." She turned it over in her hand. "A Saint Christopher medal. You're not a Mormon?"

"No. It's just my brother-in-law ... well, my sister is one of them now too." She tossed her head toward the back of the house.

Marie took a needle-nose pliers out of her briefcase and began to work on the chain. "Catholic then?"

"No. Davie gave that necklace to me ... That was before he ..." More tears.

"Yes, Davie. Are you sure you don't want to file a missing person report?"

"I don't see what good it would do."

"Well, give it some thought. We can always do it some other time." She placed the repaired necklace on the table. "See? An easy fix."

"Thanks so much." Garnet started to cry once again. Just as Marie was wondering if she could simply get up and go, the call came in. Another body had been found in Santa Rita Park.

•••

Who names their daughter after a semiprecious stone, Marie wondered as she waited in the drive for the air conditioning to go from hot to cold. Dismissive. Not as pretty as a Ruby, so let's just call her Garnet. Marie had to admit, the name seemed to suit the woman.

She studied the house that belonged to Garnet's sister. It was a large, two-story, earth-toned affair. On either side of the narrow concrete path leading to the front entry were Texas Ranger Sages. The work of a crew of landscapers armed with hedge trimmers and leaf blowers, they'd been planted in a sea of weed-free decomposed granite and buzzed into cubes. A Lexus and a Suburban were parked in front of a three-car garage. Except for the battered truck slumped at the curb, it looked like every other house in the upscale neighborhood. As the crow flies, it was not that far from her own neighborhood, also filled with identical, but much smaller, earth-colored homes. In fact, Garnet probably bought her disposable diapers at the same Albertsons she did down on Grant and Silverbell.

Marie rested her head against the steering wheel and let the now cool air wash over her. During the hour spent with Garnet Woodward she had alternately drilled her with questions and commiserated with her as the woman sobbed. She learned that the missing David Woodward was a medium kind of a guy: medium height, medium build, medium brown hair and eyes. According to Garnet, her husband had no beard, no tattoos, and no pierces, which was hard to believe. Marie didn't know anyone under 30 who didn't have at least one pierced earlobe. She'd held and admired baby Jason, or was it Jared, petted an affable old chocolate lab who'd wandered into the room then out, but she hadn't learned anything new other than the fact that Garnet's sister and brother-in-law were Mormons. Now all she wanted to do was pick up the damn chicken and go home to her family, but that wasn't possible.

She took a deep breath. "Hey Siri, call Nick," she said to her wrist and waited for him to pick up.

"Everything's ready," he said by way of hello.

"Something's come up," Marie said, dreading Nick's response.

"So, you won't be home for the dinner? What about the KFC? It's not like I can just load up the kids and go get the chicken myself."

"I know. And I'm sorry. There's a box of chicken burgers in the freezer." She could hear him breathing on the other end. Defrost them in the microwave. "Come on, Nick. This doesn't happen that often."

"Often enough," he said and hung up.

"Shit," she said.

"That's not very nice," Siri responded.

Marie looked at her watch. "Oh, shut up, you."

Outside, it was still kissing 100. She pulled away from the curb, now feeling not only frustrated but guilty, and so tired her hair hurt. Two blocks down the road, something nudged the corner of her brain. Like a beloved but lost lyric, it eluded her. It was a common side effect of lactation, she'd once read, and her experience confirmed it. What? What? What had she missed?

•••

Marie waved to the officer on duty, Sergeant Rodney Croft. Marie had signed a birthday card for him last week and knew the paunchy, graying Croft had just turned 60, making him an old-timer, by TPD standards.

"Evening, Detective."

"Evening, Sergeant. Could you please turn up the AC?" The heat was always good for bad humor in situations where there was nothing to joke about. "So?" she said, handing the man a bottle of water.

"Thanks," Croft said, lifting up the crime tape. He tilted his head toward a woman tucked beneath the oleander hedge.

As she knelt down beside the body, it occurred to Marie that it was the same hedge that had sheltered Jacinto. The woman was young, obese, with almost colorless hair cropped close to her skull. Her left eyebrow, lower lip and the septum of her nose were pierced. The left arm was flung over her face, the right rested on a roll of bare stomach protruding between cut-off Levis and a tee shirt. The clothes were dirty but intact. There were no obvious signs of trauma. The odor of urine hung in the air.

Marie slipped on a pair of gloves and gently turned over the woman's right arm. There was no cigarette burn. The woman, she guessed, had probably crawled beneath the hedge to escape the intense heat, might have died from hyperthermia and dehydration, an overdose, alcohol poisoning or any combination thereof. Whatever the exact cause, she wasn't one of Marie's.

She placed the arm back on the woman's stomach, then stood, leaving her to rest in peaceful repose.

By the time Audrey Wallace and Meg Gupta were wrapping up their respective tasks, it was beginning to cool off. Marie had interviewed the person who'd found the body, a sweet old gent who'd been collecting cans. She gave him a granola bar and a box of apple juice, relieved that there was nothing more that she needed to do. Unless the autopsy report proved her wrong, this death was not a homicide. With a wave at Croft, who would be there until the bitter end, she headed for the Ford Explorer.

Officer Audrey, who'd been packing up her gear, called out to her. "Detective Stransky?"

Marie sighed. Could she pretend that she hadn't heard and keep on walking?

"Detective?" Audrey shouted, jogging after her.

Marie turned on her heel. "What's up, Audrey?"

"Can we talk?"

"Sure." Marie said, anxious to end the conversation right there.

Audrey looked over her shoulder. "Can we talk somewhere else?"

Marie put a little more distance between them and the sergeant. Now that she didn't have sweat running into her eyes as was the case almost every time she encountered this young woman of late, Marie noticed that Officer Audrey had become a bit thick around the middle. She glanced at her left hand. No wedding band. Was she trying to keep her pregnancy a secret? Marie had been there and knew what a lonely place that was. She pulled out two bottles of water and handed one to the officer. "Shoot."

"Thanks." She unscrewed the top and took a gulp. "We're pregnant," Audrey whispered with a little smile.

"We are? I mean you are?" Marie wondered why any of this was her business and why they were still whispering.

"I'm 16 weeks. My wife and I are so excited."

"Ah, well, congratulations." *Wife*, Marie thought, taking a long swig of water. She'd rather *partner* or even *spouse*, which would allow her to imagine a normal heterosexual relationship. As a Catholic, however lapsed, she clung to the notion that marriage was between one man and one woman, but – and this was the lapsed part – she didn't think her beliefs should dictate the behavior of others. She glanced at her watch. "So…?"

"So, you're kind of my role model here."

Marie was sorry to hear this.

Seemed like Officer Audrey and her wife, Chablis, had their entire life planned out. Chablis was biracial. Audrey was inseminated by a biracial donor. In two years, Chablis would have a baby by a white sperm donor. They would buy a house, not a big house, but a nice little house with three bedrooms and an office – Chablis kept books for her mother's real estate business and a few others, and she could work from home. There would be a big backyard, and, oh yes, they would adopt a shelter dog because pets strengthen children's immune systems. Marie had never heard Audrey utter more than the most perfunctory communications, but now on and on she went, while Marie nodded in silence. Interesting what pregnancy, especially a first pregnancy, does to a woman.

Marie, who finished off the last of her water as Audrey finally wound down, resisted the urge to warn her that plans were written not on wet concrete, but on sand. She was just beginning to fully grasp this herself.

Marie tucked the empty bottle in her briefcase and smiled kindly, though she wasn't feeling particularly kind. "And so …?"

"So, how do you manage, you know, with Lieutenant Lindgrin?" She patted her mostly flat belly. "I can't keep this a secret forever."

Ah, so this was where they were going. Marie felt a wave of sympathy for the woman. "Let me think." She'd been dealing with the man's crude, rude harassment for years. She could well imagine what he might do to a young, attractive woman like Audrey once she was on his radar. "Okay, first defense is to avoid the man whenever possible. Second, never rise to the bait; that only serves to enhance his enjoyment of what is for him a pleasant diversion. Stick to the topic at hand. And never let anger or utter amazement at his crass stupidity distract you from your focus." She paused, to let all that sink in. "I guess that's about it. Oh yeah, and if it really gets bad, slap him with a sexual harassment suit. I've been there and I'll back you up. Gotta go now. And, Audrey, congratulations. I'm very happy for you," she said and actually meant it.

●●●

Exhausted, Marie climbed back into the Ford Explorer. It was nearly dark and her watch was telling her that the right milk bag was full and the left nearly so. The bags were guaranteed leakproof, but what about the flanges? Would they hold? She imagined the pent-up milk erupting from her breasts like twin Vesuvii. She reached into her briefcase, pulled out her last packet of tissues and stuffed several into each cup of her bra.

As the AC blew a welcome stream of cold air in Marie's face, her thoughts returned to the woman beneath the hedge. After a cursory examination of the body, Meg Gupta guessed she was perhaps 20, 22 years old, the same age as Marie's son. She was surprised that the only thing she felt at the moment was disappointment that the dead girl was not one of her priorities and evidence that her guy was still around.

Disappointment, she thought. Now that was just wrong. But if the guy had moved on, would she still be a detective on the force when he returned? If Officer Audrey Wallace sued the department for harassment, she might be issuing speeding tickets by then.

CHAPTER II

*If You're Going to Walk All Over My Heart,
Take Off Your Nikes First*

Tuesday evening, June 22

The only light in the kitchen was the one over the stove. "Hello?" Marie called out as she slipped the two packets of breast milk out of her bra and into the fridge. Nick was not working in the alcove, dirty dishes from the celebratory dinner were still on the table, and the cheesy aroma of twice baked potatoes hung in the air. Suddenly, it occurred to Marie that she hadn't eaten dinner. She put the milk in the fridge then opened the oven door, hoping that Nick had left a potato for her, but no. She'd have to scrounge up something for herself.

Marie recognized the soundtrack from their well-worn CD of "Babe" and figured everyone was gathered in the living room. Before checking in to see just how much trouble she was in, she swung by her bedroom to deposit her Glock in the gun safe.

Taking a deep breath, Marie peeked into the living room. She was startled to find not only Claire and Mary Ann, but Chutney as well, all seemingly mesmerized by the pig and the henpecked sheep farmer. Now what was Chutney doing here? Had there been some sort of emergency. "Hi, guys," she said. "Where's Daddy?"

"Out in the garage," said Claire without turning her head away from the action on the screen.

"And Catherine?"

"In her room."

Ah, no emergency then. Relieved, she went to check on Teresa and Nichole. Both were soundly asleep in their respective cribs. She leaned in and kissed Teresa's salty temple, noted she'd been put to bed without a bath, then looked in Nichole's crib. The baby was sucking on her fist. Soon she would wake and need to be fed.

Marie padded down the hall, knocked on the door of the big girls' room then opened it a crack. "May I come in, Catherine?" There was a grunt that Marie took for permission. "How're you feeling?"

"Terrible," Catherine said, stuffing a book under her pillow.

"Cramps? Did Daddy give you Midol?"

"Yeah, and he got out the heating pad too, but it still hurts."

"I know, but you'll feel lots better tomorrow." She smoothed the hair back from her daughter's face. "I'm sorry I missed your dinner."

"It's alright."

"No, it's not, but it couldn't be helped. Would you like a little back rub?"

"No thanks… well, maybe you could scratch my back," Catherine said, rolling over onto her stomach.

Marie smiled. It seemed like years since Catherine requested what had once been a nightly ritual. She lifted up her daughter's pajama top and started skimming her blunt nails lightly over the girl's shoulders, aware that she hadn't told her the whole truth about her promise to God. Whether she was protecting Catherine or herself from that deep hurt, she couldn't say. Some other time, perhaps, she'd have the courage, energy or will, whatever it was she currently lacked, to resolve that.

"So, what were you reading just now that you didn't want me to see?" Marie asked.

Reluctantly Catherine pulled a paperback book from under her pillow. "It's not as bad as they say."

"Vampire Princess?" On the cover was a voluptuous young woman with blood-red lips wearing what appeared to be a prom dress. Marie opened the book and scanned the first page. Her eyes seized on the words *freaking dork,* not great words, but better than the alternatives. "Not exactly on your summer reading list." She handed the book back to her daughter and began inscribing lazy circles across her back. "So, how come Chutney, I mean Chelsey, is here?"

"Claire spent the afternoon with Chelsey and when her mom brought her home, Dad invited them to dinner."

"Oh, that's nice," she said, trying to keep the irritation out of her voice. "So, I guess Dad and Toni are out in the garage."

"Yeah. He's spotting her on the free weights, or something."

Or something, Marie was thinking.

Out in the garage, Nick was indeed spotting Toni—spotting her tight little spandex-wrapped ass as she executed squats with 100 pounds of iron across shoulders, a lot of weight for someone who probably weighed 115 with her gym shoes on—but that's what Pilates can do for a girl. They were so lost in their labors they hadn't heard her come in. She noted Nick's look of concentration and tender concern. She couldn't remember when he'd last looked at her that way. A lump took form in her throat. Clearing it away, she managed a smile. "Hey, guys." The "caught in the act" look on Nick's face confirmed her suspicion. More than iron was being lifted.

•••

Marie had fed Nichole and showered. Her own dinner was out of the question. The very thought of food made her stomach hurt, or perhaps it was the thought that a confrontation was inevitable. Whichever, as she sat in bed waiting for Nick, both her stomach and her heart hurt.

"It's not the way it looked," he said, the moment he walked in the door.

"Oh? How did it look?"

"Well, I thought you may have gotten the wrong impression."

"Hmm. And what would the right impression be?"

He stared at her for a moment, then peeled off his sweaty tee shirt and shorts and tossed them into the hamper. "I'm going to take a shower."

She was tempted to let him, tempted to turn off the light and to let the whole thing go, but that would not make the hurt and the sick in her stomach go away. "So, are you sleeping with her yet?"

"Who?"

"Toni, of course."

"No, I haven't slept with her yet. Jesus, Marie, give me some credit. I'm still married to you."

The words *yet* and *still* hung in the space between them. "Seems you don't want to sleep with me."

"It's not that. Not exactly." He pressed his hands over his skull. "I don't know, Marie; I don't know what went wrong, but the feeling's gone and I just can't... I just can't get it back."

"You do know that you're quoting a song by Gordon Lightfoot, don't you?"

He stood there, naked, mouth agape, then shook his head. "You think this is funny?"

Marie swallowed. "No."

"Look. I haven't touched Toni. It's true, I don't want to sleep with you, but I don't want to sleep with Toni either. I don't want to sleep with anybody." He sat down on the edge of the bed. "Is there such a thing as male postpartum depression?"

"I don't know. Maybe."

"Well, I think I have it. I seem to have lost my libido," he said staring at his lap. "I just ... with all the kids, I just don't have any psychic space."

Psychic space? "So?" she said by way of encouragement.

He shrugged. "It feels ... I don't know, it seems kind of ..." He looked up from his lap. "It's just that every day, while you're out solving murders or whatever, I'm sitting at the computer spell checking."

"Your job is so much more than that. Very few people have the knowledge and talent to do your work. It's very ... technical and ..."

"I hate my work. It's killing me." He flung his head back. Marie thought he might actually start to howl.

"So, if you had more ... psychic space, what would you like to do with it?"

"You're going to laugh."

"I won't laugh."

He studied her for a moment as if trying to decide if he could trust her. "I want to write science fiction."

"You mean like ... science fiction books? You want to quit your job so you can write books, but..."

"I knew you wouldn't approve."

She tried not to sound disapproving. "But, don't you think..."

"You're just so judgmental."

"But I think that ..." she said trying not to sound judgmental. "I mean, I think you'd be really good at that." She figured this was the only thing she could say at the moment to avoid disaster. Figured this was certainly not the time to point out that it was his job that paid for preschool, horse and soccer camps, the trip to Disneyland last summer, the girls' college funds and all the extras that made their lives feasible.

CHAPTER 12

Weighty Concerns

Tuesday, June 22

Marie stared down at the scale. She'd gained .3 pounds. How was that possible? She hadn't even eaten dinner last night. As she stepped off the scale, Marie wondered how much each breast might weigh and if she could subtract at least some of that from the number on the scale. Her ideal weight was 155, though it had been years since she'd actually hit that mark. At the rate she was going, she'd be menopausal by the time she got back there.

As she hooked her bra, there was a painful swelling in her throat. Weight was the least of her problems. The workouts, though not helping her lose weight, were helping her to regain her energy, and Marie was beginning to miss sex. Nick's vasectomy was still a month away. She was afraid to ask what the recovery time was – seemed like too much pressure.

She fit two fresh bags into her breast pump, attached the flanges then tucked it all into her bra. Standing before the mirror, Marie ran her palm over her stomach, then grabbed the roll of fat that lapped over the waistband of her underpants. It had been just over three months since Nichole's birth. Not that long ago. She closed her eyes. Really, she needed to give herself a break, wished she could.

The coffee was ready. She could smell it. Quickly, she pulled on a her navy pants and a fresh blouse, tucked her hair behind her ears and put her face into neutral. Suddenly, Mary Ann burst through the bedroom door, Teresa Marie, waddling closely on her heels. Both were crying. "Daddy did it again," the 4-year-old wailed, hairbrush dangling just below her left ear.

"Oh my," Marie said. "Well, we can fix that. No need for tears. And what's wrong with you, little sister?"

"She's got a load in her diapers," Mary Ann answered in her father's voice.

"Well, we can fix that too," she said, wondering if Nick was now on strike.

•••

Nick had packed her a lunch. She laid it out on her desk. Six ounces of low-fat plain yogurt, a plastic container with two slices of turkey lunch meat rolled into a tube alongside half a slice of whole wheat bread topped with a skim of chunky peanut butter, and for desert, a baggie of six slender apple slices. All healthy food, slimming food. She wondered if he was subconsciously, or even consciously, punishing her.

There was a time when he would pack a little love into her ice chest, a note and a couple of cookies. Apparently, those days were in the past. Looking down at the paltry assortment, she didn't know whether she wanted to scream or cry, but she was sure she couldn't swallow a single bite of it. Nor could she swallow his "I don't want to sleep with anybody" claim. He clearly lusted after the queen of Pilates' firm little ass. She'd seen it on his face. The pressure, or maybe it was more like a weight squeezing her chest, was less about anger than fear.

Waiting for the feeling to pass, she thrummed her stubby nails on the desk. After all, there was real evil in the world. Biting down hard on her lower lip, she forced herself to picture Jacinto's poor injured mouth, Xochitl's unicorn tattoo, the cigarette burn on the tender inside of Sierra Horton's wrist.

"Get over yourself," she said. The tone, if not the words, was her mother's.

Sighing deeply, Marie looked at her watch. Nearly noon. Coco should be up and about by now. Lips to wrist, Marie said, "Hey Siri, text Coco."

"What do you want to say?" asked Siri, sweetly.

"What's up?" She tapped send.

As she waited for Coco's reply, Marie gathered up the baggies and the container and put the lunch back in the ice chest with her breast milk. Maybe later.

What had she missed? Jorgé and Xochitl killed – no obvious motive. Had Davie Woodward committed murder, suicide, both or neither? And what about Rocky and Sierra, drugged, sodomized, strangled, dumped? Was that the correct order? Was the actual murder committed before or after the women were sodomized? Did it matter?

Marie closed her eyes trying to visualize the scene. The murderer, tall and well built, posing as homeless, approaches his victim offering OxyContin laced with fentanyl. He then follows her, perhaps at a distance, until she passes out. Then what? Certainly, even if she was unconscious, he wouldn't attack on the spot. Too risky. So, he loads her into his cart. Could he do that without being seen? Maybe. And the cigarette burns, were they a test to make sure his victim was incapable of calling for help or putting up a struggle before proceeding, or his brand?

She heard a ping, and there was a tap on her wrist. She read Coco's response to her text. *Got nothing. Have date tonight. Afterwards, I'll check S R Park again. See if your guy wants to sell me drugs. Not to worry. We'll nail SOB.*

"Be careful," she said to her wrist, then called Torrance.

•••

Ruiz's Hot Dogs was the closest. Stedman and Marie sat at a folding table beneath a bright blue tarp, each with a diet Coke and Sonoran dog before them. The dogs, wrapped in bacon then deep fried, were nestled in a soft, row-boat-shaped bun then slathered with beans, cheese, tomatoes, onions, jalapeño peppers, mustard and a drizzle of sour cream. Marie took a deep breath before digging in. Sweat from the heat and jalapeños dotting their brows, only the occasional grunt interrupted their appreciative silence.

Wiping his mouth on a paper napkin, Stedman sat back in a metal folding chair that didn't quite accommodate his bulk. "Want to tell me about it?"

"Nope."

"Okay." He took a sip of diet Coke. "So, what's going on with your guy?"

Had he read her mind? "Which one?"

"Which one? The one trolling Santa Rita Park."

Lips pulled into a frown, she shrugged. "Coco's working undercover, but she's got nothing so far."

"And the kid?"

"Jacinto? Stokey came through with a snitch visa." She laughed. "Lindgrin had lots to say about that."

"I bet. The man's no fan of immigrants, especially brown ones. I wish I'd been a fly on the wall."

"Yeah, he's quite the chameleon, turned from paper white to rosy red in 10 seconds. Anyway, that's taken care of for now. Tricia Delgado at Posada de la Luz says they need his bed for incoming immigrants and he needs another place to stay. She's looking for someone to sponsor him, but so far nobody's stepping up."

"You gonna?"

"No room at the hotel. You wouldn't consider …"

"Got my hands full." He held up two meaty hands for emphasis. "So, how about the two Mexican kids? Did you talk to Garnet Woodward?"

As she sopped up the last of the beans with the last of the bun, she felt a sense of futility. Not only were the investigations going nowhere, her personal life seemed stymied as well. Across the street was Santa Cruz Catholic Church. For a moment she gazed at its stately bell tower, dome and Moorish accents. She imagined it would be cool inside those thick old walls. Perhaps she should have followed in the footsteps of her mentor, Sister Mary Ann. At the moment, the life of a nun seemed like bliss compared to the one she was living.

"Marie?"

"Yeah?"

"Did you talk to Garnet Woodward?"

"Nada there either," she said, knowing there was a little nag wanting to play peekaboo. She was too tired to play so she didn't bother mentioning it.

"Well, that woman sure can cry. Crocodile tears?"

"Oh, I think the tears are genuine. Whatever's going down with that husband of hers, she has a lot to cry about. Anyway, that's all I got, which is not enough to name David Woodward as a person of interest in the murders of Jorgé Montenegro and Xochitl Salcedo."

"Even though he is."

She took deep breath then a sip of diet Coke. "My marriage is in big trouble, Torrance."

"Oh, yeah? You wanna tell me about it?"

"Nope."

"Okay." He wiped his mouth once again with finality and started to gather up the debris from their meal.

Marie looked down at her empty paper plate. Now that the Sonoran dog was nothing but a rusty smear, Marie regretted giving in to temptation. As Stedman gathered up the trash, she took another sip of Coke, rubbed her tired eyes with her knuckles, then stared out into space for few beats. "Nick thinks he has male postpartum depression. Is that even possible?"

"I don't see why not. I'd be depressed if was responsible for bringing up five little humans in this world what with climate change, those poor immigrants crashing the border, all the haters and folks walking around, guns on their hips and don't even get me started on Russia, China, North Korea and Iran."

"I'm responsible for our kids too and I'm not depressed, at least not about that."

Stedman picked up a remnant of jalapeño and popped it into his mouth. "As I see it, Nick's pretty confined there, working from home."

"Yes, but …" Cupping her face in her hands, she took another deep breath, another sip of Coke, another deep breath. "He doesn't want to sleep with me. I don't think he loves me anymore."

"Oh."

"Any suggestions?"

Stedman shrugged. "Just hold on, I guess. Give him some space and hold on."

A single tear slipped from Marie's eye and rolled down her flat cheek. "And I'm fat."

"You're not fat; I'm fat. You're just big-boned."

"Thanks Torrance, but I'm big-boned and fat."

•••

Marie checked her email and scanned the activity and call logs. Satisfied that there was nothing that needed her immediate attention, she focused on the problem of Jacinto. She had promised Tricia Delgado that she would look for another place for him to stay. More than once, it had occurred to her that Tucson had a school for the deaf and blind that might be a good fit. It had a residential program, and Jacinto could definitely benefit from the training that they provided. The only catch, of course, was that he was not a legal resident of Arizona. Who would foot the bill for his tuition? "Hey Siri, call the Sonoran Academy for the Visually and Hearing Impaired."

While she waited, Marie made a mental note to tell Nick how much she loved the Smart Watch he'd given her. She needed to pay more attention to the positives like his qualities as a father and a helper, thank him for making the morning coffee and her lunch every day. She needed to focus on that … and … and … not the way he'd looked at little Ms. Tight Butt.

•••

Stedman got the call just as he was about to go off duty. Lights flashing, he pulled off St. Mary's and into the Food City parking lot, where a small crowd had gathered around a skinny old lady who had a kid pinned to the ground. She had him by the hair and was grinding his face into the asphalt, all the while yelling, "Help, help. Call 911."

He leaped from the car. Even as he peeled her off the boy, her skinny arms continued to windmill. "Calm down now, ma'am."

She continued to flail. "Help, help. Somebody call 911."

"Somebody did. I'm a police officer," he said and the woman stopped throwing punches.

"Phew. What took you so long? I'm about worn out here. Don't know how much longer I could of fended him off."

The kid looked to be no more than 15 and was as skinny as the old lady. "That smelly old bitch broke my face."

"Watch your mouth, son, and stay right where you are."

"Everybody take a deep breath." As he did, Stedman became aware of a ripe odor emanating from the old lady. It smelled like that oozy kind of cheese white folks think is so tasty; to him it smelled like booty crack. Trying not to wince, he addressed the crowd. "Okay, all ya all, move along now. Nothing here that concerns you." The bystanders stepped back a few paces. He let go of the old woman's arms and took the notebook out of his pocket. "I'm Officer Stedman. And your name, ma'am?"

"Valery Stork, but call me Val." Tuffs of hair bristled at the corners of her mouth. She ruffled her steely gray hair and rewarded him with a sweet smile.

"He tried to steal Tito." She pointed to a wire cart filled with assorted shopping bags, both paper and plastic, blankets and a stained pillow.

"Tito?"

She reached into the pile of blankets and pulled out a warty little chihuahua. "This here's Tito. He's my therapy dog. No one can touch him but me."

Stedman looked down at the kid on the ground. "Son?"

"I didn't touch her mangy little dog, I just …"

"Liar. He tried to make off with my dog, cart and all." She turned to Stedman. "Do you have any idea how much a trained therapy dog is worth on the black market?"

"No, ma'am."

"Enough to keep that punk in dope for a year, that's how much." She rubbed her shoulder. "When I get home, I'm taking two Aleves, no matter what the directions say."

"And where's home?"

She made a vague gesture in the direction of the Santa Cruz River.

The kid craned his neck so he could follow the proceedings, pricks of blood dotting the road rash on his right cheek.

"You really did a number on this kid. May I ask your age?"

"Old enough to know better." She cocked her eyebrow and smiled. "Too young to care."

"Okay, so where did you say your home is?"

"Wouldn't you like to know?"

"Actually, I would like to know if you intend to press charges."

"Who said anything about pressing charges?"

After he offered first aid to the boy, who figured he didn't want to press charges either, he considered the situation. Obviously, Ms. Valery Stork was a few cards shy of a full deck and probably not as old as she looked. Life on the streets was hard on both body and soul. It was nearly dark and in good conscience, he couldn't just let her wander on down to the Santa Cruz.

"How would you like a hot meal?" He offered.

"You buying?"

Overcoming his reluctance, Stedman had loaded the odiferous Ms. Val, dog Tito, cart and all into his squad car. Though it had been late, he figured if he showed up in person, Las Hermanas was more likely to find room for one more. Fortunately, he'd been right.

Now he rolled down all the windows. Before clearing the call with dispatch, he wrote up the particulars concerning Ms. Valery Stork and Tito on the patrol car's computer terminal then made a few additional notes in his little book for his own record.

Once he finished his shift, his plan was to take a pizza to Abby, a tradition. They'd first connected over a pizza delivery and a murder attempt. He'd been assigned to her case and when he'd called her *miss*, she'd taken great offence, thought he was being dismissive, which had been true. It didn't take long before she made him aware of his mistake.

Abby was no little miss.

Yes, a little quality time with Abby would be good, but before that, he thought he'd just swing by Garnet Woodward's, see if that old truck was still out front.

It was gone. Stedman had a hard time picturing Garnet Woodward, who was so small and scrawny she looked like she'd just stepped out of the dust bowl, driving that big old truck. Could she even see over the steering wheel?

He rang the bell. After a few minutes, he rang again and a woman, looking almost as anemic as Garnet, opened the door a crack.

"Good evening, ma'am. I'm Officer Stedman," he said, offering her his card.

"I know who you are," she said eyeing him, one brow cocked and loaded.

Unmoved by the woman's wary reception, Stedman nodded. "I'd like to speak to Ms. Woodward, if I may."

"She went out to buy some diapers. Any word about her husband?"

"No ma'am. Just checking in with Ms. Woodward."

"I guess you could wait in your car if you really need to speak to her."

"That's alright, ma'am. Some other time. Just tell her I stopped by, please."

He took out his notebook and jotted down the date and time, but didn't enter this call into the computer. This wasn't his business, except, of course, it was.

After ordering one pizza with everything but pineapple, he called Abby to say he was on his way. It had been a long day. He looked forward to a quiet evening. Pizza first, then he'd help her out of her wheelchair and into the bed. She could do that for herself, but it seemed more romantic to pick her up and carry her to bed. He was at the age where sex wasn't an imperative, but if Abby wasn't too tired … well, he looked forward to that too. He hadn't told her loved her yet. Too risky.

As he pulled into the Pizza Hut on Sixth Avenue, he wondered about Garnet's shopping habits. It was nearly 8, kind of late for a diaper run. Sure, you don't ever want to run out of diapers, but that seemed to him mighty poor planning. It had been what, three, four weeks since the baby was born? By now, the woman should have a better handle on the number of diapers a newborn needs every day. He remembered clearly, after his daughter's birth, Clarisse had packages of diapers stacked three-deep along one wall of their bedroom. Seemed like a small thing, but it did niggle at his brain.

•••

Coco La Batt perched on a tall stool at a small round table sipping ice water. For a Tuesday night, the Hotel Congress was hopping. Besides being old, the hotel's main claim to fame was that gangster John Dillinger had stayed there. She could hear the buzz of several foreign languages, German and others less recognizable. Despite the heat, Europeans, especially the young and the hip, came to Arizona because it was cheap, and the centrally located Hotel Congress was a good deal.

She checked her watch. Jake, a decorous older gentleman, was a bit prim. His wife had Alzheimer's, or so he said. True or not, it didn't matter. He was sweet, solicitous, avuncular, even. He was late, but unless he'd suffered a heart attack, which was a possibility given his age, she figured he wouldn't miss their date. It would be leisurely. He'd have a glass of wine, she cranberry juice and lime over ice. They'd talk politics, the environment, the awful state of the state. When he finished his wine, he'd clear his throat; that would be her cue. Afterward, he'd ask her to join him for dessert downstairs. They had a chocolate mousse cake that she adored, so usually she did.

She'd been eyeing a well-dressed, older man at the bar. Nice shoes, spoke of money. He'd been hunched over a beer for the past 10 minutes and she wondered if he was waiting for someone. Now, as if he had felt her eyes on his back, he turned and looked straight at her. Never one to miss an opportunity, Coco smiled and raised her glass.

As he approached her table, she could see that he was not as old as she thought. True, his hair was silver-gray, but it was thick, his face tan and smooth. He was tall and a bit paunchy, but she could tell that if she pressed her hand onto his stomach it would be firm. If it weren't against her ethics—her ethics mostly being determined by how much she owed on her Visa—she would give him a freebie.

"May I buy you a drink, miss?"

Expanding her chest, Coco smiled. "I'd like that, but I'm waiting for a friend." She looked at her watch. "Well, he's late. If he's not here in five minutes, I'll join you at the bar. How's that?"

"Let's wait and see then." Smiling, he resumed his station at the bar.

Not a minute later her date waved from the foyer. He took forever to cum, but was adoring and more importantly, he always paid more than she charged. Before joining him, Coco swung by the bar. "I come here often." She handed him her card.

Pursing his lips, he studied it for a moment. "Private detective."

"Among other things." She shoved her hair back and to the side. "Maybe next time, hmm?"

•••

By the time Coco had dressed down and gotten to Santa Rita Park it was past midnight, the right time if you're looking for a little action. She pulled into the 7-Eleven on the corner of Park and 22nd Street. Despite the warmth of the night, she was wearing an oversized hoodie that came down well below her butt. She didn't want to attract attention as she walked the three blocks to the park.

For several minutes she studied the men, some huddled in small groups smoking and jiving in pools of overhead light, some already splayed out beside their gear. Where had they gotten their shit, she wondered? One man quietly nodding on a picnic table beneath an Aleppo pine drew her attention. Slowly, she approached.

"Hey man," she said, throwing off the hood of her sweatshirt.

He was thin and still youngish looking maybe 25, certainly no more than 30. In another year or two, she figured, he'd be old or dead. He looked up at her with a goofy smile. "Hey, beautiful."

"Hey yourself," she said returning his smile. "Say, I'm looking for a friend. Tall, blond guy, built. He's done me a few favors in the past and I wonder if he's been around lately."

"Does he have a name, this guy?" he said, putting a hand on

Coco's hip.

"Hands off." Coco tried to back away, but the man chuckled and using both hands now, drew her toward him.

Instantly, she thrust her index and middle fingers into the soft depression between his Adam's apple and collarbone. Coughing, he flailed backward onto the table.

"I said hands off!"

She glanced around to see if anyone had caught that move, but no one seemed to think the man's sudden collapse was anything but ordinary. She decided to move on.

After circling the periphery of the park once then crossing it on the diagonal, she considered her next move. There'd been some action earlier, it appeared, but there were no women about now and no one pushing a roller bag matching the description Marie had given her. She took a seat at a concrete picnic table beneath a light. Maybe he'd come to her. In both her lines of work, patience was key. It was kind of a Zen thing. Pulling the hood of her sweatshirt over her head, she leaned back against the table and took a deep, cleansing breath. She would simply sit and wait and watch until dawn.

CHAPTER 13

God Will Provide
(and make sure what's provided
is damn well-needed)

Wednesday, July 8

Neither of them danced. How ironic that now she and Nick were waltzing around about who would take him to the hospital for his vasectomy. Marie had insisted her mother wanted to take care of Nichole, Teresa and Mary Ann and that she would take him to the hospital herself. This, of course, was a lie. Marie had yet to mention Nick's vasectomy to her mother.

Skeptical, Nick insisted that it was stupid for her to miss another day of work when Toni could drop him off at the hospital and take care of the kids. Well, that was just not going to happen.

"Hey Siri, call my mother." While she waited for her mother to pick up, she pulled out the ground turkey she'd defrosted the night before.

"Hello, Mother? I need a big favor."

"Oh?"

"Yes, Nick's decided to get a vasectomy and …"

"What! You're going to let him get a vasectomy?"

"He's an adult, Mother. I don't *let* him do anything."

"Well, once he's neutered I suppose …"

Ignoring the comment, Marie charged on. "So, Mother, I'm taking off work so I can go to the hospital with him. It's just outpatient, but I want to be with him. Will you take care of the kids for a few hours? It would just be Nichole, Teresa and Mary Ann."

"You know I'm not very good with little girls."

Marie knew that very well. She's always supposed her mother's pregnancy had been an accident, that neither her mother or father had wanted a baby.

"Mary Ann is so active," her mother was saying. "And what about Teresa Marie? Is she still in diapers? I mean, shouldn't she be potty-trained by now?"

"She's only 2, Mother. We'll get around to it pretty soon. So?"

After considerable wheedling and guilt tripping, her mother had given in. Most mothers would have been delighted to help out. Why was hers so withholding? As she pondered this, Marie took up her excellent Japanese chopping knife, quickly reducing a small yellow onion to a dice so fine that even the most sensitive pallet could hardly discern it in the meatloaf. A green pepper met the same fate.

And why did Marie still expect her mother to act any differently? When she was little, the woman never pulled her into her lap to read to her or offer comfort, rarely kissed her, rarely touched her at all except to nudge her to hurry along. She never spanked her or sent her to her room either, rather offering correction though disappointed sighs. Eyes heavenward, her mother often implored God to explain what she had done to deserve THIS. It was never clear to Marie whether THIS referred to her behavior or her person, just as it was never clear to Marie how eating the last spoonful of canned peas, which always made her gag, would help starving children in places like Bangladesh.

Marie scraped the green pepper and onion into the bowl with the turkey. She closed her eyes for a moment. Only when Catherine was born and she couldn't stop kissing her tiny hands and feet, the pulsing soft spot on the top of her head, had it occurred to her that the problem was her mother's, not hers.

Well, the woman was never going to become the mother Marie wanted and she needed to accept her for who she was. Marie dumped in a can of marinara sauce, two eggs and a cup of breadcrumbs in the bowl and kneaded them into the mixture with her fingers, thinking *easier said than done.*

And then there was Nick. She crushed a pile of Italian seasoning between her thumb and palm and sprinkled it over the mixture. Even though Marie had serious misgivings about his desire to write science fiction, she'd been trying to provide him more *psychic space* so he could, or at least so he couldn't blame her if he didn't. He'd moved his workspace into the garage where there was less distraction. He was out there now, presumably banging away at she knew not what, because he would not discuss it.

Marie massaged a small can of chopped olives into the mix, while two of the biggest *psychic space* consumers were at the kitchen table patting playdough into cookies. The third was asleep in her carrier on the counter,

As she slapped the turkey into a loaf, she could feel her irritation recede. She dumped the meatloaf onto a baking pan, ringed it with quartered potatoes and carrots and slipped it into the oven. "There," she said, washing her hands of the mess.

She kissed the crowns of her daughters' heads, then she picked up a cookie and pretended to take a bite.

"No, Mama," Mary Ann protested. "They're not ready yet."

"Ah. Sorry, sweetie." She put the cookie back on the table and began to straighten the kitchen.

"Can we put our cookies in the oven too?" Mary Ann asked.

"How about in the toaster oven?"

She provided the girls with a tray, which Mary Ann carefully began to fill.

"Me do," said Teresa, grabbing a flattened playdough cookie in her fist.

"No!" Mary Ann cried. "You're ruining them."

"Me do, me do," Teresa insisted, bunching a cookie up and flinging it to the floor.

"She's ruining them," Mary Ann cried, trying to wrest another smashed cookie from her sister's fist.

Teresa started to wail, Mary Ann started to wail, then Nichole chimed in.

"I guess that's it for the cookies." She picked up the struggling 2-year-old, who immediately plunged her hand down the front Marie's shirt. Sniffing the air, she extracted the hand then deftly pulled out the back of Teresa's pull-ups with an index finger and took a peak. Sighing, she had to admit that her mother was right. It was past time to begin toilet training.

She looked from Mary Ann to Nichole, both red-faced now. Surely, Nick could hear the girls screaming.

"Come on, girls. Let's get everybody cleaned up and then we'll all have a real cookie." Picking up the baby carrier, she figured she might have more than one.

•••

The sun was hovering just above the Tucson Mountains when Coco pulled onto I-10 heading south. Her car, a 2013 Camry, was not the car of her dreams – that would have been a vintage Mustang, preferably red—but it was so bland, not to mention dirty, that no one ever looked twice at it, and that served her purposes well, especially when she was out on a repo. Earlier, Kent, the used car manager at Dealer's Toyota, had called to say he had a job for her. The man gave her all his business—one, because she was good at it, and two, because she let Kent think that someday she might deign to sleep with him.

One Tomás Muñoz had missed a single payment of $349 on his 2017 Toyota Tacoma. Kent was a sleaze to be sure. He'd bragged that he could peg the ones that were overextended, offering them deals that were hard to refuse. Once a payment was missed, he'd repossess the car. He said he could flip the same car three times easy, pocketing the down payment and the monthly payments with each buyer until they defaulted, which, according to Kent, he knew they would. To be sure, Coco had no use for the man, but the money was good considering the amount of time it took to repossess a car and Coco liked the adrenaline rush she got from this kind of a gig.

Earlier, she'd swung by the dealership to pick up a duplicate key and the particulars. Though she never attempted a repo until well after midnight, she always conducted a reconnaissance in the daylight, greatly reducing the chance of a screwup.

She took the exit at Irvington onto 17th Avenue, thumped over two speed bumps, then took a right on Louisiana. It was a working-class neighborhood. By the look of the houses, some folks worked harder than others. She slowed as she approached the address Kent had given her. The house was a low-slung slump block, like all the others on the street. Unlike the others, a bedsheet substituted for a curtain in the front window – never a good sign.

The Tacoma was parked in the carport. She was in luck. Even though he'd received the default notice Mr. Muñoz hadn't taken the precaution to park it elsewhere. She paused a moment to double check the license plate. Later, she'd come back when everyone in the neighborhood was most likely to be asleep. She'd park her car around the corner then come for the truck. Tomorrow she'd deliver the truck to Kent and he'd give her a ride back to the dusty little Camry nobody had noticed. Simple.

Coco drove around the corner, got out, and surveyed the left back bumper. Before her sobriety, she'd backed the Camry hard into a mailbox. She got a cheap repair on the bumper, but ever since, like when she went too fast over a speed dump, it tended to rattle loose. Sure enough, the bumper looked like one more rattle was all it would take. She thumped it into place with her fist then got back into the car.

It would be hours before she needed to move on the truck so there was plenty of time to pick up a class at Capoeira Baiana. Capoeira, where karate meets samba. She'd been taking classes for over three years now and had an on again, off again thing going with João, who owned the studio. A hard-body Brazilian vegan who did not drink, drug or smoke, João had thick dreadlocks that swept across the middle of his back with every head turn. When he sweat, the man looked like he was carved out of maple, and tonight, after class, she'd have time to make him sweat.

•••

João had a little apartment in the back of Capoeira Baiana. They hadn't bothered to shower after class. What would be the point? The old swamp cooler, chuffing and chugging, blew damp air across her skin as he bent her over the back of the leather love seat, squeezing her nipples almost to the point of pain, almost. She breathed in the scent of the imported sandalwood soap he favored and beneath that the musky funk that wreathed his body like a vapor.

João had thought to take her from behind. Coco thought differently. Capoeiritas all had nicknames. Her *apelido* was *A Malandra*, the wily one. As if to prove the name was apt, she twisted before he could land, then pushed him off with a foot to the chest. He wheeled back. His uncircumcised penis, she noted with satisfaction, had lost some of its starch, the glans receding into the foreskin.

"*Balança, beleza, balança,*" his voice a baritone, his smile bright in the dimly lit room.

Now the *ginga,* both rocking back and forth, upper bodies swaying like twin cobras as they searched for an opening. Coco was the first to strike with a swirling kick, her heel coming within inches of her opponent's jaw. João, ducked, feinted to the right, then spun to the left, locks like a spray of dark water. She could have grabbed a handful of that magnificent hair and brought him to his knees, she knew how to do it, but that was not part of the game they were playing.

João, all bone and muscle, executed a kick. His heel grazed Coco's breast like a kiss. She ducked, then spun out of reach, feinted, ducked, spun. Coco crouched, three points on the ground, then kicked back, heel first. As her foot passed João's face, he snatched it out of the air then licked the arch just to remind her that she may be *A Malandra*, but he was *O Mestre*

In a series of sweeping kicks, left, right, left, Coco backed the *mestre* against the bed until he had no choice but to fall back, his head and torso a silhouette against the white sheet. Quickly she moved in for the takedown, pinning him between her legs. His hands smoothed over her hips before grabbing her buttocks. "Ah, *meu bem*."

Panting, she resumed the *ginga* to the rhythm of the *berimbau* that echoed in her head. As she rocked forward and back, she wondered if she could love this man. She didn't think so, but Coco did love winning, and João always let her win.

Coco hadn't meant to sleep. João was snoring softly as Coco quickly gathered up her clothes. She had told Kent that she'd deliver the repo by morning and it would soon be that. With only an hour or so of dark left, a shower would have to wait.

Just as she was zipping up her jeans, skintight and black, João rolled over then sat up. "What, *beleza*? You're leaving me now?"

She pulled a sleeveless black hoodie over her head. "Sorry, *amorziño*. Got another gig."

"Next time, then," he said, collapsing back onto the pillow.

•••

Coco, body covered in a salty, post-coitus residue, drove with all the windows down. She retraced the route she'd taken earlier. To her relief, the truck was still in the carport. As planned, she parked the Camry around the corner.

The neighborhood was dark, the only sound faint Banda music emanating from somewhere down the street. Holding her breath, she slipped the duplicate Kent had given her into the lock. As she opened the door, a troop of chihuahuas came yipping out from behind the house. Instantly, a light snapped on in the carport and a stout, middle-aged woman flung open the screen door.

"What the hell do you think you're doing?" she yelled.

Coco could have run, but then she'd have to abort the mission. Instead, she decided to stall.

"Oh, I … I'm sorry," Coco stammered. "I was just looking for … a… um … place to sleep."

"What?" she shouted. "You homeless or something?"

"It's only temporary. I just need to get off the street for a couple of hours. I mean, he… well …" Coco did not know how to finish the sentence. Fortunately, the woman who was now standing next to her, arms folded over an ample chest, finished it for her.

"*Ay, mija*, I know what it's like to be chased from the house in the middle of the night. Is he looking for you?"

Coco nodded.

"Then you better come inside, quick."

Coco was now totally into her new role as abused spouse. "I didn't even have time to clean myself. I'm just lucky I got out with this." She pointed to the small leather fanny pack that served as a purse when she was out on a repo.

"No worries, *mija*. You can shower here." The woman, her name was Inez, put water on to boil, set out two cups, a jar of Folgers instant and a can of Carnation milk, sweetened and condensed. "You want a PB&J sandwich, *mija*?"

"I don't want you to go to any trouble."

"It's no trouble."

Coco was hungry. "Well, that would be very nice. Thank you."

"So, your man kicked you out. My Tomás, my second husband and not the *carbón* who kicked me out of my own home, tried that once and I chased him with this very knife." She pointed to a butcher knife lying on the counter. "I learned from number one how to handle number two. Now, Tomás is gone. Somebody at La Bamba – have you ever eaten there?"

"No."

"The food is great. Anyway, Tomás was making pretty good money working in the kitchen. He's a good cook, Tomás; I'll give him that. Anyway, somebody must have gotten jealous and reported him to *La Migra*. Now he's back in Mexico. We had our difference, Tomás and me, but I miss him, I miss his cooking and, of course, his money." She laughed. "Like we Mexicans say, *Nadie es perfecto.*"

"That's so true."

"You speak Spanish?"

"Not much."

"Well, Tomás was not perfect, but I loved him. Celia, that's my daughter from number one, she and my baby granddaughter live with me now. Celia works nights cleaning office buildings and I clean houses during the day." She poured boiling water into the cups then set out a loaf of Wonder Bread and jars of peanut butter and grape jelly on the table. "Help yourself, *mija*."

As Coco slammed together her sandwich, Inez stirred the milk into her coffee. "I just thank the Lord that Tomás didn't have the chance to take the truck with him. Without it, how would we get to work? We had to skip the last payment on that truck cause Celia got real sick and had to miss a couple of days of work. Never before have we skipped a payment, but there was the rent to pay and the electric, food, diapers, so many things, we had to choose. It's hard, but God will provide."

And you, *mija*? You want to call the cops on that man of yours? You sure can use my phone."

Coco shook her head.

Inez looked at the clock on the stove. "Time to get Celia from work. Usually, I take the baby with me, but if you'd keep an eye on her, I wouldn't have to wake her. Have another PB&J sandwich; I won't be long."

Celia, who like her mother was sympathetic, had given her a pair of clean bikini panties, the kind you buy at Walmart eight in a package. While the young woman slept, Coco showered, then carefully washed her own, a lacy Victoria's Secret thong, and hung it to dry in the shower. Celia, who unlike her mother, was slender, would look good in them.

By the time Coco came out to the kitchen, Inez had already gone to her first job and the house was quiet. She imagined that at any moment, the baby would start to wail and she wanted to be gone by the time Celia was up. Quickly, Coco made herself another PB&J sandwich then took her check book out of the fanny pack. Taking care not to drip grape jelly, she wrote a check to Dealer's Toyota for $349 and left it on the kitchen table under the jar of peanut butter. Kent wouldn't like it, but she knew just how to appease him.

For Coco, it was usually all about the money, but sometimes it wasn't.

CHAPTER 14

Cut and Dried

Thursday, July 10

Marie had just finished writing up her report on what was most likely a drug deal turned sour. It could have been somebody wanting something for nothing, a disgruntled client or competitor, or a case of wounded pride, all common factors in drug related homicides. Whatever the motive, somebody shot an 18-year-old dealer once in the face point-blank. No witnesses, or at least none willing to come forward. Even worse, from Marie's perspective, the kid was shot in one of those little alleys off Fourth Street, which meant there was scant evidence that a crime had been committed other than a boy with no face lying in a pool of his own blood.

Although she felt pity for the boy's family, it was hard to work up much enthusiasm for the case. At 18, the kid already had a long rap sheet, and in the world of dealers and dopers, the killer might become a victim himself before she could find out who he or she was. Still, Marie figured something would break. There might be an anonymous call fingering the killer, or one of the associates would get arrested and exchange information for a plea deal, or perhaps the killer simply wouldn't be able to keep his mouth shut. Marie was certain that one way or another, there would be some sort of closure; one might even call it justice. Another thing that Marie was certain of was that underlying everything in these gang and drug related killings was an entrenched hopelessness, and that, more than the killing itself, left her feeling despondent.

She glared at her computer screen. Equally disheartening, the two cases Marie was most invested in were stalled and she had no confidence that resolution would come any time soon. On the surface, the murders of Jorgé and Xochitl and the Santa Rita Stalker killings had nothing in common. But there was one very practical characteristic they shared and that was the crime scene. As in the case of the young drug dealer, there was no enclosed space, no bedroom or kitchen with bloody footprints to study or fingerprints to lift. The fact that the bodies of the victims in the Santa Rita Park murders had been dumped compounded the problem. The actual crime scene was yet unknown and without that, there was no context, and little physical evidence other than DNA and the condition of the body. Of course, there was Jacinto. If ever they were to find a suspect, he could ID him.

As for the murders in Julian Wash, it was damn hard to lift a print off a mesquite, and a thorough canvasing of the area produced not one fiber or hair that did not belong to the victims. The weapon was a Colt 45. There was a person of interest, whose location was unknown, his association with the murder nothing more than a feeling in the gut.

Before she became totally demoralized, she needed to get out of her head and away from her desk. She hadn't had any contact with Garnet Woodward for a week. She decided to leave the station a bit early and swing by Garnet's on the way home to let the woman know that she had not been forgotten. Sometimes keeping the pressure on yielded results. At any rate, it was clear that what Marie needed most in both cases was a bit of dumb luck.

The call came in, but Marie had learned over the years not to be the one to pick up the phone so near the end of her shift. Moments later, Ed Johnson pounded on the carpeted wall of her cubicle.

"Knock, knock," he said with a grin. Johnson, a recent transfer from burglary, was as dull as his name. Reluctantly, she'd partnered with him a couple of times. The man wore no wedding ring, and Marie pegged him as divorced. Chubby. Always dressed in a cheap blue blazer, his concave butt in wrinkled khakis. Johnson was a frump, his only endearing quality.

A visit from Ed at any time of day was bad news. Late in the day, it was especially bad news. "Lindgrin wants us to take the call," he said still grinning.

"Oh?" She did not look up from her computer screen. "Somebody dead?"

Johnson shrugged. The man had no sense of humor.

Since Torrance's demotion, Marie preferred to work without a secondary, but ignoring preferences was just one of the ways Lindgrin had for asserting his dominance. Sighing deeply, she checked the breast pump app on her watch. "Okay. I'll need a minute."

On her way to the restroom, cooler in hand, she figured Garnet Woodward would have to wait another day.

•••

Marie was too familiar with the Palms Apartments. The descending sun cast a golden light on the two tall palm trees that did, in fact, flank the entrance to the parking lot, roosting pigeons cooing amorously from between their fronds. On the way to number 43, they passed a small, kidney-shaped swimming pool. A suspicious murky green, it was worthy of an inspection by the health department.

Standing by the door to number 43 was the first responding officer, Sergeant Tanya Moreno. She was a stout, immaculately groomed woman with over 20 years of experience on the force, and Marie was happy to see her.

The officer nodded and offered a tired smile as they reached the second story landing. "Sorry," she said. "The victim didn't seem dead enough to the paramedics, I guess, so they loaded him up and took him to the hospital." Shaking her head, she added, "DOA."

Marie nodded. "Figures. It's been that kind of a day. So, who called 911?"

Moreno cocked her head. "He's inside."

Marie poked her head in the door, grateful to discover that the air conditioner was on full blast. A boy, 15, 16 years old, was sitting on the couch, head in hands. A woman, who could only be his mother, sat next to him, an arm around his shoulder. The woman's eyes were nearly swollen shut and beginning to purple. Her lower lip was so torn she'd probably need stitches, and her nose bloody and off center left.

"Why didn't they take her to the hospital?"

"She wouldn't go," Moreno answered.

"I see." Marie left Ed to write up the particulars.

From the doorway, she took a moment to study the room. It was easy to mess up a crime scene. One misstep and you were tracking blood across the floor.

Every crime scene told a story. She could see it unfold as she stepped into the living room. A knife lay on the kitchen counter; the blood on it already turned brown by the cool, dry air. Next to the sink was a Styrofoam tray of raw chicken wings, half a head of iceberg lettuce, a tomato and a small pile of diced onion. Picking her way around the pool of blood that covered much of the worn linoleum, Marie took a dishtowel from a hook aside the stove. Just above the stove, a spray of blood told its own little story. From its configuration and direction, Marie guessed it was from the woman's nose. She could almost see the man striking the woman from the right side, her head twisting with such force to the left, that the blood splattered on the wall a bit like wind-driven rain. She filled the towel with ice from the refrigerator then returned to the living room.

"I'm Detective Marie Stransky," she said, handing the makeshift icepack to the woman.

The crime scene tech slipped under the tape. Marie was relieved to see that it wasn't Officer Audrey. As he began to unload his equipment, Marie turned to the woman and her son. "Let's go someplace quiet where we can talk." She knew interviewing a suspect so close to the murder weapon was a bad idea. "How about the bedroom?"

•••

"What do you think?" Detective Ed asked when she emerged from the bedroom.

"Pretty cut and dried," she said and waited for a laugh. When it didn't come, she merely sighed.

Mom had been almost pathologically passive, and the boy, if he didn't get a break and some serious intervention, would probably end up an alcoholic wife beater like his dad. By the time Marie had interviewed both, by the time the crime tech had taken meticulous measurements, photographed the scene and mom's face from every angle, by the time they'd taken the boy to the Juvenile Detention Center and had seen that the mom had gotten to the hospital, and by the time they'd gone to the morgue for the post mortem and written up the report (she practically directing Ed's every keystroke) it had been nearly midnight. Though Marie would get a bump on her next paycheck from the overtime, it wouldn't nearly compensate for the loss of family time and sleep.

As she had explained to Johnson, the crime scene told the story. Mom had been making dinner; dad had come home and started beating on mom for whatever reason had entered his alcohol-saturated brain. The boy, having witnessed this countless times, had simply had enough. By the condition of the mother's face, the so-called victim had been a pretty brutal guy. From Marie's point of view, the bastard had gotten off easy.

Most likely the case would go down as self-defense. A bit problematic was the fact that the victim had been stabbed in the back. More problematic, he'd been stabbed five times. Still, it could easily be argued that the boy faced a credible threat of great bodily harm at the hands of his father. This was one of those cases, and there had been a half-dozen over the years, where she felt less concerned about the fate of the victim than the redemption of the killer.

Homicides in conjunction with domestic violence were usually a slam dunk.

Lindgrin, she figured, had tagged her for the call just to put it to her. She would not be the primary on this case because he wouldn't want her to get credit for solving anything if he could help it. No, Ed, his little sycophant, would land this one.

CHAPTER 15

Equipment Failure

Friday, July 10

Marie had spent the better part of the morning going over the notes she'd dictated into her watch, writing her own report of the stabbing then filing paperwork outlining yesterday's shift, detailing every hour spent in overtime. She'd eaten her sensible lunch — cottage cheese and blueberries, apple slices and exactly one tablespoon of peanut butter, which was never enough to spread on the number of apple slices Nick supplied — and was now becalmed in the mid-afternoon doldrums.

Marie's head nodded as she struggled through the activity logs. Sitting up straighter, she bit the inside of her cheek. Still, within moments, she drifted off again, jerking awake as her head toppled painfully to the side.

"Ouch." Rubbing her neck, she got up, stretched, then cast her eyes about for something to do that was more compelling than the activity logs. At the moment, there was nothing.

She'd heard that today was Audrey Wallace's birthday, the big 3-0. Marie was surprised the woman was that old. She knew people would be gathering in the coffee room around a sheet cake probably provided by her ... she found it hard to even think the word *wife*. Though Marie was in no mood to celebrate, she was not one to miss a piece of chocolate cake, so, after the happy birthday song had been sung, after the cake had been cut and distributed and just as the birthday girl was packing up the remains, she poked her head in the door. "Anything left?"

A glowing Officer Audrey turned and smiled. "Oh, Detective Stransky. I was hoping you'd make it."

"Sorry, I missed the celebration. I'm just so busy."

"No worries." The woman put a large piece of cake on a paper plate and handed it to Marie.

"Thanks," she said. "I'm just going to take this to my desk and eat it there. Like I said, I'm so busy."

"Oh, before you go, could we take a picture together, sort of to mark the day?" She took her phone out of her pocket.

Marie did not want her picture taken in her current state of fatitude and she really did not want her picture taken with Officer Audrey, who made her feel fatter by contrast. But manners prevailed. Obligingly, she held out the evidence of her lack of willpower on the plate in front of her so it could be documented. Marie smiled bravely as Audrey snapped the selfie.

Cake in hand, Marie returned to her desk. For some moments, she stared blankly at her computer screen as she shoved forkful after forkful of cake into her mouth. When every crumb was gone, her eyes widened and she smiled.

"Hey Siri, call Garnet Woodward," she said tossing the paper plate in the garbage pail beneath her desk. After a couple of rings, a woman answered.

"Hello, Garnet? Marie Stansky here."

"Oh yeah. Hi."

"Ah, Garnet." Her tone was light, matter of fact. "Sorry to bother you, but just for my records, is this your sister's phone or your cell?"

Marie ended the call. Garnet's answer had scratched the itch that had been just out of reach for days. Now energized by chocolate, Marie considered what that answer might mean.

What with people taking cell phone pictures of their dinner plates, it was certainly odd that Garnet didn't have at least one of her and Davie mugging for the camera in happier times. If, in fact, the woman was lying about not having a single photo of her husband to round out the missing person report, chances were good that she was also lying about her husband.

Was Davie Woodward a suicide? Marie didn't think so. Although there might be other explanations for the man's apparent abandonment of wife and newborn, only one was of interest to her. Still, she had nothing concrete to justify naming Davie Woodward as a person of interest in the murders of Xochitl Salcedo and Jorgé Montenegro.

Marie was about to pack it in for the day when her watch rang. Though she didn't recognize the number, she pressed accept. "Yes," she said, waiting for the robocall.

"Is this Detective Stransky?"

"Yes," she said, waiting to be hit up for a donation.

"It's Flor. Remember me?"

"Oh, Flor. Sure. Rocky's friend. We met at Las Hermanas."

"Right. I'm still here. Sorry to bother you so late, but I've been thinking a lot about Rocky and I remember there was this one guy. He gave her some OxyContin in exchange for a blow job. He was a doctor or maybe a nurse, something medical, I can't remember exactly what. I never saw him, but she said he was good looking. Rocky got her drugs from different sources, but this one stood out for her, I guess, because he didn't seem to be the type who needed to buy sex. I don't know if this helps."

"Thanks, Flor. Anything you might remember about Rocky and drugs, especially OxyContin, is helpful. Call me anytime."

Marie flung her briefcase into the passenger seat of the Explorer then rolled down the windows. The humidity was up and sweat was already running down the side of her face. Cumulous clouds were piled up just east of the Rincon Mountains and shafts of gray rain were visible across the valley. A common observation about the monsoon was that it was raining everywhere but here. Somebody, somewhere would be doing a happy dance in the puddles.

As Marie pulled out of the TPD lot, she considered the possible value of Flor's information. By Flor's account, Rocky's john was a good-looking health professional with access to drugs, not a man who appeared to be homeless as Marie had assumed. Could the man with the roller bag that Jacinto saw in the vicinity of both body dumps be Rocky's handsome john? Maybe he was trying to blend into the homeless population not to lure his victims, as Marie had thought, but to dump their bodies without anyone's notice.

Her watch chimed. She checked her app. The right bag on her breast pump was full, the left nearly. Well, she'd take care of it as soon as she got home.

Nick met her at the kitchen door. "There's someone here to see you."

At first Marie was irritated. Her watch had been chiming intermittently and both bags had now reached capacity. As she headed for the living room, she couldn't imagine who would want to see her at this time of day, then her knees buckled. Nick caught her under the arm.

"Sorry, it's not Francis. It's your mom. She's here with some guy she wants you to meet."

Her mother, looking snappy in a crisp navy blouse and white capris, was sitting on the couch holding hands with a tall, broad-chested man. He had a full head of white wavy hair, but his eyebrows and trim mustache were brown – Just for Men Brown, Marie concluded.

Her mother smiled at the man then turned her smile on Marie. "I'd like to introduce you to someone I met on eBay."

"Facebook, Ruthie," the man corrected.

Ruthie? Marie had never heard anyone refer to her mother as Ruthie.

"Silly me. That's what I meant." The woman was blushing like girl.

Such a display, Marie thought, could only mean one thing. Her mother was in love with this guy. And Facebook! She'd seen her mother's Facebook page – not that they were friends: widowed, retired banker, no mention of a daughter or grandchildren, and her picture was at least five years old!

Taking the man's hand, her mother squared her shoulders and leveled her gaze at Marie. "Ask the girls to come into the living room."

"Why?"

Her mother bristled. "I want them to meet their grandfather, that's why."

Marie was confused. Nick's father had died over two years ago. Nichole began to cry and her watch began an incessant chiming, compounding her confusion.

Impatient, the woman waved her hand. "Never mind, dear. That can wait."

Dear? Her mother never called her dear.

Ignoring the now wailing baby, her mother continued. "I want to introduce you to a very special person. This is James Conway. Marie," she said, tears filling her eyes, "Your father."

The man rose from the couch arms opened as if to say *ta-da* or perhaps he thought she'd run to into them for an embrace, or maybe it was a bid for forgiveness or a simple gesture of helplessness. Whatever, the expression on his face was not giving away his intentions.

Marie stuck out her hand. "How do you do?"

"How do you do?" her mother asked, tears evaporating before they fell. "Is that all you have to say to your father?"

At that moment the flange on her right nipple exploded, breast milk quickly saturating the front of her blouse. "Excuse me, the baby..." she managed to say.

Marie barely made it to the toilet before throwing up. She flushed then rested her forehead on the cool porcelain. When was the last time she'd cleaned the toilet? she wondered, not that it made any difference. She could not have moved even if she'd wanted to.

There was a soft knock on the door. "Marie?" Nick pushed the door open a crack. "Are you okay?"

"Not really," she said, her voice reverberating within the toilet bowl.

"Well, don't worry, honey. You go take care of Nichole. Let me take care of them."

The words *honey* and *care* penetrated the surrounding miasma of humiliation and anger and there was something else. Grief? Yes, grief, she supposed it was. How else to account for her tears? The father that never was, but suddenly is, and the son that was, but is gone, coalesced into a single ache.

Marie needed to haul herself off the floor, clean up and feed the baby, but she would allow herself a few more minutes to consider this newly surfaced emotion and the words *honey* and *care*.

CHAPTER 16

Murphy's Law

Saturday, July 12

Coco lived in a neglected but once elegant three-story house converted into apartments. Hers, located under the eaves, was cold in winter, hot in summer and so small she had to store her extensive shoe collection in the trunk of her Camry, each pair bound together by a thick rubber band. She could pay less for more elsewhere, but it was in Armory Park, a ritzy neighborhood, and Coco found the close proximity to old wealth irresistible. It came furnished, and most importantly, she could afford it, just.

She shared this space with Angelo, an elderly peach-faced lovebird, who was dozing on her shoulder as she tried to read herself to sleep. The book she had chosen, a history of the Spanish in the New World, though boring, was not boring enough, apparently, because it was nearly 4 a.m. and sleep would not come. Food might help. She'd lunched late and well at Vivaci's with a client then skipped dinner.

Sighing, she put the book aside and rose from the single bed that was also her couch. Angelo, now awake, nibbled her earlobe. Coco turned her head and kissed him squarely on his sturdy little beak.

A floor fan pushed damp air around the kitchen, which was also the living room, which was also the bedroom. Above the sink, a window looked west on the Tucson Mountains, now silhouetted in the predawn light. She kept it cracked open to facilitate the circulation of air from the swamp cooler that partially occluded the other window on the opposite side of the room. There was a small stove, which she never used in summer, a tiny table and chair, a loveseat and side table with a reading lamp. A little fridge squatted in the corner.

She took out mayo, a carton of cottage cheese, a rib of celery, a couple of limp green onions, tops turning slimy, and a small jar of capers from the fridge. Coco didn't know exactly what a caper was, but she was pretty sure it qualified as a vegetable. She rinsed one off and offered it to Angelo.

The tuna was in a freestanding cupboard that might have even been an antique. The plan was to mix all the ingredients together and stuff them into a tomato. Healthy, filling, cheap, and hopefully sleep inducing.

As Coco was opening the tuna can, there was a great thump on the landing outside her door. Startled, Angelo fluttered and Coco slopped tuna on the counter. "Damn," she whispered. Listening hard, she tucked Angelo down the front of her tee shirt then crept over to the bed where her LadySmith revolver nestled in the holster hanging from the metal bedpost.

If trouble awaited, Coco decided that confrontation was her best option. She flung open the door, snarling and brandishing the little revolver. There slumped on the landing was a mound of flesh. The mound groaned and rose up on one elbow.

"Auntie Colette? Can I use your shower?"

•••

Her niece, a chubby, lackluster University of Arizona freshman who'd been retaking algebra in summer school, perched miserably on the bed.

"Please don't tell Mom, and for God's sake don't tell Grandma."

"What is it that I'm not supposed to tell them, Becka? I'm not supposed to tell them that you got so pissed that you threw up all over your U of A tee shirt? Got so pissed that you couldn't even find your car? Thank God you couldn't find your car. How did you even get here?"

The girl sank onto the loveseat. "Uber."

"Uber?" She sighed. "Okay. Uber." Angelo peeked cautiously out from between Coco's breasts. "They didn't have Uber in my day."

Becka began to sob.

Coco squeezed in next to her niece. "Okay, honey, take it easy," she said looping her arm around the girl's meaty shoulder. "I'm not going to tell on you this time."

"Auntie Colette? There's something else."

"I'm listening."

"I'm all gooey down there."

Coco tightened her grip on her niece's shoulder. "Okay."

"I think ... something happened."

"Becka. What do you remember?"

Wailing, the girl flung herself back on the bed, bumping her head on the wall. "Ough! Shit. Please, Auntie Colette, don't call the police."

"Becka, did some guy rape you?"

"Maybe it wasn't rape."

"Were you conscious?"

"Not exactly."

"Then it was rape."

"But Auntie Colette, if you call the police they'll call Mom."

"You're 18, Becka. They won't call anyone you don't give them permission to call."

"But nobody's going to believe me. He's like this super popular guy, really good looking. Everybody likes him. And me?" She took the edge of her soiled tee shirt, found a clean spot and wiped her nose. "Look at me."

She did and it reminded Coco of her younger self, before she'd lost 30 pounds, before she'd had her hair foiled and her teeth whitened.

"Auntie Colette. Who's going to believe he'd even want to have sex with me?"

"I believe you," Coco said, though the girl was probably right. Twenty years ago, she'd been assaulted at a party. Back then, it wasn't called rape: It was called "getting what you deserved." She'd never reported it because *who would have believed her*. Coco wasn't so sure that things had changed all that much since then.

"So, here's my take, sweetie. You probably are not the first girl this slime ball has raped." She let her niece chew on that for a minute then added: "And if you let him get away with this, you won't be the last."

"So, I have to be the hero?" Her voice quavered. "I'm not like you, Auntie Colette."

Coco had never thought of herself as heroic and was surprised that anyone would have such a notion, especially anyone in her family. "Hero?"

"Yeah, like the dog thing?"

"What dog thing? Oh, the dog thing." She'd been about to go into Nine Inch Nails for a mani-pedi when she saw the dog, a golden retriever, prostrate on the front seat of a minivan. "That wasn't heroic. It must have been 180 degrees inside that car. In Tucson, it's against the law to leave an animal unattended in a car."

"Well, I wouldn't have had the nerve to smash the window."

"You would have if you'd seen that poor dog."

"And you're a private detective. Grandma says a lot of things you do you can't even reveal."

Coco managed a wry smile. "Grandma's right about that." Her niece was now sitting, shoulders slumped, chin cradled in her right hand, eyes at half-mast. "Becka, you still with me?"

The girl straightened. "I'm not like you, Auntie Colette!" she yelled. "Can't I just take a stupid shower? I just want to take a shower and forget about it."

"The thing is, Becka. You won't forget it, ever."

"It was my fault for getting drunk."

"It was his fault for raping you while you were drunk."

Then again in a small voice. "Auntie Colette, promise not to tell, but I wasn't even a virgin."

"Makes no difference. He raped you, Beck. Listen, let me tell you a little story. Back when I was at the police academy, there was this party. I'd been drinking, not much, just a few beers and a swig of Old Crow, but back in the day it took surprisingly little to make me drunk. I'd just come out of the bathroom. A guy I kind of admired, you know, he was good looking and built, started to kiss me in the hallway and I kissed back. Sound familiar?"

Becka shook her head, but she was paying close attention.

"In less than 10 seconds his hands were under my nice fluffy sweater. When I protested, he laughed and pushed me into a bedroom. After he'd raped me, I felt dirty and humiliated and guilty. Sound familiar yet?"

Again, Becka shook her head, but her lips were trembling and tears had begun to fall. She wiped them away with the hem of her tee shirt.

"I didn't tell anyone – well, I told one friend at the academy, but her response … let's just say it only reinforced my feelings of worthlessness. After a few days of pretending I had the flu so I could just stay in bed, I stole some of mom's Valium and chugged it down with some of Dad's vodka. I woke up in my own puke. I took that as a sign from God that I was supposed to continue my life as if nothing had happened. That was on a Sunday. On Tuesday there was a mandatory urine drop at the academy. Imagine my surprise when I failed.

"The head instructor told me I tested positive for benzodiazepine. I said, 'What's that?' 'Sleeping pills, like Valium or Librium,' he said. And did I have a prescription? Well, that was that. I was kicked out of the police academy and things spiraled downhill from there. End of story. That's why you need to go to the police, confront your attacker and take back your power."

The girl's chin jutted out as if she were ready to take a punch. "Can I take a shower now?"

Still half drunk, Becka lurched into the bathroom. Coco, who was determined to collect the soiled panties in case her niece changed her mind, followed close behind. She steadied the girl as she peeled off the smelly tee shirt, steadied her as she stepped out of her shorts and panties. Coco was about to help her into the shower when she paused.

"Becka?"

"What now?"

"Hang on a minute. I want to show you something." Quickly, Coco retrieved her cell phone and took a photo of the girl's buttocks, which were covered with livid hand prints. She held out the phone so the girl could see them for herself.

"Call the cops, Beck. I promise to hold your hand the entire time."

•••

Marie scrolled down through her notes. The Santa Rita Stalker had struck twice within a two-week period, but nothing since June 15th. The CODIS report indicated that four out of eight hits were in Tucson. Two were in San Diego. He hit Pensacola once in 2015 and once in Orlando in 2017. Maybe they were outliers. It appeared that sometimes there were months between killings, but a body left in a dumpster could easily end up buried in a landfill. Perhaps his victims numbered more than eight. Had her guy moved on or was he still lurking around Tucson.

She opened COPLINK, an interface integrating data sources from police departments across the nation. For a moment she considered the best way to define her search then entered *strangulation/drug overdose, W/F, age 16 to 40, prostitute, anal penetration.* She thought to add *burn on wrist*, but that would narrow the search and there was no telling if the killer had burned every victim. Maybe mashing his cigarette on the wrist of his victim was a more recent refinement. She read back though her list of attributes and removed the *W*. So far, all the known victims were white, but that didn't mean he'd been excluding woman of color.

Within seconds, there were a half-dozen hits dated after June 15. First, she scanned by location. None were in San Diego, Pensacola or Orlando. Next, she studied the description of the victims. All had been strangled, all had OxyContin, fentanyl or both in their bloodstreams. One had turned up in a dumpster behind a Circle K in La Mesa, California, drugged, sodomized, but not strangled. There was a burn on the inside of her right wrist. Bingo, but now what?

Her guy seemed to run through some kind of cycle, yet she could not predict where or when he might kill again. One thing Marie had learned over time was that chaos theory, which she had labored to understand as an undergrad, could be applied to murder, especially serial murder. One small, unforeseen event could throw everything off kilter. All Marie could do at the moment was sit tight and wait for that event. It may even have already occurred.

"Damn." Now that the guy had moved on, she'd have to call Coco off the case. She printed out her notes and stuffed them into her briefcase.

Suddenly furious, Marie closed her eyes. She did not want that man in her house ever again. If she could manage it, she wouldn't have her mother in the house either, at least not for a long time, but Nick's vasectomy was set for July 22, and somebody had to take care of the girls. It was either her mother or Toni. "Hey Siri, call my mother," she said to her wrist.

"It's me, Mother."

"I know it's you."

"About last night…"

"You don't have to apologize."

Marie took a deep breath. "Actually, that's not why I called."

"Oh? You know, Nick was really rude."

Marie was glad to hear it. "Well, we were both tired and it was … you shouldn't have … you should have … a warning at least. Anyway, that's not why I called."

"Oh?"

Her mother was clearly affronted. "I wanted to talk to you about babysitting while I take Nick to the hospital. Remember his vasectomy? You were going to babysit?"

"Yes, I remember and we're really looking forward to it."

"We?"

"Yes, it will give Jimmy a chance to get to know his grandchildren, the little ones at least."

Dear God, now it was *Jimmy*. "About that man."

"Your father?"

Marie refused to call him father. "You say he found you on Facebook."

"Yes, he …"

"Think a minute, Mother. What does your Facebook page say about you?"

"Well…"

"On it you are a retired banker and a widow, not a bank teller and a … single person. There is a picture of your charming condo. You on the patio with your potted petunias, you by the pool with friends drinking margaritas at sunset, you on the golf course living the good life."

"So?"

"It makes you a target. You appear to be a wealthy widow, no apparent family. What do you actually know about him?"

"A lot. He was the CEO of a big electronics company in New Jersey and quite well off. His wife died three years ago of some sort of cancer, I think it was, and …"

"Says who? Think of your page. A person can post anything they want about who they are on Facebook. Does he have children?"

"Other than you? A daughter. There's a picture on Facebook. She could be your sister … well, she is your sister. You both look a lot like your father."

"Siblings? Cousins?"

"Good lord, Marie. I don't know. The man's only been in town for a week."

"A week. My point is that you don't even know him. You haven't seen this guy in over 38 years, Mother. He left you." She paused a beat. "He left me."

There was a long silence. "He didn't even know about you."

"You didn't tell him you were pregnant?"

"I was going to but …"

"But he left you before you could? Were you even married?"

Another long silence. "No."

"Oh." Marie closed her eyes so she could process that single word. "So … all these years you lied to me." Marie was so angry now, she could hardly think. "I don't want that stranger in my house."

"He's your father."

"He's a stranger, Mother, and I don't want him around my children." If she didn't hang up immediately, she would explode. "I've got to go now. Oh, by the way. You don't have to babysit the kids. I'll make other plans." Marie hung up without saying goodbye.

"Shit," she whispered, eyes stinging. "Shit." She'd forgotten about Murphy's Corollary: Just when things start to come together, they fall apart again.

For no other reason than to make herself feel better she googled American Sign Language. Within seconds, she was watching the ABC song with the hand shapes for the alphabet on YouTube.

CHAPTER 17

No Good Deed Goes Unpunished

Saturday, July 12

"So, the bastard's moved on. Okay, Marie, some other time then."

Coco placed her cell phone back in the charger, Angelo riding on her shoulder. Feeling the pinch of her generosity, she considered that very bad timing. She was out the $349 car payment and the 15 percent she would have received on the resale of the repossessed Tacoma – she'd have to do more than show a lot of cleavage if she wanted to do business with Kent ever again – and now this.

Coco put a sunflower seed between her lips. Angelo sidled up her shoulder and plucked up the offering then skittered back down her shoulder to eat it.

She sighed deeply. Well, she knew how to live within limited means; she just didn't like to. And she was overdue for a bikini wax. Now that would have to wait. What she needed was another source of income. Lately, she'd been looking into telephone sex. It didn't pay as well, but it paid and with her cell phone, she could do it anywhere.

For sure, it had been a hell of a day and it wasn't even noon yet. As promised, she'd held her niece's hand throughout the interview and the forensic exam. She'd administered two Advil and a bowl of Cream of Wheat, and Becka was finally exhausted enough to sleep. Not so Coco.

The whole thing had brought up ·a lot of bad juju. She took a deep cleansing breath, then another, but it did nothing to dispel the palpably negative energy that surrounded her.

That party. She remembered it all too clearly. Lots of beer and at least one bottle of Old Crow passed from mouth to mouth. Marie had been there briefly with Nick, but neither was into parties where the major entertainment was drinking. The sex was rough and definitely nonconsensual.

Next day, she had confided in Marie.

"Were you drunk?" It had been Marie's only question; she hadn't even asked who. For years, Coco had resented, no hated that the woman she'd thought was a friend had tacitly judged her and found her guilty of "asking for it."

Coco dusted the air above her head, dusted it off her shoulders and wiped down her arms with her hands. But the bad juju still clung to her like a funk. She longed to wash it away. A beer would be good, vodka better, a Quaalude best of all.

Coco plucked the bird off her shoulder and ran her lips across his feathered back. It was time to call her sponsor. She hadn't needed to do that in over a week.

•••

Marie hadn't worn her sports bra for … well, she'd been six months pregnant with Teresa when she quit working out, so over two years. It was way too tight, but comfort had no place in the room, which was the garage, which was the workout space, which felt like an oven. She was already sweating heavily and hadn't even begun yet. She took a sip of ice water then stepped onto the treadmill, setting the pace to a 15-minute mile. After five minutes, she set her watch for 15 minutes then turned the machine up to a 10-minute mile. For the first time in over two years, she was running. It felt bad, but not terrible. She took another sip of water, then dribbled a bit over her head and down the front of her bra. She could do this. She would do this. How would she let Lindgrin know that she had run 1.5 miles? It would have to be something subtle, something that would allow her to rub his nose in it without seeming to rub his nose in it.

She checked her watch. Only 14 minutes to go. Mind over matter, she told herself, then willed her thoughts away from her breasts, which, despite the bra, were bouncing painfully.

The vasectomy was less than a week away. Catherine, who was totally on board, had agreed to take charge of Claire and Mary Ann while she took Nick to the hospital, babies in tow. She had wanted to stay with him during the surgery and recovery, but that was just not possible. The only decision left was whether to take a vacation day or a sick day. A vacation day could be denied. Better make it a sick day. Lindgrin would give her a hard time, but explaining the real reason for her absence was out of the question. Perhaps she could tell him she sprained her ankle while running 1.5 miles.

Marie's lungs were burning. She eyed her watch. Still 11 minutes to go. Another sip of water, a little over her head, old running shoes slapping rhythmically on the rubber treads, she could do this.

Unbidden, her thoughts turned to her mother. Predictably, after she'd hung up, Marie's anger had turned to guilt. Her mother had been almost 30 when Marie was born. She'd always been so self-sufficient, it was hard for Marie to imagine her as a woman in love, vulnerable and abandoned, needing compassion rather than scorn. Certainly, her mother hadn't shown much compassion when Marie had most needed it. And what about the man who fathered her? Marie was surprised to discover she could harbor so much resentment toward a man she didn't even know, so much anger.

Now Marie, a familiar voice played in her ear. Sister Mary Ann often started her gentle chides in that manner. Panting now, Marie knew exactly how the woman would have completed the sentence. *Forgiveness trumps anger.* She would have also pointed out that Marie's anger always turned itself around and bit her in the butt.

Whether it was anger or guilt or both, the emotion served to spur her on. At last, her wrist chimed. Dripping, Marie stepped off the machine. Hands on knees, she gulped hot air. Forgiveness. Everything all at once?

She took a moment to catch her breath then looked at her watch. Late, but not too late. Hey, Siri, call my mother.

"Hello, Mother. It's me."

"I know it's you."

"So, why didn't you tell him you were pregnant?"

After a long silence, her mother answered. "He was married."

"Oh." It was all she could think to say.

"Marie?" Another long silence. "I love you, Marie."

"I know, Mother. I love you too," she said as if it were an undisputable fact.

CHAPTER 18

If You Live in the Desert,
Never Curse the Rain

Sunday, July 20

Below the Aleppo pine, the air was hot and thick, the sky closing in like the walls of a padded cell. In the distance, lightning flashed. "One thousand one, one thousand two," they chanted. Before they made it to 10 there was clap of thunder.

Rain was inevitable, which was good because it would cool things down, and bad because it was Sunday and Las Hermanas was closed to anyone who hadn't secured a bed there, and the library was closed and all the places they might go to avoid a soaking were too far away to get to before those clouds cracked open. That left them with Santa Rita Park and the elements.

Like the circling of wagons before an attack, Pappy, Elaine and Brittany gathered their packs and the roller bag together. With a series of bungee cords, they secured black plastic garbage bags over the top to protect them from the rain. Around them other makeshift shelters were being assembled. Some were complicated structures involving shopping carts, garbage bags, cardboard and canvas; others were as simple as an umbrella covered with a beach towel. One minimalist stepped into a garbage bag and pulled another over his head. There were a number of concrete table and bench units in the park, but the city, in its characteristic disregard for the homeless, had cleverly designed them so no one could crawl beneath to escape sun or rain.

Again, lightning flashed. "One thousand one," they began. The boom came at one thousand six. "About a mile away," Pappy noted, and the women, kitten in tow, crawled into their dark little cave.

"Probably shouldn't be under this tree," Elaine observed, as the first pats of rain fell on their garbage bag roof.

"Should have thought of that sooner," said Pappy.

For a moment, lightning brightened the interior. "One thousand one," they began. The boom came at one thousand three and the rain fell, each drop big enough to half-fill a shot glass.

"I wonder if it hurts to be struck by lightning," Elaine said.

After a moment's consideration, Pappy said, "Might not be a bad way to go."

"Be quick," Elaine added.

"I was struck by lightning once and died," Brittany said. "I don't remember if it hurt or not, but Jesus came to me and sat right on my chest and said, 'No you don't, little girl,' so I didn't … die that is."

"Well, wasn't that nice of him." Pappy said, matter of fact.

"Yeah, that was the first time he saved my life."

"When was the second time?" Elaine asked.

"Second time was when I started to walk in front of the SunTran. He grabbed me by the arm and held me back."

"That was me held you back," said Pappy, beginning to get annoyed.

"No, first time I wanted to walk in front of a bus, is was Jesus that stopped me. You stopped me the second time."

"Oh," Pappy said, mollified.

The women huddled closer together then lapsed into silence as they waited for the rain to cool the air and the next bolt of lightning.

It was a typical monsoon rainstorm, the kind everyone had been waiting for, the kind that cooled and scented the air, the kind you didn't want to be caught in.

Marie pulled her Dodge minivan into the parking lot of the Sonoran Academy for the Visually and Hearing Impaired. In keeping with her vow to give Nick his psychic space, Marie had loaded the girls up to "help" run errands. She had actually bribed Catherine and Claire with a trip to Bookman's where they could each spend up to five bucks on used books, in exchange for helping with the repeated loading and buckling, unbuckling and unloading required anytime they transported the entire family, minus Nick, anywhere. Rain hadn't figured into her plans.

Their first stop had been Target. As arranged, Catherine and Claire had shepherded Teresa and Mary Ann, while Marie ran around the men's department, Nichole content in her carrier, scooping up a package of Fruit of the Loom boxers, a half-dozen cotton gym socks and a pair of rubber shower shoes. She selected four pocket tee shirts in assorted colors, then pondered the Bermuda shorts. She didn't know if young men in Honduras wore those, but young men in the United States did, and if there was a God in heaven, Jacinto would be staying here. She figured a size 28 waist might work. He would need a belt. She quickly located one made of webbing that would do.

In the past couple of days, she'd memorized the alphabet in American Sign Language, not particularly useful given her limited Spanish. She'd also learned the signs: *hello, how are you, sad, happy, yes, no, sorry*, figuring that Jacinto too would have learned these signs by now.

Marie pulled the van into a handicapped space close to the entrance. "I'll only be a minute," she said into the rearview mirror. Catherine, riding shotgun, looked stoic, Claire, sitting in the way back by herself, was bored, the little girls squirmy in their car seats and Nichole, secured in her carrier, angelic.

The rain was coming down so hard now everything on the other side of the windshield was a blur. Confident that the downpour would make it unlikely that a concerned passerby would report her to the police for child neglect, or occupying a handicapped space illegally, Marie gathered up her Target bags and made a run for it. By the time she reached the entry, her tee shirt was soaked through and her hair pasted to her scalp.

Jacinto was waiting for her in the reception area. Marie hadn't seen him since she'd dropped him off at the school. He'd filled out a bit since then. A little puddle had formed at her feet and she was pleasantly chilled as she stood in the air-conditioned room.

Hello, she signed, raising her hand to an invisible cap. He returned her greeting, a faint smile on his face.

How are you, was her next sign, but he looked puzzled. Perhaps she had made a mistake. She tried again. Clearly confused, Jacinto shrugged, the international sign for *I don't know*. Slowly she mouthed ¿*Como estas?* After a moment's consideration, his hands went up to his face, palms inward, right hand higher than left, then his hands drew down. Jacinto was sad.

Bookman's was the next stop. With lightning precision, Claire and Catherine unbuckled Teresa and Mary Ann while Marie grappled with the Nichole's carrier. By the time they walked into the chaos of the used bookstore/toy store/music store, everyone was soaked but Nichole, who was still sleeping soundly.

"Okay girls, I'll meet you up front in 20 minutes. I'll subtract 50 cents for every minute you're late." Claire and Catherine set off practically at a run. Marie scanned the shelves filled with children's books and quickly settled on "Make Way for Ducklings." She found a spot out of the main traffic pattern then set herself and the carrier down. Immediately, Mary Ann nestled against one breast, Teresa, the other. Teresa's little hand began to snake down the neck of Marie's blouse. She plucked out the hand and began: *Mr. and Mrs. Mallard were looking for a place to live.*

•••

The moment everyone was buckled back into their respective places, Nichole began screaming. Marie closed her eyes, breathed in through her nostrils and out through her mouth three times.

"Claire, please pass out the juice boxes and peanut butter crackers from the diaper bag."

Marie jumped out of the car, plucked Nichole from her carrier then sat next to Claire in the way back seat.

Marie offered the baby her damp breast, while Claire, frowning, studied the blurred landscape on the other side of the window.

The only sounds were the rain, the slurping of juice, the crackle of cellophane and the thup, thup of Nichole at her breast.

"Well," Marie said brightly, a drop of rain poised at the end of her nose, "Isn't this cozy?"

Their last stop was Albertsons. While Marie stood in line at the checkout with Nichole perched on top of the full cart, including fried chicken and a half gallon of fudge ripple ice cream for a belated celebration of Catherine's first menses, the girls waited by the entrance. Catherine held a thumb-sucking Teresa in her arms as Claire distracted Mary Ann with all the treasures found in the machine with the claw that for the price of 50 cents might, but probably wouldn't, grab a cheap plush toy from the pile of cheap plush toys. Everyone looked damp, messy and exhausted.

A trim and meticulously groomed woman who was waiting her turn behind Marie craned her neck so she could peer into Nichole's carrier.

"What a lovely baby. How old is it?"

"She's 14 weeks."

"Only 14 weeks? She's a big healthy girl, isn't she? Your first?"

Surprised and a bit flattered by the notion that this could possibly be her first baby, Marie chuckled. "My fifth." She pointed to the bunch standing by the entrance. "They're mine too."

"Really?" The woman looked at Marie at if she were personally responsible for global warming, then turned her attention to the magazine rack.

By the time the groceries were stored in the way, way back and all the girls were buckled in, blue shone through the cracks in the clouds and the steamy fragrance of wet desert rose all around them. Marie thought of Nick, constructing the first pages of his sci-fi novel and determined their outing a success despite that fact that the wet desert smell was quickly being displaced by the stink of dirty diaper. The diaper would have to wait.

Marie was about to pull out of the parking lot when she spied Garnet Woodward, infant carrier in one hand, case of Bud in the other, trudging toward her truck. Why would Garnet be taking a case of beer to the home of her Mormon sister and brother-in-law?

"Catherine, honey, would you hand me the sunglasses in the glove compartment?"

"There's no sun. What do you need sunglasses for?"

"Just hand them to me, okay?"

Marie slipped them on, figuring they were the only disguise she needed, then waited for Garnet to load up the baby and the beer. When the truck began to back out of the parking space, Marie pulled out too.

Minutes later, when Marie turned right onto Silverbell Road instead of left, Catherine protested, "Mother, in case you hadn't noticed, you're going the wrong way."

"Yeah, I know, I'm just taking a little detour."

"It stinks in here, the ice cream is melting and you're taking a detour?"

"Just a little one." She hoped.

By the time they got home the ice cream had indeed melted, but she was pretty sure Davie Woodward had been found.

CHAPTER 19

Dumb Luck

Monday, July 21

Marie was uncertain how to proceed. She'd tailed Garnet until the woman pulled into a dirt lot alongside the Santa Cruz River, just west of I-10. Marie had kept driving for a hundred yards or so then executed a U-turn. As she drove past the lot again, Garnet, beer and baby were picking their way north on a path alongside the riverbed.

It was convenient to the interstate and a Circle K, so homeless folks set up camps along the banks of the mostly dry river, though during a kickass monsoon storm, that wash could quickly turn dangerous, cocoa colored waters roiling and swift. She wondered if Davie Woodward knew that.

Garnet had described her husband as medium: medium height, medium built, medium brown hair. Well, medium or not, Torrance would be able to ID him. Feeling hopeful, Marie called him right after eating the breakfast that Nick had laid out for her: a single poached egg atop whole wheat toast—no butter—an orange cut in wedges and a glob of cottage cheese.

•••

They met at the Circle K. As a courtesy, Marie had notified the Pima County Sheriff's Department that they'd be in the homeless camp along the Santa Cruz River north of Tucson looking for a possible murder suspect.

Neither Marie nor Stedman was in uniform. Just in case things went south, Marie had her holstered taser beneath her maternity blouse, it was now a bit roomier. Stedman had tucked his Glock in the small of his back under a faded Hawaiian shirt. The plan was simple. Drop down into the wash and take a look around. If they came across Davie, Stedman would act surprised. That was it. That was their plan.

Marie pulled the Ford Explorer into the dirt lot. Thanks to yesterday's rain, the air was cool, clean and redolent with the resin of the straggly creosote bushes that dotted the terrain. They took the dirt track that paralleled the riverbed. The narrow year-round stream of treated sewage effluent that was part of the county's aquifer recharge project had been augmented by the rain. It fed a ribbon of green that was restful to the eye in an otherwise sere landscape.

Stedman pointed to one of several braided paths that led down to the river. "So, I'm thinking that I'll just put out the word that I'm looking for somebody, not Davie ..."

"You're looking for your brother."

"Yeah, that'll work. My brother, Lawrence."

"Good. Rhymes with Torrance so that won't be hard to remember." Marie trailed behind Stedman, eyes to the ground. "Watching out for rattlers?"

Nudging his glassed up the bridge of his nose, Stedman surveyed the trail ahead. "I am now."

"So, if we run into Davie, who am I?"

"My brother's wife. Your name is ... Louise. For some reason, I've always liked that name."

"Louise? Okay." Marie unhooked a catclaw that had snagged her blouse. "I smell coffee."

"Good sign." Stedman patted the front pocket of his shirt. He'd bought a pack of Winston's at the Circle K. He opened the pack, tapped two out, and threw them into the brush.

"Why did you do that?"

"So, when I offer some dude a cigarette, it will look like I actually smoke."

"Do you even have matches."

He patted his pants pocket. "Got a lighter."

At first there was only an assortment of blankets and clothing piled on the bank and draped over brushes to dry. Slowly, some of those piles, though motionless, took on human forms. Others huddled beneath shelters made of plastic tarps suspended between mesquite branches. Two men sat around a small cook fire, Styrofoam cups in hand, socks steaming on creosote branches close to the flame. One had a thick, gray beard that covered his chest and a good deal of his paunch. The other had a narrow face with a thumb-sized thatch of flame red between lower lip and chin. Clearly, neither was Davie.

Though they glanced up at the approach of Stedman and Marie, neither seemed surprised or particularly interested.

"Morning," Stedman offered.

The men nodded, guarding their cups. Only the cigarette pack that Stedman pulled from his pocket seemed to tweak their interest. He offered one to each.

For a moment, The Beard studied the interlopers, rheumy eyes resting on watery blue pouches. "Thanks." He took the cigarette and stuck it behind his ear. The other man accepted the smoke wordlessly, lighting it with a twig from the fire.

"Nice morning," Stedman said, and regretted it. When all your gear is sopping wet, it's probably not a nice morning.

"Say, I'm looking for a fellow … my brother actually. I heard he was camped somewhere along the Santa Cruz. I was wondering …"

"What's he look like?"

Stedman turned to Marie. "Louise?"

"Huh? Oh, my husband? Well … I'd say he's, hmm, 6'4", weights about 240. He's got dark hair and a beard." She looked at The Beard and amended her description. "A short beard."

"You got a picture?" The Beard asked.

Marie took a moment to find a picture of Nick, then held out her cell phone.

The Beard looked from Stedman to Marie, then back to Stedman. "You say this is your brother?"

Stedman frowned. "It's complicated, man."

"Yeah, I know all about complications. Anyway, he looks kinda familiar. Maybe seen him somewheres, but he ain't here."

Stedman pushed his glasses back in place. "Well, thanks anyway, man." He looked around the camp. The bundles were beginning to pick themselves up. A woman crawled out of a cardboard box rainproofed by layers of black plastic. In the distance, a man slipped into the brush to pee.

"So, Lawrence isn't here, Louise, but don't give up hope. We'll try another camp."

Looking sad, Marie nodded.

Stedman started back up the riverbank then turned. "Take these, man." He handed the pack of cigarettes to The Beard. "I'm trying to quit."

They remained silent until they were back in the dirt lot. "Well, that was a waste of time." Marie said, climbing behind the wheel.

Stedman slid into the passenger seat. "Not at all. You see the guy heading into the brush?"

"Yeah."

"That was Davie Woodward."

Rather than take 1-10 back into town, Marie went under the freeway and headed west to Stone. From there it was a straight shot to the station. As she drove, Marie was eating the maple bar she'd gotten back at the Circle K. She wasn't going to indulge, but Stedman wanted one and seeing his weakened her resolve.

She was feeling less hopeful than when she left the house. After all, what exactly did they have? Only that Davie was living, or more likely hiding, in a homeless camp. Garnet was lying about his whereabouts.

Did Garnet even know why Davie was in hiding? Marie doubted it. Still, the woman must realize that Davie was in some kind of trouble even if she didn't know the exact nature of that trouble.

How to proceed? They needed to get a hold of Davie's Colt to determine if it was the murder weapon. They could not do that without something concrete that would allow them to claim him a person of interest

Squinting into the sun, Marie took another bite of her maple bar as she considered her choices. She could scare Garnet with talk of aiding and abetting. Would that force some kind of admission? Possibly, but it could also backfire. Threatened, Garnet might run directly to Davie, Davie might flee, Garnet and baby Jared or Jason in tow. Now that would make him a person of interest and provide a reason to put out an APB on him, but it would also put mother and babe in danger.

No. Marie had to think about possible unintended consequences. There had been too many of those already, starting with the landlord who evicted the Woodwards and a six-pack of Bud, and ending with the death of two kids.

At least for the time being, Marie needed to keep it low key. Maybe Garnet would come around on her own. Marie figured it was time to pay her another visit, keep the pressure on. Possibly in her state of chronic sleep deprivation, anxiety and general postpartum doldrums, the woman would spill more than tears. Weak as it was, that was the only strategy she could think of at the moment.

She felt a little buzz on her wrist, her mother. Reluctantly, she pressed the green button on her watch and accepted the call.

"It's me."

"I know, Mother. I'm just on my way to the station."

"I hope you're not driving and talking on the phone."

"I'm on speaker, Mother. I have both hands on the wheel." This was not true. She had one hand on her maple bar. "Do you have a cold? You sound congested." There was a long silence. "Mother?"

"Jimmy's gone."

"What do you mean gone? Like back to New Jersey?"

"I suppose. I don't really know. Yesterday I called and called, left a dozen messages. I was worried. So, first thing this morning I went over to his apartment. The manager told me he'd left. Seems he was renting the place by the week. Seems like he never …" Her mother started to cry.

While her mother sobbed into the phone, Marie took another large bite of the maple bar. Burned twice by the same flame, she thought as she chewed.

Her mother blew her nose. "I think he was … overwhelmed."

"By what?"

"Well, by seeing you and your family. And then you and Nick were so rude."

"So, it's our fault."

"That's not what I'm saying."

"Sounds like it to me." There was a long pause. Marie took a deep breath. Arguing with her mother changed nothing and ultimately left Marie feeling bad. "Mother?"

More silence.

"I'm sorry, Mom."

"Why should you be sorry? Isn't this what you wanted?"

"No. I just wanted you to be careful. Seems like …"

"Well, you were right."

"I'm sorry anyway."

"You don't sound sorry."

"Maybe not in the way you'd like me to be, but I am."

A deep shuddering intake of breath.

She thought of her mother's Facebook page. "Come on, Mother. He's not worth a single tear. Seems to me that you're lucky he bugged out. Better sooner than later." Marie was about to mention the possibility that Jimmy was a conman looking for the wealthy widow with no family that she presented on damn Facebook. To her mind, the fact that she and Nick had scared him away was strong evidence. Instead she said, "And all these years, you've done very well on your own. Nice condo, good retirement."

"I have. I've made a good life for myself without him. I raised a successful daughter and have five nice grandchildren."

Marie was pleasantly surprised to hear this. She'd spare her the reminder that the number of grandchildren was six.

Her mother continued. "And it's not as though he was the only man in my life. Remember Harvey?"

"Of course. Everybody liked Harvey."

"If he hadn't been such a booze hound I suppose I might have married him."

Another big sigh. "It's just, I thought, well… maybe this time Jimmy … I just don't know what I'm going to do."

"I guess you could unfriend him."

•••

As she walked down the hall to the bathroom, Officer Audrey spotted Lindgrin leaning against the door frame of his office. Seeing him standing there for no apparent reason reminded her of her senior year in high school when she had to pass through a gauntlet of athletic types who felt it was their duty to audibly assess every girl who walked by. It had always made her stomach sick and her armpits sweat. She felt that way now. Her first impulse was to turn around. Instead, she clenched her teeth and proceeded down the hall.

Lindgrin slowly looked her up and down. "Tell me you're just getting fat," he said as she passed by.

"Pardon me?"

"Looks like you're pregnant."

Remembering Marie's advice, Audrey didn't engage.

"So, I hear you're a dyke, I mean a lesbian, or should I say gay? I want to be PC here. How'd you get knocked up?" He sucked his teeth contemplatively. "Artificial insemination? Just don't tell me TPD insurance covered that abomination." Shaking his head, Lindgrin went back into his office slamming the door behind him.

Audrey looked around the hallway to see if anyone else might have heard the man. Finding it empty, she hurried into the bathroom. She took the waste bin into the stall with her, thinking she might throw up while she peed.

•••

Before Marie had a chance to open her computer, Officer Audrey was standing by her desk. What now, she thought.

Audrey grabbed Marie by the forearm. "Can we talk?"

"Sure. What's going on, Audrey?"

"I just threw up."

"My goodness," Marie said, thinking *why are you telling me this*? "I hate morning sickness."

"It wasn't morning sickness, Detective Stransky."

"Please call me Marie." Wishing Audrey gone, she sat at her desk and opened her computer.

"It wasn't morning sickness, Marie. It was Lieutenant Lindgrin. Just now, he was lurking in the hallway."

Marie turned away from her computer. The woman had her full attention now.

For years, Lindgrin had been putting it to Marie about her pregnancies and appearance, always implying that she was too fat and too stupid to be a detective. Now he was targeting Officer Audrey. The fact the Lindgrin wasn't Audrey's direct supervisor didn't matter, the man had created a hostile workplace. She figured he must know that. Carl wasn't stupid. He was a sexist racist asshole, but he wasn't stupid.

The thing that Marie found most puzzling, most grating, was that a pig like Lindgrin had been promoted to the head of the homicide division. How had that happened? Certainly, it had nothing to do with his people skills. The creep factor alone should have sunk him.

•••

Marie had told Audrey to document the incident and she would do the same. If they were lucky and things went as planned, it would be the first nail in Lindgrin's coffin. If things didn't go as planned, it would be the first nail in hers.

Midmorning Ed Johnson pounded on the wall of her cubical. "Knock, knock."

"What now, Ed?"

"Unattended death. Carl wants you on it, and me, of course."

"Of course," she said, thinking *make-work*. Any cop on the beat could handle an unattended death, so why was Lindgrin sending them? Did he simply want to saddle her with extra work? She wouldn't be surprised. Was it now her assignment to keep track of Ed Johnson, or had the new detective been assigned to keep track of her? That wouldn't surprise her either.

•••

As Marie pulled back the cotton crochet blanket that had been tucked just beneath the chin of Mrs. Gloria Carroli, age 86, Ed Johnson stood quietly by, wrists crossed at crotch level.

She was neat as a pin, Mrs. Carroli, cotton nightie with a sweet floral print primly covering her knees. Sniffing the air, which smelled faintly of lemon, she lifted the nightie and peeked beneath. White, white, white cotton panties. "Hmm," Marie said.

Johnson snorted then yawned. "Jesus, my right ear is plugged. Allergies." He yawned again, bottom jaw wagging from side to side.

"I hate it when that happens," Marie said, wishing that the guy would just disappear.

Marie pulled on latex gloves. Gently she tried to turn the woman's head. The skin was room temperature, the body in full rigor. There were reddish pouches under her eyes, and her mouth was open, just. Marie glanced around the room. It was as tidy as the woman on the bed.

In the bathroom, dentures were marinating in a glass of pale blue water, a damp washcloth was spread flat on the counter, the toilet was flushed, and on the back of the toilet a can of air freshener, lemon scented. Marie lifted the lid on the laundry hamper. It was empty.

Johnson poked his head into the bathroom. "How do you spell Cannoli?"

"Cannoli? Why ... Oh. The woman's name is Carroli, Ed. C-a-r-r-o-l-i. Gloria. G-l-o ..."

"I know how to spell Gloria." He keyed in the name carefully on his iPad. "So, what do you think?"

The cleaning lady, who had a key, said the door was locked when she arrived. There were no signs of trauma, the woman looked like, well, like she might wake up any moment, and she was 86. It seemed obvious to Marie that Mrs. Carroli had died in her sleep. "Gee, Ed. I don't know. What do you think?"

He yawned hugely. "Every once in a while, I hear a humming noise. It's driving me nuts."

"Allergies can do that."

Marie left Detective Ed, thumbs busy on his cell phone, and went into the living room where the cleaning lady had been waiting, eyes red-rimmed but dry. Her name was Ruth Shuman. A wiry little woman with a cap of permed white hair, she appeared to be nearly as old as her employer. "Ms. Shuman, could you go over the events of this morning?"

The woman sniffed. "Sure. I come in at 8 as usual. As usual, I put the coffee on. Mrs. Carroli and me, we like our coffee first thing. I straighten up the kitchen a bit while I'm waiting for the coffee, put out her meds and such."

"What kind of medication was Mrs. Carroli taking?"

"Oh, couldn't say for sure. There's six of 'em, pills that is. I can show you."

"A little later. Please go on."

"I get the pills ready. Today is Monday, which means laundry, and I'm thinking it might rain. It said so in the paper, and I wanted to get it out and in – we always line dry – before that started."

"How long have you been working for Mrs. Carroli?"

"Oh, since my retirement." The woman looked up at the ceiling. "I'd say, 15, 18 years. See when I retired – I was a custodian at Tucson High School for many years and all the stairs were just killing my knees. So, I says, 'Ruth, it's time to retire,' but when I did, the pension and my Social, well, I could get by, but I wanted a few extras. I like to go to the casino once in a while and every summer I go to San Diego. Got a friend there and ..."

"I see. So, when you found Mrs. Carroli ..."

"At first, I thought she's just sleeping in. I want her up so's I can change the bed and get the laundry out, see. I says to her, 'Morning, Mrs. C.,'—that's what I call her, Mrs. C.—but she doesn't move, so

I say it again only louder. When she still doesn't move, I take a closer look and see that she's passed, poor soul."

"And then?"

"And then I call her daughter up in Phoenix and she tells me to call 911. The daughter said she's coming down, but I don't know exactly when that will be."

"Umm, Ms. Shuman, did you ever touch the body?"

"Well, sure. Mrs. Carroli is … was a very particular lady, very fine, and she wouldn't like anybody to see her …" Her voice dropped to a whisper. "When I got close, I could tell she'd soiled herself, poor soul. Now, she would not want anyone finding her like that. So, while I waited, I cleaned her up a bit, you know. Changed her nightie and unders. Cleaned up the bedroom and bathroom a bit like she likes it. After so many years, I figured, well, I owe her that bit of respect."

Marie and Detective Ed had hung around until Meg Gupta, arrived for pickup. Despite the obvious fact that Gloria Carroli had died of natural causes, there would still have to be an autopsy.

"Nothing fancy," Marie informed Johnson. "Just bare bones."

He didn't smile. Hopeless, she thought.

Marie determined that Detective Ed would draft the report then she'd go over it before it was entered into the log.

It was nearly 2 by the time she spread the contents of her ice chest out on her desk. Today there was one slice of turkey lunchmeat and one slice of low-fat cheddar cheese wrapped around a dill pickle and a little jar of baby applesauce. Teresa had stopped eating baby food when she was 9 months old. She looked at the expiration date on the jar. Thanks to modern preservatives it was good for another five years. She pushed it aside.

She was about to go to the vending machine for a Butterfinger to supplement her lunch when she noticed that there was a message from Jorgé Montenegro's mother. Seems the woman had collected Jorgé's effects, but the only thing of real value to her was missing – the Saint Christopher medal she'd given him on his first Holy Communion.

CHAPTER 20

A Person of Interest

Tuesday, July 22

Garnet Woodward was packing the truck as Marie pulled up to the house. Fortunately, babies increased a person's belongings significantly and the process had taken more than the 10 minutes it would have otherwise, given the paucity of the Woodwards' belongings.

Marie hopped out of the Ford Explorer. "What's up, Garnet? Looks like you're moving out."

Obviously abashed, Garnet took a few moments to gather her thoughts. "My sister... she ... um ... found us another place to stay."

"Really? Is that a good thing?"

Garnet nodded. "I guess. We ... we don't much get along, me and my sister."

"I see. So, where are you going?"

"Well, I'm not going just yet, at least ... well ... not right this minute."

Marie smiled her encouragement. "How's the St. Christopher's medal holding up?"

Garnet pulled it out from under her tee shirt. "Good. Thanks again for fixing it."

"It was a gift from Davie, right? He Catholic?"

"Davie, well ... he doesn't go to church or anything like that, but yeah."

"So, when was it he gave you the medal?"

Garnet shook her head then busied herself rearranging the stuffed garbage bags in the back of the truck. "Don't remember, exactly." She opened a bag, peered inside, closed it. "Listen, I've got lots to do here, maybe you should ..."

"Sure, you've got my card. If you hear from Davie, give me a call. Let me know all's well."

The woman nodded. With both hands, Garnet swiped the sweat off her face, then wiped them on her jeans.

There was a pleasant, post-rain breeze. It was a bit muggy out, but even Marie found nothing to sweat about.

Seemed Davie had gotten spooked. Maybe he'd spotted Torrance. A Hawaiian shirt wasn't much of a disguise for someone as distinctive as Torrance.

•••

Marie was in a hurry. She'd already given Torrance a heads-up. Now she needed to get Lindgrin's okay. He was not one to reward initiative and it didn't seem politic to do anything that the man could complain about to the chief later, like not following the chain of command.

His door was ajar. She pressed the record function on her watch, knocked, then entered.

Lindgrin looked up from his computer. Sighing, he closed the lid. "To what do I owe this interruption?"

"Remember the two Mexican kids found shot in Julian Wash about a month ago?"

"Two gangbangers?"

"Turns out, it was likely a hate crime, or something to that effect.

Anyway, I've got a person of interest and I want to bring him in for questioning."

"So?"

"So, I need to take Officer Stedman with me."

"Stedman, that fat …? Take Johnson instead."

Clearly, Lindgrin's unspoken slur was meant to goad her. She wouldn't give him the satisfaction of a reaction. "I need Stedman. The man's hiding out in a homeless camp, and Stedman, who encountered him earlier while supporting an eviction, can ID him."

Another huge sigh. "Okay, but take Johnson along too."

Marie nodded. She didn't ask why she was being saddled with Johnson. She was pretty sure she already knew.

Reluctantly, Marie had donned her Kevlar vest beneath her blouse. It was hot and tight, but necessary. If she was correct, Davie Woodward had already committed two murders. He was armed and desperate, for sure, and afraid, most likely.

Following protocol—with Detective Ed in tow, she was especially mindful of protocol—Marie had notified the sheriff's department that they were again going into a homeless camp outside TPD's jurisdiction. Since Davie was only a person of interest, there was no need for a warrant, and she doubted a deputy would bother to show.

By the time she and Johnson arrived at the Santa Cruz River, Torrance was waiting for them. There was no sign of Davie's truck. She hoped that meant that Garnet had yet to arrive rather than that they had already left.

"So, what's the plan?" Detective Ed asked.

Marie and Torrance exchanged looks. It was a reasonable question. Unfortunately, there was no clear answer. As if this weren't the case, she said, "First, we need to determine if the person of interest, Davie Woodward, is in the vicinity." That sounded good.

"Then?" Detective Ed asked.

As a homicide detective with nine years of experience, Marie figured she should share her finer strategies with the neophyte. "We play it by ear."

Johnson nodded as if that were a perfectly good answer, and the three hurried down the path to the riverbank. As they neared the camp, they paused. Two men were still sitting around the little fire. One was The Beard.

Stedman raised his chin in their direction and whispered. "That's our guy."

"Which one?" Johnson asked, again quite reasonably.

"Younger guy, plaid shirt."

Marie touched Johnson's arm. "You stay up here. I need you to watch out for trouble coming from the other men in the camp. If our guy runs, you'll be in place to stop him."

Chewing lightly on the index finger and thumb of his left hand, Johnson nodded.

At their approach, The Beard rose and stepped away from the fire. Davie stood as well, but held his ground.

Marie hung back, allowing Torrance to make first contact. Far from average, Davie now had a scruffy beard, more rufous than brown. His eyes were a swampy green. He had a white scar that bifurcated his bottom lip and a nose that listed a bit to the left as if it had once been broken. Although the hunting knife was still strapped to his leg, he was not carrying the Colt, at least not anywhere that she could see.

"Remember me, Davie? Officer Torrance Stedman, we met some time ago."

"I remember you."

Marie stepped up. "I'm Detective Marie Stransky, Mr. Woodward." She didn't extend her hand. "Lately, I've been talking with your wife, Garnet. Watched her with your son. What's his name again?"

"Jared?"

"That's right, Jared. Sweet little fellow. Anyway, seems like Garnet cries a lot." She paused to let that sink in. "Seems she's worried about you. Thought you might have committed suicide, but," she shrugged, "well, obviously that's not the case." She waited for a response.

Great cumulous clouds had begun to close in over blue sky. Reasonably sure she had a winning hand, Marie figured it was time to lay out her cards. "A big problem, Mr. Woodward, is that Garnet is wearing a Saint Christopher medal known to have belonged to a kid by the name of Jorgé Montenegro. He and his girlfriend were both shot with a Colt 45 down in Julian Wash on Sunday, May 24. According to Garnet, that was the day you were evicted. Same day, you disappeared."

"Am I under arrest?"

"No. We're simply asking you to come into the station and answer a few questions."

"And if I don't go with you now?"

Marie sighed deeply. "Let's put it this way. We know that Garnet has been coming to see you. She even brings you beer. Aiding and abetting after a crime are felonies. And there's the St. Christopher medal. That's receipt of stolen goods." She waited a beat to give him a chance to think.

"You've put her in a pretty bad situation, Mr. Woodward. If she goes to jail, what would happen to Jared? I guess Garnet's sister might take him in." She sighed again. "Kind of breaks my heart, and I'm thinking Officer Stedman and I are really the only ones who know about the St. Christopher medal and how your wife has been coming to see you, and I'm thinking … Well, Garnet is the last person in the world who deserves all this trouble. Maybe if you come into the station now, if you could help us out here, well, that stuff about your wife being an accessory after the crime could just be … forgotten."

There was a pleading look on his face, as he sunk to his knees. "I didn't mean to kill them."

Stedman took a step forward. "We know that, Davie."

"Garnet didn't have nothing to do with it; didn't know nothing about it."

Stedman nodded. "Where's the Colt?"

"Sold it."

"I see." Stedman quickly read the man his rights.

Suddenly, Davie grabbed the knife from the sheath at his leg. Both Stedman and Marie drew their weapons. For a moment, Davie held the knife high, as if trying to decide, then plunged it into his gut once, twice. Before he could strike a third time, Ed Johnson came storming out of the brush and caught him from behind in a half-nelson. Stedman stepped in and wrenched the knife from his hand.

Marie sprinted up the path. Back at the Ford Explorer she turned on the flashers then waited to guide the EMTs back to the place Davie Woodward was bleeding into the sand.

•••

The wind had picked up. Marie inhaled deeply, then again. The resinous scent of creosote filled the air. In these parts, it was synonymous with rain.

Marie followed close on the tail of the ambulance. She and Johnson would wait at Northwest Hospital until they were relieved by a uniform.

Marie hated to admit it, but she'd been wrong about Detective Ed, at least as far as his usefulness went. He was still a stooge.

"You did good, Ed," was all she could manage.

"Thanks. Means a lot coming from you."

If old Ed was trying to butter her up, he'd have to try a lot harder, she was thinking. "Nice half-nelson," she said.

"Was on the wrestling team in high school. Four years. My senior year we won the state championship."

"Hmm. Imagine that."

"Yeah, it was great. I've kind of let myself go these past few years. Got to get back into shape."

She could identify.

He rubbed his hands together. "Man, that was amazing. Never got that kind of a rush in burglary."

"Oh yeah?"

"Amazing. I recorded the whole thing on my phone."

Marie shot the man a weary glance. "Why did you do that?"

"Just because … because it was so amazing, like on TV or something. Obviously, I couldn't tape the attempt at hari-kari, but I got the guy's confession, if you need it." Johnson chucked. "Man, did he ever spill his guts."

The corners of Marie's mouth twitched up. Detective Ed had a sense of humor after all.

•••

By the time Marie got home, dinner was well over, Nichole asleep, the little girls in bed and Nick barely talking to her. And no, he had not set a plate aside for her.

In boxers and tee shirt, she stood in front of the open fridge enjoying the cold air. Even Nick's sour mood could not dim her satisfaction. Call it a gut reaction, experience, attention to detail, whatever, she'd been right from the moment she spotted the unicorn tattoo on Xochitl's shoulder. And Stedman was the best intuitive cop she'd ever worked with. She'd be sure to tell Lindgrin all about it, go out of her way to rub the man's nose in the fact of Stedman's brilliance.

She shoved ketchup, mayo and milk to the side. Nothing. Gazed into the meat tender. She did not feel like turkey lunch meat and low-fat orange cheese.

Yes, they'd gotten it right. Davie would live to go to prison. And poor, loyal Garnet. Marie would minimize her involvement. Certainly, there was no need to say she'd witnessed the woman going down to the Santa Cruz with a case of beer. She would have to retrieve the St. Christopher medal. She'd do that tomorrow. That was the evidence needed to seal the deal.

Maybe a couple of pieces of toast. She pulled out a loaf of whole wheat bread. Hidden beneath was a zip-lock bag with two pieces of pepperoni pizza. How old were they? She'd have to think about it. Had it really been two weeks since they last had pizza?

She took her prize to the microwave.

CHAPTER 21

V-Day

Thursday, July 24

"So, it's settled. You're going to be Grandma Ruth's helper."

"Helper? You know how that'll work."

"Yes. That's why I'm paying you five dollars an hour. It's only Teresa and Mary Ann. Claire will be in summer school, and Nichole will come to the hospital with me."

Catherine sighed. "Is all this really necessary? I mean, you're 38 now and Dad's even older. Can't you two just stop doing it?"

Marie looked at her daughter then at the ceiling trying to decide just how much information an 11-year-old needed to know about her parents' sex life.

"People have satisfying sex lives well into old age."

A look of surprise then revulsion came over her daughter's face. "Really?"

"Really. I'll probably be fertile … you know, still having my period, for another 10 or 15 years." Marie paused to allow her daughter to absorb that. "As much as we love all of you, we can't afford any more babies. As you've pointed out more than once, we don't have enough bedrooms as it is, and there's college to think of. So, after much thought, your father has decided to have a vasectomy."

"But won't it hurt?"

"Well, yes, but the pain is temporary; a baby is forever." That's that, Marie thought, hoping the part about having a satisfying sex life well into old age would once again become a possibility after Nick recovered from the vasectomy. "And please don't discuss this with Claire."

"So, you want me to lie to Claire?"

"No. I told Claire that Dad's operation was like a hernia repair. And that's the truth."

"And what are you going to tell Mary Ann?"

"That daddy has an owie."

Catherine's head dipped. "Whatever. So, what's a hernia and how is it like a vasectomy?"

Marie was struggling with that answer when the landline in the kitchen rang. "Hang on." She hoped it was her mother calling and that it would take so long that Catherine would lose interest in hernias and vasectomies.

"Hello." Only silence on the other end, but unlike a robocall silence, she felt a sense of occupied space on the other end. "This is the Stransky-Grace residence. Hello?" More silence, then nothing. Marie put the phone back into the wall charger and surveyed the kitchen. "Hmm." She hated calls like that.

In order to avoid being caught in what she considered a white lie, Marie loaded a few dishes in the dishwasher, wiped the counters, then took out the broom from the slender space between the wall and refrigerator. As she was sweeping the floor, Catherine flopped down at the kitchen table. "So, what's a hernia and how is it like a vasectomy?"

•••

Marie sat in the nicely padded chair in the mother's nursing room at Northwest Hospital, one hand holding Nichole to her breast, the other a Butterfinger to her mouth. She took a small bite and closed her eyes, enjoying the dual sensations, the baby tugging at her nipple and the sweet, crunchy chocolate in her mouth.

Nick was in recovery and in an hour or so, she'd be taking him home. She felt relieved and hopeful. She gazed into the baby's sweet face, dark lashes against her smooth cheek and was already nostalgic. Nichole would be her last.

Tears began to well. *Don't be stupid*, the inner voice scolded. A few tears, not many, fell. Marie stuffed the last of the Butterfinger into her mouth, but found it hard to swallow.

The baby withdrew from her breast and stared up at her mother, clear-eyed and intense, then a smile. "Happy baby?"

Marie moved on to the changing table. Nichole kicked her legs and cooed merrily. "Yes," a smiling Marie encouraged. "I know exactly what you mean."

Considering the current danger of being caught in a lie, Marie had decided to take leave rather than call in sick. When she told Lindgrin she needed to take two days, he'd been particularly nosy as to the nature of Nick's medical emergency. Hernia, she had told him, and he actually sneered, as if a hernia were a blot on Nick's virility. What would he have thought if she'd told the truth.

The image of Lindgrin interrupted her maternal bliss. He was a serial harasser; but Audrey's complaint alone would not be enough to bring the man down. Marie had a vague plan involving a bit of deliberate provocation on her part, but nothing would likely cause him to say anything to her that was worse than he already had. Would that be enough?

She put the baby back in the carrier. Marie had tucked two Butterfingers into the diaper bag. She'd skipped lunch and the second one was calling her name.

Nichole seemed content to play with her toes. Marie sat back down with her Butterfinger, nibbling slowly to make it last. There was something tickling her memory, something involving Coco.

Back in June, when she had suggested they hire Coco as a decoy, Lindgrin had been so … What was it he said about her? Something about back at the academy, how she'd been a boozer and a slut. The woman she knew back then was neither of those. Now, what made him form that opinion? She looked down at Nichole, "Sweetie," she said, as a memory began to bubble up to the surface.

Suddenly, Marie felt a wave of shame-induced nausea. Lindgrin certainly seemed to have that effect on women.

"Call Coco La Batt," she said to her wrist.

•••

Marie was in the kitchen putting together chicken salad for dinner, a family favorite. She'd poached the chicken in a bath of bay, carrots peels, onion bottoms and celery tops, salt and a generous grind of pepper right after she'd helped Nick into bed yesterday. With her excellent Japanese knife, she had cut it into bite-size pieces and was just starting in on the celery when the doorbell rang.

Marie looked through the peephole. Standing on the porch was a smiling Toni in a sawed-off tee shirt and cutoffs that barely covered her pumpkin ass. Marie opened the door hip width and stood there stolidly in that space. Toni's smile faded momentarily then brightened.

Guido padded out from the living room, woofed a couple of times, then pressed against the backs of Marie's knees. She commanded her own smile. "Well, Toni, what a surprise."

"Hey Marie, how's our boy?"

Our boy? Marie thought, a sour taste in her mouth. "Nick's doing okay. He's asleep right now," she lied. He was actually in the living room watching "Star Trek reruns on the couch with Catherine, Claire and Mary Ann. Not 15 minutes ago, she'd taken a picture of them, they'd looked so cute.

"Well, I was just …" Toni thrust a carton with the Frost logo on it into Marie's hands. "A pint of chocolate hazelnut gelato."

"How thoughtful." Marie stood in the doorway and waited, daring the woman to invite herself in.

"So… umm, tell him I hope he has a swift recovery. Tell him I said hey."

"Sure thing, Toni. Bye-bye." Marie shut the door.

Gelato from Frost was expensive. They never bought it. Chocolate hazelnut. Now how did Toni know it was Nick's favorite? Standing over the kitchen sink she opened the quickly melting gelato and began spooning it into her mouth and continued spooning until the carton was empty.

She went back to the celery, chopping with machine-gun speed. When she finished the celery, she turned on the three green onions, rapidly reducing them to a mince. As she was scrapping them into the bowl. Nick appeared in the doorway.

"Heard the doorbell ring. Who was it?"

"Toni." Marie flung two fistfuls of cranberries, followed two of walnuts into the bowl.

"Oh."

Marie couldn't quite read his expression. Sheepish? Embarrassed? Guilty? All of the above? "Yeah, she brought you a pint of hazelnut gelato." In went a glop of mayo, an equal glop of plain, low fat yogurt, and a generous spoonful of Dijon mustard.

"Really? That was thoughtful of her." He opened the freezer. "Where is it?"

"I ate it," she said, stirring everything together.

"The whole carton?"

"Yup."

"Oh." He turned and walked slowly, painfully, back to the living room.

Marie pulverized a palmful of dry tarragon and mixed it into her very excellent chicken salad.

After a dinner Marie barely touched, Nick went to the bedroom to sit on an icepack, she presumed. She cleaned the kitchen, bathed the little girls, settled them into bed with "The Cat in the Hat," then went to the garage to do penance. Turning the floor fan on high, she directed it away from Nick's makeshift desk and onto the treadmill, placed her bottle of ice water in the holder and stepped on, setting the pace at a 10-minute mile. She would run for 30 minutes then do upper body on the Power Tower.

Forty-five minutes later, she'd sweated through her sports bra, underpants and socks, tee shirt and shorts. She stepped on the scale. One hundred seventy-nine point seven pounds. Ten down, 25 to go. Parting her breasts, Marie looked down and there they were. "Long time no see," she said to her toes. Progress was being made. She drained the now tepid water.

She'd blow a good-night kiss to Claire and Catherine – too sweaty for hugs – jump in the shower then feed Nichole. With any luck, Nick would be sound asleep by the time she climbed in bed beside him.

Marie snapped off the garage light. "What a big sad mess!"

"That's too bad," Siri observed.

"Shut up, Siri."

CHAPTER 22

Sometimes You're the Nail,
Sometimes the Hammer

Friday, July 25

Even though it was sticky-hot, Coco had insisted on tacos at Seis, a take-out restaurant with little tables scattered about a courtyard that was lovely in winter. She was already waiting at a shaded table, one of a few hardy souls who refused to let the heat of July come between them and an excellent fish taco.

Marie was scheduled for weekend duty, and this was the only day she had off in the next 10. Figuring that sooner was better than later, she agreed to meet despite the fact that it was currently 96 degrees in the shade. She set the carrier on a chair.

"So, this is the newbie," Coco said, looking cool in a sleeveless cotton shift that barely reached mid-thigh. She took hold of Nichole's big toe and gave it a little wiggle. "Cute."

The women studied the menu for a moment.

"Want to split an order?" Coco asked.

"Fried or grilled?"

"Fried."

Marie got up to place the order. "Mind keeping an eye on Nichole?"

Coco eyed the baby, who was happily sucking on her fist. "Not at all."

As she stood in line, Marie tried to formulate her apology. She'd given it a lot of thought, but so far everything she'd come up with rang hollow. She was sincerely, even profoundly sorry. How to convey that? Nichole began to fuss. She placed their order and hurried back to the table.

"Sorry. She must be hungry."

"You going to feed her now?" Coco asked with an expression of concern.

"Not to worry." Marie reached into her diaper bag then held a bottle of breast milk aloft. Happy to have the distraction, she plucked Nichole out of her carrier.

Coco looked at her watch. "Are you still using that machine?"

"Yes, if you mean the breast pump."

A young woman brought their order to the table: three fish tacos, a side of *calabacitas*—squash and corn sprinkled with cheese—a small bowl of murky black beans and an extra plate. Coco slid one taco and the *calabacitas* onto her plate. "You can have the rest. Need to watch my bread and butter," she said patting her flat tummy.

"Right." One thing Marie appreciated about Coco was that the woman never made any pretenses about how she really made her living. Marie shifted Nichole into the crook of her left arm, bottle propped up against her breast then tackled a taco: crisp cod, battered, fried and sauced, nestled between two soft little corn tortillas. She closed her eyes and chewed. For a few minutes the women ate in silence.

Coco put her half-eaten taco down then pushed her plate aside. Once again, she looked at her watch. "I've got a hair appointment across town in 45 minutes, so I'm in kind of a hurry. What's on your mind, Ms. Detective?"

Marie carefully wiped her mouth on the too small napkin while she formulated her response. "I owe you an apology."

"Oh yeah? It wasn't your fault the bastard left town?"

Marie felt the heat rise from her chest to her cheeks. "Not for that. She wiped her mouth again. "Carl Lindgrin, remember him?"

Coco tipped her head. "Go on."

Marie bit into her second taco as she organized her next sentence. "As I recall, there had been a number of macho assholes at the academy, but Carl stood out."

"That he did."

"When we were at the academy, you told me that you'd been assaulted at a party."

"Raped," Coco said without expression.

"At a party."

"That was a million years ago, Marie. It didn't matter to you then. Why should it matter to you now?"

"It matters because, like I said, I owe you ... well, apology is too small a word."

Coco nodded.

"I have no excuse. All I can say is that at the time I was in deep denial about some shit of my own. Maybe when you have more time, I'll tell you about it. Anyway, that's a totally separate issue."

Coco remained expressionless. "So?"

"So, for years Carl's been harassing me about my weight, my pregnancies, my ineptitude and stupidity. I pretty much just put up with it, but now he's started in on a young woman, a crime tech, who is pregnant with her first."

"And this has to do with me because?"

"Because I want to nail the guy."

"And you think I'd make a good hammer?"

Marie nodded.

"I suppose you want a letter or something."

"A letter to the chief or Human Resources."

"I'll have to think about it."

"Of course." Marie took a last bite of her taco, then pushed the plate aside. "I know you're short on time..."

"I've got time, Marie. Tell me about your own shit."

•••

Looking for Target's best deal, Marie quickly sorted through packs of boxers. The academy had emailed informing Marie Jacinto needed additional underwear. The headmaster was pleased to report that Jacinto was adjusting well. He had begun mobility training. He'd been issued a bus pass, a watch and a set of printed cards: *I cannot hear or speak. I can read and write in Spanish,* they read. Attached was a bill for the cards and the watch.

He'd already successfully completed a solo bus trip to the zoo. Marie doubted that Jacinto had ever been to a zoo. She could imagine him walking along the shaded paths, amazed by animals he'd never seen before, some he'd probably never known existed.

Smiling at the vision, she selected a packet of Fruit of the Looms and a six-pack of tube socks. Two pocket tees, one navy blue, the other forest green so as not to show the dirt, rounded out the underwear purchase.

The elastic on her own underwear was shot. It would be better to buy new ones after she'd lost another 10 pounds, but the only thing holding up her underpants was her outer pants. At the rate she was going, she couldn't wait that long.

She set Nichole in her carrier on the floor while she scanned Target's selections of cotton eight-packs, $8.99. Her legs, sturdy, but slender at the knee and ankle, were her only vanity. The underpants she liked were cut high on the thigh, which made her legs look longer. They were hard to find in size eight.

Marie stood shoulder to shoulder with a woman. She looked to be about 40 with a cap of perfectly coifed white-blond hair and a face so smooth and tight it looked like an invisible hand was tugging on if from the back of her head.

The woman grabbed a pack of size fives. Her hands, spotted and veiny, didn't match the face. Sure, Marie thought, cosmetic surgery could take years off the face, but what do you do about the rest? What about the flaccid skin under the arms, or the spray of broken capillaries across the thigh? Marie had those already. They looked like the road map of a midsize American city.

The woman snagged another pack then hurried off on rhinestone-studded sandals. Her polished, navy blue toenails and bunions matched up with the hands. Yeah, 70 at the very least.

After several minutes, Marie pulled out a package with the cut she liked in assorted colors. Really, that was all she needed. She picked up the baby carrier and started for the checkout when a nightgown caught her eye. It was a silky pale blue trimmed in two inches of white lace.

It had only been two days since Nick's vasectomy. She'd googled vasectomy. A person could resume normal activity after six to eight days, she'd read. Did normal activity include sex? She hadn't asked Nick about that, but she was ready for sex now, had been for weeks. Of course, she understood that they should wait until it was determined there was no sperm in Nick's semen. She understood that would take six weeks at least. They could use condoms, but Nick would probably not want to chance it. She understood that as well. What she didn't understand was why, after 15 years of marriage and five children, she couldn't talk to him about it.

As she rubbed the sheer fabric between her fingers she could feel the heat rise to her face. Grotesque. Such a light and lovely gown would look grotesque on her.

Back at the van, Marie secured a fussy Nichole in the backseat. She was about to climb into the driver's seat when she felt, more than saw, a figure rush up behind her. Before she could turn to face her attacker, he delivered a blow from behind that sent her head crashing into the driver's side window then yanked so hard on her purse strap that she fell backward. With the speed of lightning the man, young and wiry, began to climb over her into the car, purse in hand.

Before he could pull his leg in, Marie scrambled to her knees and slammed the door. The guy howled. Back up on her feet, Marie opened the door and slammed it again. The next instant, she was hauling him, cursing and writhing, out of the car by the leg that she hoped was broken. She gave the leg a yank and a twist. He tried to roll out of her grasp but she quickly pinned him to the ground.

"Get off me, you fat bitch."

A crowd had formed, but no one was stepping up. "I'm Detective Marie Stransky," she panted, yanking back his head. "You're under arrest for assault, attempted theft, carjacking and kidnapping." She said this, though she had no cuffs, no gun, no way to actually subdue him other than her weight on his back.

"Under arrest?" said Sri. "Can I help?"

"Call 911." After a few rings the dispatcher picked up. "Detective Marie Stransky—S-t-r-a-n-s-k-y—needs assistance with an arrest at the Target on Oracle."

Marie bounced a bit to remind her assailant that she was still on top. Finally, security sped up in his golf cart. The guy, who must have weighed 300 pounds, parted the crowd like the prow of an icebreaker. "What seems to be the problem?"

Marie looked at the man, shook her head. "Don't suppose you got a pair of cuffs on you."

•••

Marie had just walked in the door, her pants torn and bloodied at the knee, a bruise rising on her forehead where it hit the window. She set Nichole and the underwear on the counter. Just as she was about to drop her pants so she could clean and bandage the abrasion, the landline in the kitchen started to ring. No one ever picked up the landline but Marie. She thought to simply let it ring, then thought again.

"Hello." There was no response, but just as before, she had the sense that a living, breathing person was on the other end. That sense made her stomach do a little flip.

"Hello? This is Marie Stransky speaking." Silence on the line. "Francis?" she asked, just before the caller disconnected.

Marie recalled how both Señoras Salcedo and Montenegro had claimed *a mother always knows*. At the time, she'd been skeptical. Now Marie felt certain that the person who'd been on the line was her son. Knew it was only a matter of time before curiosity would drive him to call again. When she put the phone back in the charger, her hand was shaking.

•••

Coco guided the Camry into the parking lot adjacent to the train station. Adjusting the rearview mirror onto her face, she ran a tube of frosted-pink over her lips. She smiled at her reflection then slipped out of the car, dragging her oversized purse along. Inside was a little beaded coin purse filled with assorted condoms. There was a bottle of K-Y Jelly, hand lotion, hairbrush, toothbrush, extra panties, cell phone, wallet and water bottle. In its own easily accessed zipper pocket was her LadySmith revolver with the polished walnut butt she so loved the feel of. She had a strappy little black leather harness, custom made, that secured the butt of the gun between her breasts for easy access, but it was Jake's night. The old gent was a gun control advocate and found it … well, off-putting.

All afternoon she'd been chewing on Marie's request. She'd like to nail Lindgrin, but what was in it for her? Other than satisfaction, she couldn't see the advantage. There would likely be negative publicity, and people would dig into her present as well as her past. She could predict how her family would react and it might hurt business. But Becka had called her a hero. The girl had been pretty heroic herself when she filed charges against the guy who raped her. She might not peg Lindgrin for herself, but for Becka, maybe. No need to decide right now, she figured.

On bare feet, she ran around to the trunk and popped it open. For a moment she surveyed the selection of shoes stored there, then grabbed a pair of white stiletto-heeled sandals to complete her costume: black, faux-leather miniskirt, black sleeveless tee with a deeply scooped neck, large silver hoop earrings that brushed her shoulder if she tilted her head and a series of bangles that went from her left wrist halfway to her elbow.

She slipped on the sandals then slammed the trunk closed, which loosened the bumper. She thumped it back in place. Bending over at the waist, she shook her head, giving her hair a rumpled, just-out-of-bed look, then crossed the street to the Hotel Congress.

Coco was early, a bad habit. She positioned herself on a stool at a high round table in the middle of the bar, which was also the lobby.

It was early by Hotel Congress standards. Outside, the band was just arriving and there were only a few people scattered about.

He was sitting at the bar as though he'd never left, silver hair groomed to perfection, blue oxford shirt rolled up over tanned, muscular forearms. Only his shoes were different. Tonight, he was wearing gray Adidas. They looked brand new. Coco tilted her head in his direction and smiled. He dug into his wallet and waved a card, hers she presumed. He'd saved it. How sweet. She slipped off the stool.

Hand on hip, Coco dipped her chin a bit off center, tucking her frosted lips into a little smile. "You again? What a coincidence."

"A nice coincidence, I hope."

Coco swooped her hair over to one side. "Definitely."

"I just got back in town. Are you busy?"

"Will be, but if you have no other plans, I'd love to join you later." She looked at her watch. "Say, 9:30, 10?"

"Fine."

"Do you have a card? I could call your cell."

The man fished in his wallet. "Damn. I must be out. My name is Dave, by the way. I'm in pharmaceuticals." He picked up a cocktail napkin and jotted down his room number. "I'll be in my room." He handed her the napkin. "No need to call."

Coco tucked the napkin into her bra then placed her hand in his. It was smooth, cool to the touch. Playtime, she thought, imagining his hand smoothing over her breasts and belly. "Well then, Dave in pharmaceuticals, I'll see you later."

"Really?"

"Absolutely." Coco returned to her perch. She didn't want Jake to catch her flirting. A wounded ego, might take twice as long to finish. And tonight, she'd forgo the chocolate mousse cake. She had another dessert in mind.

•••

"Give me a minute, honey. I'm a little tense."

Coco sat back on her haunches. This was work, not play. Dave was not what she had imagined. Ah well, her Visa wouldn't know the difference.

He zipped up his pants then opened the little fridge. "Would you like a drink?

"Vodka, tonic, rum and Coke, Seagram's?"

"No thanks." She was surprised to see a pack of cigarettes on the bureau. "You smoke?"

"Not much and only outside." An odd little smile lifted the corners of his mouth. "Want one?"

She shook her head. "No thanks."

"As I said, I'm in pharmaceuticals. I could set you up with a little something? What's your pleasure?"

Her pleasure was to go home and go to bed. "No thanks, Dave."

"Sure?"

"Positive."

"Okay. Excuse me." He headed for the bathroom. "I'll be ready in five."

"You know, Dave, it's getting late."

"Late? I thought we'd party for a little while."

"I'd like that, but I told the babysitter I'd be home by 11."

"You've got a kid?"

Coco smiled brightly. "Little girl; she's … 2."

"What's her name?"

"Nichole," Coco answered without hesitation.

"Why don't you call the sitter and tell her you'll be late. I'll make it worth her while."

"I can't do that, Dave. Her mother wouldn't like it."

"Too bad."

"Well, this won't take long, promise." He went into the bathroom and closed the door.

Viagra, Coco thought. This could take forever. She looked around the room with its vintage décor: a rotary phone that probably didn't work and old timey radio that probably did. She'd never tried either. A silver dollar money clip was on the dresser, a crisp twenty visible, probably all twenties, she figures, fresh out of the ATM. She shook her head. It simply wasn't worth her time. She dressed quickly, there wasn't that much to put on and grabbed her purse. Just as she got to the door, he came out of the bathroom.

Frowning, he tilted his head. "Please don't rush off. Really, this will only take a minute." Smiling, he crossed the room then stepped in close.

Coco braced herself for an unwanted kiss. Instead, she felt a prick on her shoulder. "Ouch!" She was momentarily confused then it all came into sharp focus: the cigarettes on the bureau, the pharmaceuticals, the "just back in town." Dave was Marie's guy. Now he was her guy. She groped inside her purse, but couldn't grasp the zipper on the pocket containing her gun. She was fucked. Oh well, here we go, she thought as she crumpled to her knees.

Coco could feel his arms beneath her. Felt him pick her up and lay her face-down on the bed.

He didn't know how long he'd been sitting on the edge of the bed clutching his skull, as he waited for the squirrel to stop banging against his ribs. When it finally did, he went into the bathroom and washed his face.

All the rooms at the Hotel Congress were on the second floor. Years ago, there had been a fire. The hotel had been rebuilt, but for some reason the old elevator had never been replaced. Though inconvenient, this worked in his favor.

By the time he'd done his business and packed up, the band, this one playing zydeco, was revved up. No one would hear as he bumped the roller bag down the emergency stairs.

•••

The Weird Sisters said good night to Pancho Villa and his horse and made their way to the west side of the library. It was not yet midnight and still too muggy-hot for comfort, but there was no reason to wait for quiet to bed down. There would be no quiet for hours and they were tired, too tired to mind heat and noise. Besides, their usual spot by the library was a bit removed from the downtown action.

In no time, Elaine, Brittany and Pappy had cached their gear behind a planter, laid out their arsenal – rocks in the knotted knee sock, Sting, the sharp, number 2 pencil with duct tape hilt, and the red, stiletto-heeled patent leather shoe. They layered the blankets that would insulate them from the heat, and settled down into their guarded, fitful sleep.

Pappy drifted off to the clack of wheels on concrete. Some other homeless soul seeking refuge, she figured. Some minutes later, she roused to the smell of cigarette smoke, breathing deeply, savoring the aroma. She had a cigarette rolling machine in the bottom of her bag, but currently lacked the disposable income to buy tobacco and the fancy filtered cigarette tubes she preferred.

Fingers to her lips, Pappy inhaled deeply on an invisible cigarette, exhaled the invisible smoke. "Christ," she whispered. Maybe she'd just get up and see if she could bum one off the son of a bitch who'd disturbed her fragile sleep. She was about to, when she heard a muffled mewing.

Please, not another goddamn kitten, she thought. Pappy looked at her companions. Brittany's lips fluttered in her sleep. Elaine, who'd taken charge of Lil' Bit, was asleep as well. But there it was again, a strangled mewing, coming from the grassy little hill not 50 feet away. It took Pappy a moment to realize that this was not another kitten, but a muffled, human-in-distress whimper. Her hand found the sock of rocks. "Elaine, Britt. Wake up," she hissed.

•••

"What now?" Elaine wanted to know. "She can't walk."

They had pulled the woman out from under the dead weight of her attacker. Now, Brittany knelt beside her head. "Well, we can't just leave her. Maybe we'd better call the cops."

"We could do that," Pappy said. "But I forget to plug my cell phone into the current bushes."

"That joke is older than you are if that's even possible," said Elaine.

Gently, Brittany patted the woman's face. "Hey. Wake up." The woman made a smacking noise with her mouth, but her eyelids remained at half-mast.

"So?" Elaine insisted.

"So, we wait until the buses run. By that time, she should be able to fend for herself. If she can't and if we don't see a cop along the way, we'll take her with us to Las Hermanas."

Elaine hooked her thumb toward the man. "What about him?"

"What about him?" Pappy said. "If he wakes up before she does, I imagine he'll just crawl back into his hole."

Pappy took the woman under the arms. "Grab her legs. We'll take her back to our spot for now." The woman moaned softly as the three half-carried, half dragged her into the dark shelter of the pepper tree.

CHAPTER 23

Good Luck Has It's Down Side

Saturday, July 26

The sun was still low on the horizon as the three women made their way toward the bus stop, supporting the fourth. Pappy pulled her new roller bag; why should she leave it for the cockroach? The kitten rode on top in its carrier and on top of that, the woman's sandals, high heels stuck through the holes in the carrier. With one hand, Brittany pulled her bag while she and Elaine propelled the woman forward, arms twined across the woman's back. All four were sweating.

"You'll feel better after you've had a shower and a change of clothes," Elaine offered. "And we'll get some ice for your mouth and then we can have breakfast."

Pappy steadied the sandals atop the carrier. "When the cockroach wakes up, he'll have a hell of a headache," she said in an attempt to console.

"I think it's best that you don't mention you've been raped," Brittany suggested. "Been there done that. They put you on a metal table, probe your cavities and insert a device to track your every move. Once they've done that, they forward your numbers to the CIA and the FBI."

"Never happened, Brittany," said Pappy.

"How would you know? You weren't even there."

The woman, too shocky for conversation, allowed herself to be steered, barefoot, down the sidewalk. They stopped, grateful for the bit of shade provided by the bus stop shelter. The four sank down onto the bench, shoulder to shoulder, to wait.

•••

Officer Wallace was already at the scene taking photos of the victim from every conceivable angle. Marie smiled, and flashed a V for victory in her direction, before stepping under the crime tape, where Torrance stood, quietly sweating, as he entered the particulars into his notebook.

"Morning, Torrance."

"Marie."

The sun glanced off the wall of the library, harsh. Marie shaded her eyes with her hand as she studied the white man lying face-down on the green grass, butt crack peeking out of his trousers, oxford shirt hiked up to his armpits. Bits of white skull stood out against the now black blood that covered his head.

"Hmm," Marie said, extracting two pairs of latex gloves from her briefcase. "This is interesting." She pointed to multiple puncture wounds on the torso and knelt down beside the corpse. "What do you make of this, Torrance?"

Stedman leaned in. "Not a knife, not a fork, not a spork. Could be..."

"Got a pencil?"

Stedman reached into his breast pocket.

Marie slipped the pencil into a finger of the glove then into one of the smaller punctures on the upper torso. "Pretty good fit. Goes in about an inch, I'd say." She slipped the pencil into another hole. "About the same diameter and depth."

"What about the big ones?"

Marie pulled a Stanley PowerLock tape measure from her briefcase and measured several of the larger punctures. "Each one is just about 15 centimeters across." She plunged her gloved index finger into a hole in the buttocks, sinking it in nearly to the knuckle. She held up her finger then looked at her tape. "I'd say 35 centimeters maybe. The diameter of the wound seems to narrow as it goes down, so I don't know if I hit bottom. What do you make of that?"

Frowning, Stedman shook his head. "Let's roll him."

He was a big man, muscular and a bit paunchy. Officer Wallace stepped in and the three turned him over. Wallace snapped half-a-dozen more photos then backed out of their way.

The man's pants were unzipped and his cock dangled sadly over the top of his plaid boxers. His right cheek was discolored by pooled blood beneath the skin where it had rested against the ground. Under his nose was a smear of blood. Otherwise his face was unscathed. "Looks like blunt force trauma, rather than any of those puncture wounds, was the cause of death."

"Yup."

Grimacing, Marie sat back on her heals and pointed to the man's pockets. "You do it."

"What is it with you and pockets?"

Marie shrugged.

Stedman pushed his glasses back up the bridge of his nose then reached into the man's right pocket. There was a white handkerchief, neatly folded, ironed and apparently unused, in the left a room key to the Hotel Congress. He held the key up for Stransky to see, then handed it and the handkerchief to Officer Wallace, who dropped it into an evidence bag. "No wallet."

He patted down the pockets. "Wait. There's something else." He plunged his hand back into the left pocket. "A money clip. Nice." Stedman handed her the clip, which was adorned with a Walking Liberty half dollar.

Marie thumbed through the bills. "All twenties. Looks like this guy made a recent trip to an ATM." She handed the clip to Wallace, who counted the bills and dropped the clip into the evidence bag.

"I guess the perp got the wallet but missed the clip." Stedman picked up a stiff arm then let it drop. "Full rigor."

Still kneeling as if in silent prayer, they turned their attention back to the body. Almost simultaneously, they rocked back on their heels. Once again, Wallace stepped up and the three turned the body back over.

"You know what I'm thinking, Marie?"

"You're thinking this is totally weird."

"There's that and the clothes." Stedman ran a finger along the sharp crease in the man's pant leg. "He's pretty well put together, don't you think? And that hanky."

"Fastidious." The sun was beating down on Marie's head. Sweat made her scalp itch. She tried not to scratch.

"And you're thinking this guy was a john."

"Yeah. Why else would a guy dressed like that be here at night?" Stedman pulled off his gloves then took out his own clean, white handkerchief and wiped the sweat from his brow. "And the money clip, the hotel key. He could easily have walked over here from Hotel Congress looking for action. Maybe sex, maybe drugs."

"So, let's just say this guy was a john," Marie suggested. "Let's just say he was getting ready to put it to a prostitute, and the woman's pimp …"

"Could have been a guy he was about to screw, or maybe we've got it backwards. Maybe it was rape and robbery."

"Could have been. Let's just say somebody struck from behind with something handy, a rock or a …"

"A pipe or a wrench, multiple times."

"Yeah. So, he takes the wallet, but misses the money clip …"

"Right, but …"

"Exactly. Those puncture wounds." Marie squinted her eyes as if that might bring clarity. "Could be something a pimp or even the prostitute might do if they were sorely pissed. But with what?"

Torrance shrugged. He stood, then helped Marie to her feet. "After we've been to the hotel, maybe we'll know a bit more about what went on here and why."

Shading her eyes from the sun, Marie perused the scene one last time. "What's that?" She walked over to a planter and plucked an object impaled on the thorns of an aloe plant. Smiling, she held a condom aloft between thumb and forefinger. "Whether the victim was a john or he was raped, we've got two sets of DNA in one." Wallace produced a zip-lock bag and Marie dropped it in.

"Marie, someday I wish you'd explain to me why you've got no problem picking up a used condom, but can't stand to put your hand into a dead man's pocket."

"Can't say, Torrance. Something about that just creeps me out."

"Hang on," Stedman said. "I forgot to check the shirt pocket." He prodded the pocket with his thick index finger. "Something, a card, maybe." He pulled it out, read it. "Uh oh," he said, then handed it to Marie.

She looked at it. For a minute, Marie thought she was going to throw up.

•••

By the time the Weird Sisters escorted Coco through the front door of Las Hermanas, the drug was wearing off. She was simultaneously bereft and furious.

"You'll feel better after a nice, cool shower," Brittany said.

"And a good breakfast," Elaine added.

Coco shook her head. "Where's my goddamn purse?"

"There wasn't a purse," Pappy said.

For the first time Coco noticed the burn on her wrist. "Jesus!" Coco pushed her hair off her face, eyes sweeping the reception area. "I need to use the phone," she said to the sweet-faced old lady at the reception counter.

"I'm sorry but..."

"This is serious shit. Give me the goddamn phone."

"I'm sorry, but..."

Coco reached over the counter and grabbed the phone.

Pappy placed a restraining hand on Coco's wrist. "You can't do that. You're going to get us all kicked out."

Coco jerked her hand away and dialed. Turning her back on the women, she waited for Marie to pick up.

"Thank God, my ass," Coco said. "You told me he was a homeless dude. Blond hair, you said. You said he'd moved on." She paused for a response.

"Where am I?" she asked the woman behind the counter.

"Las Hermanas Women's Hostel, but …"

"Las Hermanas," she yelled into the receiver. "You better get your ass over here quick, Marie, before I …" Coco picked up a ballpoint pen that was lying on the counter. "Before I gouge somebody's eyeball out."

Coco handed the phone to Pappy who smiled apologetically at the woman behind the counter then replaced it gently on the counter.

"I'm afraid I must call the police," the woman said, not unkindly. She was used to dealing with women who were flipping their lids. "It's policy."

"Not to worry," Coco said. "They'll be here shortly." There was a chair next to a potted philodendron. Fuming, Coco sank down in it to wait. After a few minutes, she began to cry.

Coco slid into the front seat of the Ford Explorer. "First, you need to take me to the Hotel Congress to get my purse."

"Hang on a minute, Coco. First, YOU need to tell me how your card got into the shirt pocket of a man found bludgeoned to death on the library lawn this morning?"

"What?"

"OK, let's back up."

"How did you get to Las Hermanas and where are your shoes?"

"I can't quite remember the details, but I met a man at the Hotel Congress. God, yes. That reminds me. I need to have a forensic exam."

"Okay. Were you raped?"

"He drugged me first."

"The man at the Hotel Congress?"

"Yes. And look." She turned her right wrist over. "Hurts like hell and it's going to leave an ugly scar. And I need a forensic exam to provide me with evidence for my lawsuit."

"You're going to sue? Who? The man's dead."

"Dead? How the hell did that happen?"

"Bludgeoned. And there were weird puncture marks all over his back and buttocks."

"I'll be damned." Coco stared into mid space for a moment. "Doesn't make any difference. I'm still suing."

Mildly amused, Marie asked, "Who?"

"I'm suing you in particular and Tucson Police Department in general."

Thinking Coco was kidding, Marie smiled. "Do what you must, but I'd like you to reconsider suing me. I can't afford a lawyer."

"Tough shit! Eight months sobriety, Marie. Eight months!" Coco started to cry.

Marie pulled the car over to the side of the road. For a moment she just watched the woman sob. "Jesus, Coco. I so sorry. But, he forced you, surely this doesn't count."

"Yes, it counts!"

"How can that be?"

"It can be because part of me enjoyed it. What if I relapse?"

"Coco. You've come so far. You're not going to relapse."

"How the fuck to do know?"

"I understand that you're …"

"No you don't."

"I think I do, at least some."

"You can't possibly. Goddammit, Marie. I hate you!" Coco pounded her fist on the dash, alternating sobs with curses.

While Coco cried, Marie tried to piece together the series of events. The guy had likely used fentanyl laced OxyContin to drug Coco in the hotel – that would explain her rage – then he must have transported her somehow to the library grounds. Did he rape her before or after? The guy's pants were down, so maybe he raped her, or at least tried to, maybe before and after. He burned her wrist with a cigarette to see if she was still alive, in which case he would strangle her. At least that was her theory. But who had bashed the man's head in and how did Coco get to Las Hermanas? One thing she knew for sure: The woman was lucky to be alive.

Marie sat quietly and waited for Coco to play herself out. After several minutes she sat up, shoved her hair back then released a long, shuddering sigh. "My wrist! He was about to kill me!"

Marie nodded. "I know. You're a lucky woman."

"Lucky?" Coco sighed deeply. "If I had any more luck I'd be dead."

Marie nodded again. No sense in trying to argue with that logic. She waited a moment then asked, "Can you start at the beginning? I'm totally confused."

"You mean about why I'm going to sue or how the guy got killed?"

"First, how the guy got killed."

"I know how it began, I know how it ended, but I remember nothing about the middle."

"That's okay. Just tell me the beginning and the end."

"Okay, but I really need my purse. It might still be at the hotel."

"Officer Stedman's at the hotel right now. If it's there, he'll have it."

"Okay. Then I have to go to my apartment to check on Angelo."

"Angelo?"

"Angelo, my lovebird. He's been alone all night long. After that you can take me to the hospital."

•••

After she had taken Coco to check on Angelo, after she'd taken her to the hospital, after she had taken her to the station to pick up her purse and make a formal statement, and after she had dropped the woman off at the train station parking lot to pick up her car, Marie had gone back to Las Hermanas. She needed to interview the three women who'd taken charge of Coco, but she was too late. They had already moved on. The three were regulars, she'd been told, and she could try to catch them Monday morning; they were closed on Sunday.

By the time Marie got back to the station, it was mid-afternoon. Immediately, she started in on the paperwork. She'd be lucky if she finished it by the time her shift ended. Briefly she described the details of the crime scene, including a chronological description of her involvement at the scene, omitting, of course, the finger in the puncture wound and anything else that was untoward.

She was about to move on to Coco, tiptoeing around the circumstances preceding the attack, when she realized that she hadn't eaten lunch. Inside her little ice chest were tucked the usual apple slices, the smear of peanut butter, string cheese and a single slice of turkey. Today there were also thick rounds of unpeeled cucumber. Nothing that she wanted to eat. What she wanted to eat was a Butterfinger.

As she walked down the hall to the vending machine, she heard Lindgrin lambasting some poor soul. It was loud enough that she could hear it through the closed door.

"What good are you then?" he was shouting. "Listen, you goddamn faggot ..."

Marie continued past his door to the end of the hallway and waited. When the door opened, she started to walk back down the hallway and was surprised to see Detective Ed, red faced, emerge from the office.

Back at her desk, she nibbled slowly on the Butterfinger. The third nail? Could be.

An hour later, Marie caught him out in the parking lot just as he was getting into his car.

"Hey, Ed," she shouted. "Got a minute?"

He waited by his back bumper as she sprinted across the asphalt.

"What's up, Marie?"

"Well, this is kind of embarrassing, but I overheard your ... well, conversation is not the right word. Anyway, as I was coming back from the vending machine, I heard Carl reaming you out. I mean, I could hear him right through the closed door."

Ed's face reddened. "And?"

Marie hesitated. Just because the man was a recipient of Lindgrin's harassment, did not necessarily mean she could trust him.

"What?" His tone was sharp.

"It's called harassment. Carl is a master at it."

"Yeah?"

"A couple of us are thinking about filing a complaint with HR—hostile workplace—if you want to do something about it."

"Nope," he said flatly. "I've waited a long time to move into homicide and I don't want to fuck that up."

Marie nodded. "I understand, Ed." She felt the heat crawl up her neck and bleed into her face. She started to turn away, should have, but turned on him instead. "This may sound like something out of a B movie, Ed, but much of the work of a homicide detective takes place on a gut level. Since you don't seem to have any guts, I can't imagine a future for you in the department."

Maybe that was overkill, Marie was thinking as she walked away.

CHAPTER 24

Reunions

Monday, July 28

As she entered the dining room at Las Hermanas, Marie realized that she had met the three women when she was trying to ID Jane Doe number 4. They were sitting at a table, plates of fruit and doughnuts in front of them.

"Good morning, ladies," she said, a pleasant smile on her face. "I don't want to interrupt your breakfast but …"

"I remember you," Pappy said. "You're that detective. Is this about the woman who got raped at the library?"

"Yes."

Playing hostess, Pappy pointed to the carafe on the counter. "Get yourself a cup of coffee and have a seat, why don't you."

"And have some breakfast," Brittany suggested. "Besides cereal, there's doughnuts and fruit." She looked down at her plate. "This morning we've got apple, banana and, hmm. I don't know what that green one is, but it's good."

"Thanks. I've eaten. But it's kind of noisy in here. Maybe we could go in there where it's quiet." Marie pointed to a glass enclosed room.

"Oh, that's the library. No food allowed in there."

"Well then, I'll just wait until you've finished your breakfast."

"Don't you want some coffee?" Pappy asked. "It doesn't matter that you're not homeless, and the coffee here is great, better than Starbucks."

"Maybe coffee."

As Marie passed the serving window she spotted the tray of doughnuts. She looked around at the other women in the dining room. There did seem to be plenty.

Pets were not allowed in the dining room or the library, so after breakfast, they'd moved into the common room that served as lounge and dormitory where they'd left the cat.

"So," Marie was saying. "What you're telling me is that you subdued the man who was attacking Ms. La Batt with a sock full of rocks, a spike heeled shoe and a pencil?"

"The pencil has a kind of hilt on it that I made of duct tape," Brittany said. The kitten, who had grown considerably rounder since Marie had last seen it, was eating kibble from the palm of the woman's hand.

Marie nodded. "I see. And were you afraid for your own safety?"

Pappy looked around the table at her companions. "Well, if it hadn't been Ms. ..."

"La Batt. Her name is Coco La Batt."

"Well, if it hadn't been her, I guess it could have been one of us."

"We've all been there," added Elaine.

Nodding, Marie took the last bite of her glazed doughnut, followed by a sip of coffee laced with Coffeemate and Splenda. "Before we go on, I need to tell you that the perpetrator is dead."

All eyes equally wide, all mouths equally agape, the three women stood in unison.

"We killed him?" It was Elaine who asked.

"It will be some time before I get the autopsy report. Could be he died of some other cause. In any case, I would say you saved a woman's life and that's where my focus will be. I do need you to come into the police station with me and make a statement."

"I'm not going," Brittany said. "The last time I was in the police station they put me into an airtight room and filled it with nitrous oxide, and when I stopped laughing …"

"Didn't happen, Brit," Pappy said, not unkindly.

"How do you know? You weren't there."

"Neither were you, Brittany," said Pappy. "The only time the police picked you up was when you tried to break Los Betos' front window with your backpack. They took you to the Behavioral Center at Saint Mary's, not to jail. Elaine and I went to visit you there. Right. Elaine?"

"She's right, Brittany. They kept you there for a 48-hour observation."

Brittany sat back down at the table. "Not going."

Elaine and Pappy exchanged looks, shrugged.

"It won't take long." Marie said. "I'll take you there myself. On the way back, we can stop for Sonoran dogs at Ruiz's if you want."

"I'd rather go to Los Betos for tacos," said Brittany.

"You're not allowed at Los Betos anymore Brit, remember? How about Taco Bell, Brit. You like it there. Could we go to Taco Bell instead, Detective Stransky?"

"Anywhere you want, ladies."

"Not going," Brittany said flatly.

Marie looked from Pappy to Elaine and back to Pappy. The only weapon Brittany had wielded was a number 2 pencil. "Well, I guess it would be enough if just the two of you made a statement."

"In that case," Pappy said, "I prefer the Sonoran dog. Elaine?"

"Sonoran dog."

"Sonoran dog it is," Marie said, rising from the chair.

"Would you bring one back for me?" Brittany asked.

"No," Pappy said flatly.

•••

She was about to pack it for the day when a Butterfinger sailed over the top of her cubicle. Attached by a rubber band was a note.

I'm in.—Ed

As she opened the Butterfinger, she wondered if that meant Ed was in with her or in with Lindgrin.

•••

The sun was just beginning its downward slide, shadows lengthening in the golden light, as Marie maneuvered the Ford Explorer out of the TPD lot. By Tucson standards, it was cool. She rolled down the window on the leeward side of the car. The monsoon had greened up the desert. If you could stand the humidity, Marie thought, the monsoon season was one of the most beautiful times of the year. She released a contented sigh and pulled onto Stone.

Once she had taken the women's statements, she'd realized that Pappy's prized roller bag was the one the killer had used to transport his victims. She offered to return the bag once forensics had gone over it, but Pappy no longer wanted it. No surprise there.

The county attorney's office would review the women's statement, the autopsy and her report. The women could credibly claim self-defense. She presumed that the dead guy's DNA would match that found on the other known victims. So, even though she had very little part in making it happen, the symmetry of this case was especially satisfying. Might even call it poetic justice. Whatever, it was all but closed and she felt a great sense of relief.

Her thoughts swung to Jacinto. No closure there yet. She'd been meaning to go by the Sonoran Academy for the Visually and Hearing Impaired to see how he was doing.

She'd been fantasizing about rebuilding his life one Go Fund Me at a time.

First his eardrums. The procedure to repair the eardrum was called tympanoplasty—she'd looked it up—and it was surprisingly common. Teeth would be next. She imagined some combination of implants and dentures. But the tongue. Marie didn't know what, if anything, could be done about his poor tongue.

When she opened the kitchen door, Guido was there to greet her.

"Good old Guido," she said, giving his head a knuckle massage.

The house was quiet. She checked the refrigerator door. The note was attached by a cheesy saguaro cactus magnet. "Pizza party for Chutney's birthday." Without her. Just as well. She really couldn't stand to be in the same room with Toni. She only wished Nick felt the same. Besides, the Sonoran dog was still with her.

After depositing her gun and mace in the bedroom safe, she returned to the kitchen thinking leftover fruit salad, and noticed the phone flashing red. A message.

My name is Francis Mulvaney. This is awkward, but you … It's my understanding that you are my mother, that is my biological mother.

Can we meet somewhere for coffee?

•••

She'd written Nick a hasty note and stuck it on the fridge with the same saguaro magnet. Francis said he was without transportation, so Marie had driven back into town to the Starbucks nearest the university. There was only one young man sitting at a table by himself. He was a nice-looking kid of average build and height, with light brown hair pulled into a man bun at the top of his head. A sparse mustache filled his rather long upper lip. Peeking above the neck of his tee shirt was tattooed Chinese character. She'd been afraid that her breast pump might start humming at the sight of him, but it didn't. Odd, it had never occurred to her that Francis would look like his father. She felt a too familiar queasiness.

He stood when she came up to the table.

"Francis?"

He produced a rigid smile. "Yeah. Marie? Is it all right if I call you Marie?"

"Sure." They both sat.

"This is my treat," he said. "Order whatever you want."

My treat, Marie thought, checking her urge to laugh. Certainly, there was nothing funny happening here. "Just plain coffee for me," she said, forcing what she hoped looked like an encouraging smile. To keep them from shaking, she folded her hands and placed them on the table. "Well…"

"I'll get our coffees."

She watched him slouch to the counter. Stand up straight, she wanted to shout then took out her iPhone and placed it on the table. He might want to see pictures of his sisters.

Francis placed a large paper cup in front of her, tossed down a couple of packets of sugar. "I didn't know if you wanted milk."

"Thanks, black is fine," she said, though she would have preferred cream. She removed the lid so the coffee would cool faster, then pointed to his drink with her chin. "Frappuccino?"

He smiled. "I really don't like plain coffee all that much." He took a long draw on his straw.

"Nice rain we've been having," he said.

"Yeah. Cools things off."

"Rain's good but it makes my allergies worse."

She nodded. "Allergies." They lapsed into silence. Marie took a tiny sip of the too hot coffee while she searched her limited small talk database. "So, are you going to school?"

"I've got a semester to go for my B.A., but right now I'm working. Here, as matter of fact."

Marie smiled. With his man bun and tattoo, he certainly looked the part. "And your major?"

"Music."

Marie smiled again. "Music. What's your instrument?"

"I play the piano, some guitar, but mostly it's my voice."

She wondered if he'd inherited that from his father or from her. She'd rather he had some other major. Somehow math or science would have been easier for her to talk about. "In high school, I was in the chorus."

"Oh, right, high school chorus." His tone was dismissive. "So, you're a policewoman?"

"A detective, actually." Marie felt the need to impress. "I'm the only woman assigned to the homicide department, in fact." She regretted the last bit as soon as it left her mouth.

He nodded. "I guess you'd like …" His voice broke slightly. He cleared his throat. "Well, I just wanted to, you know, touch base."

Touch base, Marie thought, as if they ever had one. The small talk was over. "Of course."

"What I need is the medical stuff. History and …"

"As far as I know, on my side there is nothing, no heart disease, cancer, alcoholism, drug addiction, diabetes, umm. What am I missing?"

"Mental illness?"

"Nope." She tried to smile. "At least not yet." The next question would be harder to answer.

"And my father, my biological father, that is?"

Over the years there had been so many fantasies built around this longed-for meeting. Not once did she imagine a desire to flee. She supposed she could just shrug and say she didn't know. That would be the truth and their meeting would come to an end. What did Francis need to know? How much did he deserve to know? Fact was, she wanted him to know that much of what surrounded his birth and adoption hadn't been her choice. "I guess you'd have to ask your father."

"Does he know about me?"

"I would assume. I told him I was pregnant."

"What did he say?"

"Umm," Marie said, lips pursed and tucked to one side to preclude any telling expression. "Who's the father?"

"What?"

"'Who's the father?' That's what he said." For the next few minutes, really it took less than five, she explained about the chorus teacher, not everything, of course. Nothing about *little mutt* or her *finding her passion,* nothing about her vulnerability or how he had used it to groom her. Nothing that might make her seem pathetic. When she finished, she took a sip of coffee. It was still too hot; that's how brief her story was. Did she note an expression of skepticism on Francis' smooth face? Was he wondering why the chorus teacher, or anyone for that matter, would want to have sex with her? She wanted to defend herself, struggled not to. Let him draw his own conclusions.

"Do you know his name?"

"Of course." She took out a pen and wrote it on a napkin. "By now, I imagine he'd be about 60. It's possible he's still teaching."

Francis shoved the napkin into his pocket without looking at it.

She started to pick up her cell phone so she could show him pictures of the girls, then thought better of it. "Well, you have my contact info." She waited, thinking he might offer his own. "Guess I better be going. I've got five little girls and a husband waiting for me at home." When this sparked no curiosity, she managed another smile. "Oh, I noticed your tattoo. What's it say, if you don't mind my asking?"

"I don't mind," he said. He tugged down the neck of his tee shirt. The Chinese characters trailed down his neck and over his collarbone. He caressed the tattoo with his index finger. "Roughly translated, it says, 'If the sail is not raised, the boat will not be moved by a tedious wind.'"

"Good one," she said, wondering what a 21-year-old thought was tedious? By his demeanor, certainly the 38-year-old woman who gave birth to him. She had to remind herself that this was the person she'd been longing to reconnect with for years. Here he was at last and she should be thankful for that, wherever *that* might lead. "So, if you think of anything else you want to know, or if you just want to talk, we can meet again. My treat next time." The ball was in his court; she'd left hers 21 years ago.

•••

When Marie returned home, Nick was sitting on living room couch, bottle-feeding the baby. Marie almost asked him to put the bottle aside and give her the baby. She longed for her rocking chair, dim lighting and the feel of her daughter's comforting tug at her breast.

"Well?" he asked, patting the spot next to him.

"He seems like a good kid, nice looking." She had no intention of telling Nick that her son looked like his father.

"What's he do?"

"Right now, he's a barista at Starbucks, but he's about to finish a B.A. with a major in music at the U." She wasn't ready to have this conversation. "How was the party?"

"Toni forgot that it was Chutney's birthday until the last minute, so we were all supposed to pretend it was a surprise party."

"Really."

"Yeah. It was kind of a scramble. We went to Target. Catherine and Claire picked out five presents, five cards and five birthday bags to put them in. Sometimes Toni's an airhead. She only has the one kid, you'd think she could remember the day she was born." He placed the now sated Nichole back in her carrier. "You would never forget a birthday."

Marie wasn't so sure, but was encouraged that Nick thought so.

"So, tell me more about your meet-up with Francis." He stretched his arm across the back of the couch, his hand grazing Marie's arm.

Marie swallowed hard, took a deep breath, swallowed again.

"Maybe he just needs a little more time." Nick's arm tightened around her shoulder. It was this gesture that caused the dam to burst.

CHAPTER 25

Matters of Conscience

Friday, August 1

Coco awoke to sunlight slicing through the venetian blinds. A deep sleeper, João didn't stir when she rolled away from him and the light. This was the fifth night she'd slept in his bed and she resolved she and Angelo would sleep in their own apartment tonight. She'd gotten past the anger, mostly, and was determined not give in to the fear.

She wondered how Marie's campaign to bring Lindgrin down was progressing. Since her near death, she'd been thinking a career change might be in order. If the man could be brought to account for his deeds, past and present, she might apply to the police academy. Though she'd be more than a decade older than most candidates, she was in good shape and figured her experience, for lack of a better word, might work in her favor. And Marie would back her. She was sure of that.

Coco was about to get out of bed, when João moaned and rolled over, tapping his morning erection playfully against her thigh.

•••

As Marie crossed the station parking lot, she noticed Officer Audrey by the entry. When she saw Marie, the woman grinned and waved. Marie raised her right hand in acknowledgment, thinking she didn't have the psychic energy to deal with whatever was making Audrey so happy.

"It's a boy!" Audrey shoved a blurry image in her face. "See?"

Marie studied the photo for a moment, and yes, she could just make out the little scrotum. "Well, great!" What else could she say?

"We're naming him Nelson, you know, after Nelson Mandela."

"Great, Nelson Mandela, a noble man and a very nice name."

"But we'll call him Nels."

"Nels is nice."

"Yeah," Audrey said, caressing the photo with her thumb. "Umm. I have, well, a big favor to ask. I've talked it over with Chablis and we'd like you to be Nels' godmother."

"Oh my! I don't know what to say," she said, thinking she'd like to say no. "Didn't you tell me that you had a sister? Wouldn't she be …"

"Yes, Sam. I love her to pieces but she's not very reliable. She likes to travel and she's changed her college major a half dozen time. But you … well, I've always admired you as a policewoman and a mother and … I hope you'll say yes."

"I'm not very religious, I don't think I could …"

"Oh, Chablis and I don't have any religious preference. We were thinking more along the lines of a strong, positive influence in Nelson's life."

"I see, but …"

"As you know too well, there are lots of people who still question our right to marry, let alone have children. Not you. When I needed help with Lieutenant Lindgrin, you supported me, then when Ed Johnson was getting harassed, you supported him. Not only do you stand tall for yourself, you stand tall for others."

Marie was feeling rather small at the moment. In reality, far from supporting Ed, she'd bullied him into filing his complaint. In reality, she'd tried to avoid any discussion of Audrey's wife and her pregnancy. In reality, she was… well, not as bad as Lindgrin—nobody was as bad as Lindgrin—but she'd certainly been judgmental. There was that lingering Catholic sensibility. Marriage was between one man and one woman. Besides, her first responsibility was to her own children. If she became the godmother to a child of two women, well, it would expose her whole family to that lifestyle.

So what, Marie? A voice in her head countered.

She took a deep breath. Right. So what! And if she were the godmother, that would make Nick the godfather by default. Assuming their marriage survived, Nick would make a great one.

"I'd be honored," she said at last, thinking, *let God sort it out.*

•••

Other than Audrey's announcement, it had been an uneventful day. Marie had had a little interview with a guy from the Arizona Daily Star. The resulting article was to be called *Heroes Among the Homeless*, a feature with photos of Elaine and Pappy. Brittany refused to participate for fear the publicity would alert the CIA and the FBI, not to mention her parents, to her whereabouts. Marie was hopeful that something good would come their way from the article. At the very least, meds for Brittany, dentures for Elaine and a roof over all of their heads.

Ed had sent her a draft of his harassment claim, which he said he'd send to Human Resources as soon as she sent hers in. Of course, this could be a trap. Would he follow through with the complaint or leave her in the lurch?

Well, there was no turning back now that she was the kind of person who stood tall for herself and others. "Oh God," she whispered.

It was knock-off time and she was about to pack it in when she got the call.

"Marie, Stokey Stockland here."

"Hey, Stokey. How's it going?"

"Where are you?"

"At the station about to go home. You just caught me."

"Call me back when you're out in the parking lot."

"What?"

"Go out to the parking lot and call me back."

Marie was pacing in a tight little circle behind a parked patrol car. "But I thought …"

"The visa was temporary, Marie. Now that the killer is dead, ICE figures rightly that you don't need Jacinto as a witness anymore."

Of course, she knew that, but hadn't figured the killer would end up dead so soon. They needed more time. "But this kid has been through hell, there must be something …"

"There is no something."

"What do you mean, there's no something? Sending him back to Honduras is sending him back to his death."

There was silence on the line.

"We don't send innocent kids to their death, Stokey. This is the United States of America!"

"That's just it. This is the United States of America."

"That's crazy."

"Used to be that a kid like Jacinto would qualify for a humanitarian visa. But under the current administration, gang violence, domestic abuse, fear for one's life are no longer reasons for asylum."

It was Marie's turn to take a moment of silence. She had voted for the man. Up until now, she thought he'd been doing a pretty good job. "When?"

"Don't know. Soon, I imagine."

Lindgrin emerged from the building. Marie stopped pacing and squatted down behind a patrol car. "Hang on," she whispered.

The man looked at his watch, scanned the parking lot, scowled then charged back into the building.

Marie stood and resumed her pacing. "What should I do?"

"That's up to you."

"What would you do?"

"I've already done it."

"You have?"

"Yeah, I called you."

"Thanks, Stokey. Thanks, a hell of a lot."

And why is Jacinto my problem, she asked herself? The answer came immediately. *If not you, then who?*

As Marie headed back to the station, Detective Ed flew into the parking lot, zipped into a space then ran into the building. He was in such a rush, he never even saw her. What a coincidence, she thought, then tucked its possible significance away for later. She had more immediate concerns.

Despite Stokey's insistence to the contrary, Marie was sure that Jacinto had a good chance for asylum. If there was a God, and Marie was relatively certain there was, there simply had to be something that could be done. The boy just needed a good lawyer and time to argue his case. But time was one thing Jacinto did not have.

Somehow, she had to get him to a safe place. Certainly not her house. If she personally intervened, and Lindgrin found out about it, which he would if she got caught, which she would because there was no way she could extricate Jacinto from the academy without being caught, she would be demoted for sure, possibly fired, even prosecuted for aiding and abetting an illegal immigrant. On the other hand, sending Jacinto back to Honduras was the same as putting a gun to his head. Could she live with that?

"Siri, call Eva Chacon." Let her handle it, she thought, as she waited for Eva to pick up.

"Hola, this is Eva Chacon at Derechos Humanos, leave a message and ..."

Marie waited for the tone. "This is Marie Stransky. Just got word that ICE is going to pick up Jacinto Escobedo and deport him. Could be anytime. Need your help, STAT!"

"Damn," Marie whispered. It was after five on a Friday. Chances were good that Eva would not get her message until Monday. ICE worked 24/7. Chances were good that Monday would be too late. She took a deep breath then released it slowly, her mouth an O.

As she stood there in the August humidity, sweat began to drip into her eyes and down her face, down her sides. Some years ago, Marie recalled, a woman by the name of Rosa something-something was about to be deported. She was given sanctuary in a local church. How had that come about? There was a lawyer, a hero among local immigration activists, who'd handled her case. Though it had taken months, Rosa something-something was given a new hearing and allowed to stay. Even if she could remember the particulars and the name of the lawyer who handled the case, she needed to get Jacinto into a church now. There was a church not far from the academy, but she assumed that not just any church would do.

What would happen if first thing tomorrow morning she picked Jacinto up from the school, ostensibly to take him to ... the Catholic church on 22nd Street. What was it called? Santa Cruz? She liked the looks of that church. Okay so, let's say she'd take him to Santa Cruz for confession, and he simply refused to come out?

She shook her head. That was not going to work. For one thing, Jacinto had no way to make a confession, so that pretense wouldn't hold water. Hmm.

Maybe she could just show up at the school and tell them she wanted to take Jacinto out for ice cream ... no shopping. Then what? Even with a dictionary in hand, her Spanish, especially her written Spanish, was too poor to explain to him the concept of sanctuary. She needed help with that.

"Siri, call Posada de la Luz."

Quickly, Marie logged off the computer and gathered up her briefcase and ice chest. Waiting even one more day posed too great a risk. Tricia Delgado had agreed to translate for her, but under the circumstances, Jacinto couldn't stay there even one night while Marie made other arrangements.

From the car, Marie had made a call to a Padre Ted Ortiz at Santa Cruz Catholic Church, told him about Jacinto and yes, they would receive him, but no, for their sake and hers, she would not leave her name. Then she'd talked to Robert, a very nice man at Jacinto's school, told him she'd be coming by in a few minutes to take the boy out for dinner and clothes shopping. Instead, she'd take him to Posada de la Luz and from there to the church.

She pulled out of the parking lot, thinking, *No Good.* When ICE shows up tomorrow or whenever to take custody of Jacinto, the very nice Robert, if he hasn't already called the police about the missing Jacinto, will tell them that Marie Stransky, her name would be there right on the sign-out sheet, had taken him shopping and never brought him back.

She inhaled deeply through her nose and blew it out slowly through her mouth. "Okay, okay," she whispered. "There's got to be a way to do this."

The traffic was thick and she was stuck in the right lane behind a SunTran bus that was unloading. A SunTran bus! Jacinto had been training to use the city buses. She'd bring him back to the academy, sign him in, at which time he would walk back out and get himself to Santa Cruz Church by bus. No help from her!

That was as far as she got with her plan. She'd fill in the rest as needed. If she was accused of aiding an undocumented immigrant, she'd use the Catholic mother defense. However lapsed, she was a still a Catholic, and the mother part was obvious.

Now she just needed to find out what buses Jacinto needed to take to get to the church. Would they have a bus schedule at Posada de la Luz? She doubted it.

It was a stretch, but worth a try. "Siri, which buses do you take to get from the Sonoran Academy for the Visually and Hearing Impaired to Santa Cruz Catholic Church?" Marie held her breath then quickly jotted down the numbers, there were only two, as dictated by the sweet, calm voice coming from her watch.

"God bless you, Siri."

"Why, thank you. That's very kind."

Marie almost said *you're welcome*.

Layers of copper-colored clouds were glowing above the mountains in a 180-degree sunset, a monsoon season perk that made the humidity bearable, just. For a moment, Marie sat in traffic quietly enjoying the display. She knew what she had to do, knew how to do it, and was pretty sure she had the guts to do it. And so, she was at peace, at least for now.

Rapidly, the colors were deepening from copper to cayenne. There was only one thing left to do before putting her plan in place.

"Siri, call Nick." This wasn't going to be pretty.

•••

Marie and Jacinto rushed up and down the Walmart aisles, pulling toothpaste, deodorant, shampoo, socks and boxers and tee shirts from the shelves. There were granola bars, boxes of juice, packets of cheese and crackers and a sack of little mandarin oranges. They passed the steam table with chicken in a variety of forms. She handed Jacinto a container and watched as he filled it with barbecue buffalo wings.

It was now nearly 9 o'clock. It had rained lightly then stopped. As she sailed down the street, lights blurry in the wet asphalt, Marie could only hope the real rain would hold off long enough for Jacinto to catch his first bus. After that, there was only the one transfer.

Tricia Delgado had gone over the route with Jacinto and he appeared to understand. Marie was confident that the woman had done her best to explain in written Spanish what sanctuary was and why he needed it. She only wished she had the same confidence that he had fully understood what was at stake and why she was suddenly pulling him out of a place where he had food, shelter and security, and was placing him once again in the hands of strangers.

As planned, she escorted Jacinto into the academy and signed him in. She said thanks and good night to Robert, then, impulsively gave Jacinto a big hug. His arms remained at his sides and she felt awkward and exposed as if her excessive goodbye might be used against her in a court of law. She hurried out the door before her humming breast pump could further incriminate her.

•••

It started to rain again. Each isolated drop felt like a pinprick on the boy's warm skin. Hesitating, heart pounding, he stood in front of the church, its tower and dome glowing against the night. Many times, he had passed by. Many times he had thought to enter, but never had. It was only a few blocks from the park and the oleander hedge, his former sanctuary. Señora Delgado had promised that this new one would provide him with food, shelter and safety from *La Migra*. Yes, he would be cared for, but once he entered, he would not be able to leave, she had explained.

He thought of the beautiful zoo with its captured animals. It must cost a lot of money to care for them. The United States was a very strange place. Animals were not free, but they were well cared for. People were free, free to be hungry, free to live under hedges and tents made of garbage bags.

Raindrops were now bouncing off the pavement. It was that more than any other factor the drove him past the enormous statue of *Jesus Cristo* on the cross and into the church, Walmart bag in hand. Inside, it was warm and stuffy, the air filled with the familiar aroma of melted wax from the tiers of *velas* along one side of the vestibule. An old man, stiff gray hair buzzed to within a quarter of an inch of his skull, was dwarfed by the chair he was dozing in, chin almost touching his chest. He roused, rose with a grunt, then smiled.

"Bienvenidos, mijo," his lips said.

•••

"Did you even think of the consequences?" Nick was saying.

"Of course," Marie said, hooking her butt on the kitchen stool.

"Of course! Did you think about how we might survive your unemployment, how we'd pay for a lawyer, what would happen if you went to jail?"

She had.

"You put the welfare of a stranger before the welfare of your own family, Marie. Did you even think of that?"

She hadn't.

"And what if your little scheme fails and the kid is deported anyway?"

"I never thought of it as a scheme, Nick," she said too loudly, amazed that they could be so far apart on something she felt so strongly was right. She chewed on the inside of her lip to keep it from quivering. "And to my way of thinking, there is a clear difference between trying and failing and failing to try."

"The outcome is the same, Marie."

At that moment, she hated him. If words were fists, she would have loved to find the right ones to beat him bloody. "You're right, of course.

You're always right about everything." She rose from the stool and went to attend to her breast pump.

And Nick was right, she thought as she cleaned the flanges. There was no way to be on the right side of the argument. She had put herself in a very precarious place, and if things went south, her family would suffer and possibly for nothing. It was also true that if she had allowed the boy to be deported, she would have put not only the boy's life, but her soul in a very precarious place, though she wasn't wholly sure she believed that bit about her soul. Certainly, she hadn't been thinking about her soul when she dropped Jacinto off at the academy. She wasn't absolutely certain she even believed in God anymore, and if there was no God, she didn't have to worry about the state of her soul.

She recalled a theology course she'd taken in college. There was something called Pascal's wager, which essentially said that it's better to believe in God just in case he exists. At the time it made sense. Now it just struck her as cynical.

If God would allow someone like Jacinto to be deported after all he'd been through, then God was unreliable, if not downright despicable. If she believed in a God like that, she'd despise him. Then again, the boy was in sanctuary. She'd seen to that. So maybe she was part of God's plan for justice for Jacinto. She shook her head. She didn't quite believe that either.

There was one thing she was certain of. She and Nick were farther apart than ever and it was pressing hard on the place where she thought her soul, if she had one, resided.

She set her breast pump on the shelf, pulled on her sports bra, shorts and tee and headed out to the garage. Tucked in the corner was Nick's desk. A profusion of paper scraps bloomed from a wire basket. Nick never discussed his writing. Heart beating harder than was proportionate to her crime, she picked up the top scrap.

Selana: Slender, but curvaceous, pale, shoulder length blond hair, pert breasts like tea cakes topped with rosy gumdrops.

Marie picked up another scrap.

Zenith: Petit but curvaceous, multiracial, long, wavy black hair, pert breasts, like bran muffins topped with Hershey Kisses.

Bran muffins? Pert? "Hey Siri, what is the definition of pert?"

After a moment Siri responded, "Pert: impudent, saucy, vivacious."

Marie tried to imagine what an impudent breast might look like. Her breasts were definitely not impudent and certainly not vivacious. *Functional* would describe them, maybe *handy*. If she could talk, Nichole would declare them delicious comfort. And Nick? He'd never complained.

Sighing, Marie placed the notes exactly as she'd found them. Whatever Nick was working on, great fiction it was not. In fact, if the writer were anyone other than her husband, she would have laughed.

Before mounting the treadmill, she stepped gingerly on the scale. She'd gained .7 pounds. First her son, then Jacinto, then a father come and gone, and Nick with his fantasies of pert breasts. On top of all that, she'd gained nearly a pound. It was too much to support. Yanking off her tee shirt, she used it to muffle her sobs.

Dressed for his workout, Nick pounded into the garage then stopped short. "Now what?"

Under the circumstances, she thought it best to be brief. "I haven't lost any weight."

For a moment, he simply looked annoyed. "That's only because you're putting on muscle and muscle weighs more than fat."

It was the kindest thing he'd said to her in weeks.

CHAPTER, 26

The Fourth Nail

Tuesday, September 8

Marie was just about to make a trip to the vending machine when Lindgrin called her into his office to berate her for late paperwork on the Santa Rita Park Stalker, which had been ever evolving and seemingly endless due to his manner of death and the involvement of Coco and the homeless women. As Carl droned on, Marie's watch began to vibrate, which made her think of Nichole, which set her breast pump to humming.

"There's that goddamn humming again." He squinted up at the ceiling then at Marie. "What the hell? It's coming from you!"

Marie took a deep breath. She fiddled with her watch and stepped in a bit closer. "It's my breast pump."

"Breast pump? You mean like to pump your... breasts?"

"Yes, that would be a breast pump."

"That's disgusting."

His spittle misted the air and Marie took one step back. "It saves lots of time when I'm at work."

"You mean right now it's…"

"As we speak." He looked horrified. Marie wished she could take his picture. "Do you have a problem with that, because if you do …"

He drew the back of his hand across his mouth. "That's just sick. Jesus, you're sick."

"My name isn't Jesus, Carl. It's Marie Stransky. Detective Marie Stransky. Got it?"

"Get the hell out of my office you stupid cow."

Marie turned and walked out of the office, a little smile on her lips. She thought of Coco, Torrance, Ed, all the shit he'd tried to make her eat over the years. Vengeance would be sweet.

Vengeance is mine, sayeth the Lord, the voice in her head chided. In Carl's case, Marie would be happy to be God's instrument.

Marie didn't replay the recording until she was pulling out of the parking lot. The last nail in the coffin. She'd let the others know it was time to move. Coco would send three letters, one to the mayor, one to the chief and one to the Arizona Daily Star. Audrey, Ed and she would file formal complaints to HR. There was safety in numbers. Four people, assuming Ed would follow through, could not be ignored. Hostile workplace, harassment, sexual abuse.

"You're so fucked, Carl."

"That's not nice," said Siri.

"Oh, shut up, Siri."

•••

Marie was feeling pretty cocky until she pulled into her driveway. What if the old adage did not apply in the good old boy world of police work. Still, HR would be required to investigate, look at the evidence, talk to witnesses. She was a witness to Lindgrin's harassment of Ed and had a recording of her own. Audrey's complaint would be harder to prove, but the simple fact that a complaint had been filed, provable or not, added weight. Coco's accusation could not be proven either, but would gain credibility when considered along with the others.

The final report would be sent to the chief. Her stomach flipped. It was the chief who had made Lindgrin head of the homicide department in the first place.

•••

Guido was waiting at the door, as was Catherine. "How come you didn't tell me?" she demanded by way of greeting.

"Sorry," Marie said, but she felt more anger than remorse. Ice chest in hand, she went into the kitchen, Catherine on her heels. "You've been talking to your dad?"

Catherine nodded.

"I know you need to be in the loop, but the subject of your brother … well, I've had other things, police things, on my mind and it just hadn't come up lately."

"Like there has to be some sort of prompt, like, 'Gee, Mom, have you run into anybody you know at Starbucks lately?'"

No doubt about it. Her daughter was definitely an old soul.

"So, when do we get to meet him?"

Marie shrugged. "I don't know how to put this but …"

"He doesn't want to meet us." The corners of her mouth pulled down. "Is that it?"

"I don't know." She recalled Nick's words on the subject. "Let's just give him a little more time, hmmm? He knows how to get ahold of us." She put her four little bags of milk into the fridge. "Can we finish this conversation after I've changed my clothes?"

"If that means never, then no."

"Honey, I'm tired. Let me just get …" Marie gestured toward her breasts.

"So, when are you going to tell Claire she has a big brother?"

"Good God, Catherine. When I deem it appropriate."

"Does that mean when you whenever you feel like it?"

"Yes! Now will you let it go?"

"Claire has a right to know." Catherine was, well *glaring* would be too strong a word, but her look was stern, demanding. She turned on her heel then and stomped out of the kitchen.

Marie closed her eyes, inhaled deeply and congratulated herself for not blowing up, for not shouting or name calling, for not raging or crying. Though she hadn't handled the situation in the manner of a wise parent, she had acted like an adult. And really, what were her own rights? Shouldn't she be allowed to tell her own story in her own words when she chose to without pressure and guilt tripping?

Apparently not. She did need to consider Claire. There would probably be hurt feelings, possibly tears and definitely questions that Marie did not want to answer. Well, better sooner than later, she supposed. Marie quickly changed her clothes, threw cold water on her face, then went in search of Claire.

She found her at the dining room table, a fractions worksheet, an array of pencils, both colored and number 2, sharpener, spiral notebook and a ruler neatly laid out before her. Marie kissed her scalp, noting the nutty smell of her hair. "Glad to see you're getting your homework out of the way early."

"This isn't homework. It's just left over from summer school. I'm practicing."

Poor child, Marie thought. Other than a week at swim camp, she'd hardly had a summer at all and now she had nothing better to do than an old worksheet. "Oh. Well, that's … very wise. How was school today?"

"Good."

"You like your teacher?"

"Yeah, she's good."

"Well, good." Marie peered over Claire's shoulder. She was tempted to tell her that ¾ plus ½ was not ⅘, but reminded herself that was not what she had come into the room to do.

"There's something I've been wanting to tell you," Marie said, sitting down next to her daughter. "Is this a good time to talk?" Marie smiled. Now this was the way a good parent spoke to a child.

"It's okay, Mom," Claire said without looking up from her work. "I already know."

"Know what?"

"About Francis. Catherine told me." She looked at her mother then, eyebrows raised, a little smile on her lips. "When do we get to meet him?"

"Someday soon, I hope," she said, curiously deflated.

"You should invite him to dinner. Grandma could make her potato salad, you could cook corn on the cob, Dad could barbecue hamburgers, I could make a pie from scratch and we could all eat outside on TV trays."

Claire had obviously given this a lot of thought, the fact that she'd never made a pie from scratch, notwithstanding. "Sounds like a plan, sweetie. When Francis calls next time, I'll invite him to dinner."

"But what if he's a vegetarian?"

"We'll figure it out when the time comes."

Marie started to get up. "Oh, speaking of pies, let me show you something." She made two circles then cut each in half. "Now I'll cut each pie in four pieces." She shaded in three of the four pieces in one pie. Under that pie, Marie wrote ¾. "Now I'll just shade in half of the other pie." Under that she wrote ½. "See? One half is the same amount of pie as two fourths. Now count up all the fourths in both pies."

"Five."

"Exactly." Marie wrote ¾ + ½ = ¾ + ²⁄₄ = ⁵⁄₄. "And ⁵⁄₄ is the same as?"

Claire was silent for a long time.

"Do you have more than one pie?"

"Yes."

"Right." Marie figured she'd better quit while ahead. She'd struggled through fractions with Catherine, and wondered for the umpteenth time when the U.S. would join the 21ˢᵗ century and switch to the metric system. She kissed her daughter's scalp again. "Time to wash your hair. Would you like help?"

"Mom, I've been washing my own hair since forever."

"Right, again." Claire might not be a math whiz, Marie was thinking as she went to check in on the rest of the family, but her organization skills were excellent and her personal hygiene was coming right along.

She could smell distant rain. A vault of sullen clouds trapped the day's heat beneath. The heat and humidity wouldn't be so bad if Marie could just walk around naked. The relief would almost be worth the humiliation.

•••

Marie had fed Nichole then showered. It was nearly midnight, but Nick was still down in the garage working on his novel, his stupid novel as she'd come to think of it. She should be tired, well she was tired, but she couldn't sleep. Water. She would drink a glass.

Nick had been to the urologist for his six-week checkup last week. He hadn't discussed the results with her and she hadn't asked. She assumed he was good to go, but so far, nothing.

Before getting back in bed, she slipped off the boxers. Her tee shirt fell just below her hips. Marie took a long, evaluative look in the full-length mirror, something she rarely did. In the dim light, she couldn't see the spider veins on her thighs. The legs, sturdy and shapely, still looked good.

She climbed back in bed, waited, dozed then awoke when she felt his weight depress the mattress. When his breath turned light, even, she rose on one elbow. He was sprawled on his back, sheet cast aside. She was tempted to stroke his shoulders, his beautiful naked chest, but she didn't want to spook him.

"Nick?" she whispered. "Nick?"

When he was snoring softly she parted the fly in his boxers and took him into her mouth, wanting him hard and needy before he had time to think. Quickly, she slid on. He came almost immediately. For a moment, she waited for a reaction. When there was none, she slid off and slunk into the bathroom.

Maybe he never woke up. Folding her hands together, she pressed them to her lips. Maybe he'll think it was a dream.

"Dear God," she whispered. Had she really just sexually assaulted her sleeping husband?

Marie turned the cold-water tap on full blast. She took her still damp towel off the rack. Sitting on the toilet, she sobbed into the towel.

When she was finally exhausted and every tear spent, she crept back into the bedroom. As she lay in the dark, she sensed that Nick was awake. She turned on her side away from him. Chest constricted, she was afraid to inhale. It wasn't until she felt his hand smoothing down her hip that she dared a deep breath.

She awoke to the ping of raindrops on the sliding glass door. Barefoot, Marie slid open the door and stepped into the light, cooling rain. Music was coming from the house next door, faint, but not so faint that she didn't recognize Nat King Cole.

"You made a promise to be faithful by all the stars above," he crooned.

"Now you call it madness, but I call it love."

Love. It didn't always deliver on its promise. Though she no longer felt Toni was a real threat to her marriage, she could imagine somewhere down the line, maybe at a conference for sci-fi writers, he'd meet a woman with breasts like baked goods who claimed to admire his writing more than his wide shoulders and he would fall … or not. Just because she could imagine it didn't mean it would happen.

The rain intensified, rinsing the salt from Marie's face and limbs. Would there be peace now between her and Nick or was their lovemaking only a truce? Swaying, she hugged her arms.

"I can't forget the day I met you, that's all I'm dreaming of," she sang softly in her mellow alto. "And now you call it madness, but I call it love."

She didn't hear Nick, didn't know he was near until he slipped his arms around her, hugging her to him from behind. "How come you don't sing more often?"

Without answering, Marie turned in his arms. Leaning her forehead against his chin, they swayed, two refrigerators dancing in the rain.

CHAPTER 27

A Jaw Made in Heaven

Tuesday, September 15

Officer Andrey had been the first. Alex Ahumeda from HR interviewed her and took her sworn statement then moved on to Ed. Much to Marie's relief, he'd followed through with his complaint as promised. She really did need to reevaluate her opinion of the man.

Marie was the last to be called into his office. For the occasion, she'd squeezed herself into a pre-maternity blouse, which she tucked into her trousers then buttoned her jacket to hide the resulting fleshy overlap.

Ahumeda listened without expression as Marie described the conversation she'd overheard between Ed and Carl. When she played the tape of their own conversation, he stared into middle space.

"Really, this has been going on for years, years of insulting and sexist comments about my pregnancies, weight, and intelligence," she explained.

"And you're only now making a complaint."

Marie wondered if she had just been accused of overreacting, or even entrapment, which wasn't too far from the truth. "Yes, sir. Basically, I just did my job and tried to ignore it."

"What moved you to file this complaint now?" He stabbed at the paper in front of him with a pen.

"I guess the breaking point was when Lieutenant Lindgrin started making derogatory comments to Officer Wallace. He created a hostile work environment and I felt a responsibility to my younger colleague, as well as to Sergeant Johnson, who is new to the department, to try to change that." She watched closely to see if the man might blink. He didn't.

"I see," he said, tossing the pen onto the desk. "I'd like a written transcript of the recording."

"Anything else?"

"One more thing. Do you know Coco La Batt?"

"Yes. We were at the police academy together"

"That was before she was dismissed because of drug use?"

"Yes, sir. She also has worked as a decoy on two homicide cases. One within the last two months." She waited for a response. When there was none she asked, "Is there anything else you need from me?"

"That's it. We'll get back to you."

That's it? Marie thought as she exited the office. They were all fucked.

Friday, September 25

For the past 10 days, Marie, Audrey and Ed had exchanged no more than furtive glances and cursory greetings as they waited for the fallout. Then yesterday, as she crept by Lindgrin's office to the vending machine, she noticed that his desk was cleared of paperwork. Their complaints were being taking seriously, apparently. Still, the waiting seemed endless.

Marie took a deep breath then opened the file on current investigations. Last week, two hikers bushwhacking down a ravine in the Catalinas just off the road to Mt. Lemon came across the half-buried, badly decomposed remains of a young Afro-American woman. According to the medical examiner's office, she was between 13 and 17 years old and had been dead for more than a year. The death was listed as a probable homicide, the cause undetermined.

Marie studied the artist's rendering. More girl than woman, she had a sweet wide-eyed face and a shy smile. Breast pump humming, Marie was about to start sifting through cold cases, when her watch chimed. It was Tricia Delgado from Posada de la Luz. It had been nearly two months since Jacinto had entered sanctuary at Santa Cruz Church and Marie had been so caught up by her own drama, she'd given the boy little thought.

Quickly, she rose from her desk. Even with Lindgrin out of the way, it would be best to return the call from the bathroom.

"Hey, Tricia, what's up?"

Five minutes later she was on the phone with Stokey.

"Jacinto's disappeared," she said by way of greeting.

"Damn. Well, there's nothing to do about it."

"But where do you think... I mean, why would he? I'm wondering do you think his brother or his sister might have come for him?"

"Do you know their names?"

"Yeah, I've got it in my notes. I'll get back to you in a minute," she said and disconnected.

"Hey Siri, find Jacinto Escobedo." It was there in her notes from the meeting with Eva Chacon. The brother was Rigoberto, the sister, Ascención.

According to Stokey, Rigoberto Escobedo was currently living with an uncle in Phoenix. The boy had entered the U.S. just weeks before the immigration crackdown and had gotten temporary asylum. There was no record of the sister. So, maybe this Rigoberto had come for Jacinto. The question now was whether Jacinto was safer with his brother. Probably not. Was there something she could do about it? Probably not. She reminded herself of the difference between trying and failing and failing to try. It didn't make her feel any better.

"Shit," she whispered and forced her attention back to the little girl with the sweet face. She was just beginning her search through the cold cases when the Butterfinger dropped on her desk like a dead bird. She read the attached note.

Ding-dong the witch is dead – Ed

According to Ed, Lindgrin was seen pushing paperclips in Procurement, but they hadn't gotten word yet from HR or the chief about the resolution of their cases. Until then, she would not count Lindgrin out.

As Marie ate the Butterfinger, she scrolled though the cold cases, starting with those dating back two years. It didn't take her long to find a probable match. DNA would determine if the dead child was, in fact, 14-year-old DeShanna Rhodes, who went missing from her bedroom 18 months ago while her family slept. No one heard any suspicious sounds. There were no calls for help. Her window was wide open and the screen was lying in the grass beneath. The family's dog, a Rottweiler mix, had not barked.

She looked at DeShanna's eighth-grade photo. The artist's rendering had been amazingly accurate. Marie dropped the last of the Butterfinger in the wastebasket and called it a day.

She was pulling out of the parking lot when she heard the squeal of tires. Through the rearview mirror, she saw Lindgrin's Dodge Ram bearing down on her. There was nothing to do but brace for the crash. Stunned, she watched the man back up and hit her again. "What the hell?"

Dazed but undaunted, she climbed out of the car. She'd been to court that morning for Davie Woodward's preliminary and had left her taser and mace at home. Her Glock was tucked in the pancake holster on her belt, but shooting the son of a bitch seemed a bit over the top. She scanned the parking lot and noted a uniform standing some 50 yards away. How fast could he cover that 50 yards?

Carl was out of his truck and charging toward her like a Pamplona bull. From the corner of her eye Marie could see the uniform galloping their way, fists pumping air, but Carl was now no more than an arm's length away. He shuddered to a halt, red-faced and shaking like a 5.9 on the Richter scale. Marie couldn't tell whether he was trying to restrain himself or trying to figure out the best way to do the most damage.

Either way, Marie's adrenaline was surging and it was too late for flight. As she'd been trained to do at the academy, she turned her left side to him to narrow the target. When he started to go for her throat, she let him have it with a right to the jaw, putting her full weight behind the punch. Marie had never in her life punched someone in the face and was amazed when Lindgrin crumpled to the ground at her feet.

"Glass jaw," said the uniform, now puffing at her side.

"Huh?"

"Who'd a guessed the lieutenant had a glass jaw?"

CHAPTER 28

A Peculiar Alignment of the Stars
(for lack of a better explanation)

Tuesday, October 13

Marie looked around her cubicle one last time. Because of the neck brace, she had to turn her body to do so. There was only one personal item left to pack up, a photo of Nick and the girls shortly after Nichole's birth. It was stuck into the rust colored fabric that covered the wall with a pushpin. She studied it now. Nick was holding the baby and grinning as if he couldn't imagine a better life. Usually the photo brought joy, today it brought tears. Her last baby. Her last day in this little space. How had it come to this? With her left hand—the right was casted—she slipped the photo into a pocket of her briefcase, leaving the pushpin for the next occupant.

Just last week she had made an unannounced visit to the home of DeShanna Rhodes. The mother was quiet, the father suspicious. She learned nothing, not that it mattered anymore. DeShanna, with the wide eyes and shy smile, would not be her priority. Apparently, it was not in the stars.

Wednesday, October 14

The Weird Sisters had been laboring since sunrise in the front yard of a triplex, recently acquired by a businesswoman who had a number of rentals in town. She had seen the article, *Heroes Among the Homeless*, in the Arizona Daily Star and offered to let them stay in one of the units in return for maintenance.

Wearing goggles and a battered straw cowboy hat, Pappy wielded a weed-whacker in long, low arcs. Brittany was kneeling in front of a bed of cactus: prickly pear, hedgehog, barrel and assorted agaves plucking out bits of plastic debris with long metal tongs. She leaned back on her heels and watched the older woman sweeping the weed-whacker back and forth like Death his scythe. Though she was wearing heavy work gloves, spines stuck to the leather and no matter how careful she was, they found their way into her skin. She pulled off a glove and squinted at the back of her wrist where a barely visible cluster of prickly pear spines lodged in her skin. Weed-whacking looked a lot less painful, but she stayed clear of devices like weed-whackers, hedge trimmers and especially electric saws.

"It's not as easy as it looks." Elaine observed. She'd been lopping dead branches out of an old mesquite that shaded much of the yard. She drew a hand across her sweaty brow. "Takes practice."

Brittany picked at the spines, a delicate operation. She threw the gloves into the dirt and labored to her feet. "I'm too hot. I'm going to start sanding the cabinets."

Elaine preferred outside work to in, but it was getting hot. Elaine rested her lopper against the tree and began collecting the debris. "You're right. Pappy!" she shouted. "Pappy!" The woman continued her scything. Elaine shrugged. She dumped the branches into a pile by the front gate and followed Brittany into the damp, cool interior of their new digs.

They had already swabbed out the fridge and steel-wooled the oven, pumiced the ring in the toilet, scrubbed and waxed the linoleum and given the walls two coats of Navajo white. All the while, the kitten, who was now called Goldie, cage free and saucer-eyed, tore about like a crazed being. As yet, there was no furniture in their unit, but there was the swamp cooler and they had mats to sleep on. There was running water whenever they wanted it, their own bathroom, and possibly best of all, a door that locked.

When they finished rehabbing all three units, they could continue to live there, rent free, while doing maintenance on other properties. They were paid a small stipend; it was too far below minimum to be called a wage, but it allowed them to put a little aside for the catastrophe that, in their experience, lurked just around the corner.

For months, they had tried to get some sort of housing; couldn't even remember how many waiting lists they occupied or with which agencies. Now they had an address. Brittany could apply for disability, though it meant alerting the government to her whereabouts. Pappy and Elaine had already filled out dozens of job applications: Walmart, Burger King, Best Western. It was a long list. Somebody out there might even hire one or both.

Who would have thought, they thought, that killing a guy, which hadn't even been their intention, would bring such an improvement in their circumstances? It was a screwed-up world to be sure, they agreed, but they were grateful to be under a roof, grateful for as long as their luck might last, and every morning and every night they put their hands together and thanked whatever powers that might be.

In addition to the computer, there was a messy array of papers and manila folders. Gone was the photo of Carl and the governor. In its place was Nick and the girls framed in silver now. Marie smiled at it as she closed the file on current investigations. It wasn't easy with her casted right hand, but she managed, just. It didn't hurt anymore and soon she'd be rid of both the cast and the neck brace.

Just for the heck of it, she decided to conduct a Google Earth search of the area around DeShanna Rhodes' house. In moments, she had zeroed in on the house, checking out the surrounding backyards, lanes and alleyways. All the possible paths leading to the girl's bedroom window.

She held her watch up to her face. Before she went home, Marie wanted to draft a letter of recommendation for Coco. Marie had been forgiven, apparently, and now that Lindgrin was gone, rather than file a lawsuit against him and the city, Coco had decided to apply to the police academy. Given the facts surrounding her dismissal years ago, Marie figured Coco had a good chance of readmittance despite her age and encumbrances. And now—she still couldn't quite believe it—as the acting head of the homicide department, Marie was in a position to actually help make that happen.

This was not what she intended when she'd filed her harassment claim. She'd neither asked for the position nor wanted a job that would tie her to a desk. But the raise was welcome. It allowed Nick to cut back some at the Review, and he seemed more at peace as a house husband. More at peace with her as well.

Her phone chimed. It was a call from her landline. Rarely did she get a call from home and her heart raced. "Hello?"

"He's coming to dinner tonight."

"Who's coming to dinner?"

"Him! Francis, and he's not a vegetarian!" Claire didn't wait for Marie's response. "But don't worry. Dad's barbecuing chicken, Catherine's doing the corn, I'm baking a blueberry pie from scratch and Grandma's bringing her potato salad."

"Grandma's coming too?"

"Of course. Catherine didn't want to invite her, but I insisted."

"You insisted?"

"Of course. She's his Grandma too."

"Right," Marie said, thinking, *oh my God.*

"I'm so happy. I've always wanted a big brother."

"Really?"

"Sort of. Just don't be late. Bye."

Marie took a deep breath. Was she ready for this? Well, ready or not, Francis was coming to dinner and she was not to be late, though Claire had been so excited she'd forgotten to say what time late was. Marie looked at her watch. It was already 4:30. "Call Torrance," she said to her wrist. Oddly, the injuries Marie has suffered at the hands of Lingrin, had enabled her pull a few strings to get him reassigned to homicide.

He was there before she could pack up her ice chest and briefcase.

"Big favor. I've got an emergency at home."

The detective looked concerned. "What's going on, Marie?"

"Apparently, Claire is now running the show at home and she's invited my son to dinner."

"Since when to do you have a son?"

"Since I was 17." By the expression on his face, she could tell Torrance was having trouble picturing her as an unwed teen mother. "I'll fill you in on that some other time. Right now, I need you to cover for me."

"Sure."

"Oh yeah, you might want to look at DeShanna Rhodes' autopsy report."

"Sad affair. I remember when the little girl went missing. Over a year ago, right?"

"Nineteen months. I'm thinking it must have been somebody she knew."

"That's what I thought at the time, but without a body …"

"Well, now there's a body. Anyway, it will give you something to chew on while you're sitting here. Just don't leave the station until your shift is over, please. If something comes up send Frank or Ed."

Torrance looked skeptical.

"Or send them both. I don't care, just don't go yourself."

"Got you covered. You get out of here."

"Thanks, Torrance." Marie turned to go, then rummaged in her briefcase for a moment. "Something else for you to chew on," she said, dropping a Butterfinger on the desk.

Marie made her way to the Ford Explorer. Her stomach lurched as she imagined her mother, Nick and Francis in the same room. What would they talk about? What would she talk about? It occurred to her that it might be hard to have a conversation with someone who has *If the sail is not raised, the boat will not be moved by a tedious wind* tattooed on his neck. She could only hope that the girls would be sufficiently diverting and conversation, tedious or otherwise, would be in praise of her mother's potato salad and Claire's first ever made from scratch berry pie.

Fall in Tucson meant that the monsoons had finally wrung themselves out, sending temperatures plummeting to below 95 degrees. The hot, dry breeze almost felt good and there was no reason for her to feel so … Marie sighed. It was hard to know how she felt. Angry and guilty – the evil twins – plus anxious, pretty much summed it up.

She needed to shift gears. Francis was only 21. It was not his fault that he looked like his father; not his fault that she didn't love him. She doubted if she ever could, at least not the way she loved the ones she had mothered. But that was natural, wasn't it? Then why were the evil twins bearing down so hard on her. Was she afraid of her son's judgment? Yes. Nick and Catherine had exonerated her, but Marie feared Francis had already found her guilty. Guilty and tedious.

No one knew about the limits of her love but her. The family was free to love him without prejudice in her stead. All she had to do was smile.

She practiced smiling now as she pulled onto the freeway. See? No pressure. Not a care in the world, just welcome to our family, Francis, hope you … What? Don't hate me?

Her stomach had worked its way into full roil. Maybe after dinner, if she could eat it, she would ask Francis about his voice. Over blueberry pie made especially for him by his little sister who'd always wanted a big brother, she could ask if he was a tenor or a baritone. Maybe she'd invite him to bring his guitar next time, if there would be a next time. He might sing for them. She might join him. Voice was their common ground, after all, a place to start. Really, all they had to do right now was find a place to start.

ABOUT THE AUTHOR

G. Davies Jandrey has lived in Tucson, Arizona for well over half her life, which makes her a born again "Baja" Arizonan. She makes her home with her husband, Fritz, dog Tito and cat Goldie, *la traviesa*, in the desert outskirts of the city. Time spent coaching three lively six-year-olds under the auspices of Literacy Connect's Reading Seed Program brings her great joy, as does volunteering at Sister José Women's Center. She is a passionate, but not particularly gifted, gardener and canasta player.

She refers to herself as "the best southwest fiction writer you've never heard of." To read samples of Gayle's novels, both published and in progress, visit her website: www.gaylejandrey.com

ALSO BY
G. DAVIES JANDREY

A Garden of Aloes
Journey Through an Arid Land
A Small Saving Grace
Deep Breathing

ACKNOWLEDGMENTS

The Law of Unintended Consequences exists because of the encouragement and support of many people. First and foremost, there is my husband, Fritz, who must put up with months of living with a very distracted spouse. I thank Veronica Robinson, who read an early draft and was most generous with her time and observations. Bonnie Lemons read the manuscript more than once and provided not only with editorial guidance, but insights into the amazing features of her Smart Watch. Bless you. I thank Lee Sims for his careful reading. Any errors that remain, I am sure I added when correcting the errors I'd already made, and are totally mine. When in doubt about weaponry, self-defense and police procedures, I always turn to former policeman and border patrol agent, Cameron Hintzen. Friends, Diane Cheshire, Ginia Desmond, Mary Goethals and Jennie Vemich, offered encouragement. For their continued faith, patience and steady hand at the helm, I am ever grateful to production editor, Jacquie Cook, and publisher, Mary Lou Monahan of Fireship Press.

Other Titles from Fireship Press

Provincial Justice:
A Kate Mahoney Mystery, Book I
Gerry Hernbrode

Set in Tucson, Arizona, Provincial Justice is a tale of greed, lust and, of course, murder.

In another life, Kate Mahoney, was Sister Katherine in the Congregation of the Celtic Cross, under the stern direction of Mother Provincial. Now she is the principal of Saguaro Elementary, an inner-city school where the custodian wears rubber gloves on his early morning rounds to clear the playground of used needles and condoms.

When Julie Mason, the district Superintendent, is found dead in the first-grade classroom of Elijah Stewart, the teacher becomes the prime suspect. Though Kate imagines there are plenty of people who would like to see Julie Mason dead, or at least out of the business of education, she is certain that Elijah is not one of them and sets out to prove it.

Provincial Sanctuary
A Kate Mahoney Mystery, Book II
Gerry Hernbrode

Kate Mahoney, the sleuthing principal of rough and tumble Saguaro Elementary, is back again.

One hectic morning, Kate answers her office phone. In a voice that is sickeningly familiar, a man tells her that he will kill one of her students if she does not do exactly as he tells her. She does not and in turn, two of her sixth-graders, prissy Gladys and her nemesis and would-be boyfriend, Louis, disappear.

Kate's dreams catapult her back twenty years in time when she was Sister Katherine in the Congregation of the Celtic Cross. No gentle dreams, they are dominated by Mother Phillipa Manning, who issues directives from the grave, or wherever deceased Mother Provincials reside after death, to help in Kate's search for the missing children.

Cortero

An Imprint of Fireship Press

Interesting • Informative • Authoritative

All Cortero books are available through
leading bookstores and wholesalers worldwide.

CPSIA information can be obtained
at www.ICGtesting.com
Printed in the USA
BVHW092354180222
629164BV00001B/4

9 781736 620342